SHADOW
— OF THE —
DRAGON

PART TWO - ELSPETH

KATE O'HEARN

Hodder
Children's
Books

A division of Hachette Children's Books

ISBN-13: 978 0 340 94529 2

Typeset in AGaramond by Avon DataSet Ltd,
Bidford on Avon, Warwickshire

Printed in Great Britain by
Clays Ltd, St Ives plc

The paper and board used in this paperback by Hodder Children's Books
are natural recyclable products made from wood grown in sustainable
forests. The manufacturing processes conform to the environmental
regulations of the country of origin.

Hodder Children's Books
a division of Hachette Children's Books
338 Euston Road, London NW1 3BH
An Hachette UK Company
www.hachette.co.uk

For Dad,

My biggest supporter and very best friend.
I love you.

ABOUT THE AUTHOR

Kate O'Hearn was raised in the heart of New York City. Throughout her life, she has always had an active and vivid imagination. As a child walking down 5th Avenue, she would envision herself soaring among the city's canyons on the back of a wild dragon.

While in Florida, looking over the sea, she could imagine living amongst the whales and breaching in the heavy swells.

At night, a star studded sky was yet another playground.

These dreams and ideas never faded. Instead they grew until they spilled over into the books she loves to write.

For more information visit:
www.kateohearn.com

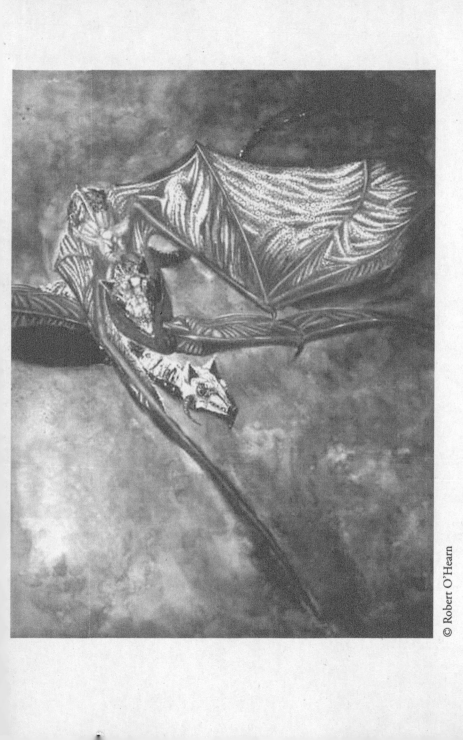

By Royal Proclamation

Here now, the six points of the King's FIRST LAW.

All royal subjects are required to memorize First Law and teach it to their children. The penalty for breaching any point of this law shall be swift and final – as described below:

Point One: Girls are not allowed to leave their homes unless escorted by their father, brothers or husbands and may never travel any further than their neighbouring village.

Point Two: Girls are never to be educated.

Point Three: Girls are not allowed to hunt, fight or engage in any activities that are considered boyish. They may not dress as boys and must never carry weapons of any sort.

Point Four: Unmarried girls are never allowed to visit the palace or approach the king.

Point Five: Girls must be matched to the boy or man they are to marry by the age of twelve. They must be married before the age of thirteen. The day after the marriage ceremony, their husbands must send confirmation to the king.

Point Six: Under no circumstances are girls *ever* to be allowed anywhere near dragons.

Penalties: Girls caught breaking any points from one to five shall be escorted to Lasser Commons where they will face immediate execution. Any girl caught breaking point *six* of First Law shall be escorted to Lasser Commons where she will be severely tortured before execution.

CHAPTER
～ 1 ～

The heavy rain that fell from the stormy skies around them did little to dampen the celebrations of the dragon riders cutting through the thick dark clouds. Everything was perfect.

'We did it!' Kira cheered triumphantly. 'We're free!'

Clutching her dragon Jinx's reins in her hands, Kira celebrated their escape from Lord Dorcon. As she laughed and waved to her brother Dane and his friend Shanks-Spar on their black dragon, Rexor, a very small part of her wished she could have seen the evil lord's face when he realized they'd escaped through Paradon's Eye.

It had been a struggle getting to where they were. Many times she doubted they would ever make it. But they had. They were safely away from Lord Dorcon and his legion of men out to capture them.

Soon, she would travel to the palace of King Arden and fulfil the ancient prophecy foretold by the great wizard Elan. It spoke of a girl, who, like her, dressed as a boy and who, also like her, had long red hair kept in braids and who rode a twin-tailed dragon. The prophecy said she would end the evil monarchy. This warrior girl, this forbidden dragon rider, would restore freedom to the land and finally end the kingdom's terrible First Law.

Kira knew she was that girl. Somehow, some way, she was the one destined to challenge First Law and destroy it. For only when it was destroyed, would she feel that she had succeeded. With the help of her beloved twin-tailed dragon Jinx, and support of her family, Kira would fulfil the prophecy.

It was just a matter of heading back to Paradon's castle to prepare to take on a king.

'Kira,' Dane called excitedly. 'Let's get back to the castle!'

Nodding and waving again, her heart fluttered with excitement that soon there would be peace in the land.

'Kira?' Kahrin said softly as she tapped her lightly on the shoulder.

When Kira looked back, she saw her younger sister sitting forward in the saddlebox looking around. 'Kira, where's Elspeth?'

Kira frowned, 'She's right behind—'

She looked back to where she'd last seen her youngest sister riding with the fox Onnie on the dragon Harmony. Elspeth was no longer there. As her frown deepened, she looked to the right, past Dane and Shanks, and then turned to her left. But no matter where she looked, she couldn't see Elspeth on the large red dragon.

Suddenly gripped with fear, she directed Jinx to fly closer to Rexor.

'Dane, where's Shadow?' Kira used her pet name for her youngest sister. 'She was right behind us, now I can't see her.'

Both Dane and Shanks turned in the saddle and searched the dark sky for signs of Elspeth on Harmony.

'I can't see her!' Dane called. 'Let's go back. Maybe she went down to Paradon's already.'

As Kira directed Jinx to turn around, she knew Elspeth wouldn't do that. They'd spent too long together on the Rogue's Mountain for Elspeth to do something without her.

'Find Shadow, Jinx,' Kira called to her dragon as panic started to grip her heart. 'Where's Shadow?'

Kira watched Jinx reacting to Elspeth's name. Despite the sound of the wind whipping around them

3

and the constant beat of the rain, she could hear Jinx starting to whine. Soon his whines turned into roars. But it wasn't a sound Kira had heard him make before. He was roaring, but it was more with fear than anything else.

Jinx's fear quickly spread through Kira and the rest of her family.

'Kira, let's go down lower,' Dane called. 'Follow us. We can't see through the storm up this high.'

Kira let Dane take the lead as her brother ordered Rexor to go lower in the sky. Behind her, she could hear Kahrin's light voice still calling out for Elspeth. With Jinx keeping close to Rexor's tail, the two dragons made their way down through the thick storm clouds. Kira could barely see the dark blur of Rexor flying ahead as the heavy mist quickly enveloped them.

When they finally burst out of the base of the clouds, Kira's eyes grew wide with shock as she got her first glimpse of the world around her.

Gone was Paradon's castle. Gone were the forests that surrounded it. Instead she looked out in fear to a world full of strange and frightening structures reaching high into the dark grey sky.

'Kira,' Shanks called back to her. 'Where are we?'

Kira look at him and shook her head, 'I don't know!

Something must have gone wrong. Paradon's spell didn't work.'

As Rexor and Jinx flew lower in the sky, they drew closer to the buildings. To Kira, they looked as grey and threatening as the skies. Between the tall structures, she saw wide roads with strange-looking carts. The carts seemed to be moving without the aid of horses, while on either side of the road she saw many people. They were looking up at them and pointing.

'Kahrin, can you see Shadow or Harmony down there?' Kira called back.

'No,' Kahrin responded. 'I can't see Paradon's castle either.'

'Kira,' Shanks called again. 'Where should we go?'

Looking around at the strange world that surrounded them, Kira had no idea how they were going to find Elspeth. 'We circle back and keep looking for Shadow!'

'Kira? Kira is that you? Can you hear me?'

Kira heard a strange voice calling her name. It was difficult to make out over the whipping winds of the storm, but it seemed close by. 'Hello?' she called.

'Kira,' the voice called again.

She looked around for the odd voice but couldn't see where it came from. But when it started again, Kira realized it was coming from the pendant around her neck. She pulled the dragon's-claw amulet out from under her top and held it up close to her ear.

'It's me, Paradon. Can you hear me?'

'Paradon? Is that really you?'

'Thank the stars!' the voice cried. 'I've finally found you.'

Kira looked forward and called to Shanks. Then she pointed to her pendant. 'It's Paradon!'

Shanks shrugged and indicated he couldn't understand her. As the wind changed direction and the rain intensified, she could barely hear herself. Searching around, she pointed to the flat roof of the tallest building nearest them.

'Land on that tower over there!' she shouted.

She then watched as Shanks instructed Dane to take Rexor down to the nearest building and land on the flat roof. Following closely behind, Jinx was soon touching down beside them.

With her back and side still aching from the recent sword wound she received while she and Elspeth were freeing the girls of Lasser Commons, she carefully undid her harness and slowly climbed out of the saddlebox. Standing on Jinx's wing, she helped Kahrin climb down as well. In the excitement of their escape she'd forgotten her wound, but now as she moved it started to burn like it did the first few days after it happened.

As she crossed over to Dane and Shanks, her fear and confusion was reflected on their faces.

'Where is Paradon?' Dane asked.

Kira held up the pendant for everyone to hear. 'Paradon, where are you? What's happened?'

The wizard's voice explained quickly. 'Everyone, listen to me very carefully. You are in terrible danger. You must leave the city now and head to the Rogue's Mountain. I'm at the top in your old meadow. Come to me and you'll be safe.'

'But where are we?' Shanks asked as he looked around at the strange, tall buildings surrounding them. 'What is this place?'

'It is the same place you've just left. Only time has changed.'

'Paradon, we don't understand,' Kira said as she looked at the confused faces of Dane, Shanks and Kahrin.

'Kira, you and the others were in the Eye far too long. You didn't just travel three seasons into the future, you travelled over three thousand!'

'What?' everyone exclaimed.

'Three thousand,' Paradon repeated. 'This is a dangerous and brutal time. There are no dragons here, only man-made machines capable of causing terrible pain and destruction. You must get on your dragons and get out of there. If they catch you, there's no telling what they'll do. I'm sure they want to capture Jinx and Rexor even more than you.'

'But what about Shadow?' Kira demanded. 'Paradon, we can't find her! I'm not leaving here until we do.'

There was a long pause and then a deep intake of breath. 'You won't find her,' he said finally. 'Elspeth isn't here. She didn't come through the Eye with you.'

'Not here?' Dane asked. 'Where is she?'

'I can't explain now. But I promise you she's safe.'

'I still don't understand. What went wrong?' Kira asked.

'I went wrong,' Paradon said darkly. 'I'm incompetent. But I promise you all, I'll fix this somehow. To do that, you must get off that roof and come to the mountain! Even as we speak, armed choppers and soldiers are heading right for you. You must go.'

'What do you mean? What are armed choppers?' Shanks asked.

'Instead of using dragons, the people of this time have created awful war machines made of metal. Some can fly. They can go faster than any dragon and are more deadly. If they catch you, there is no defence.'

'Then we're as good as dead,' Dane said.

'Not yet,' Paradon called. 'The choppers are faster than dragons, but they're not as agile. Use your skills and let the dragons do what they do best and you should be able to outfly them. But you must get moving!'

'Paradon, how can we find you?' Kira called desperately as she looked around at the strange world. 'Nothing is the same. Where is the Rogue's Mountain?'

'No further than it was before,' Paradon explained. 'This city rose up on the ruins of my old castle. I told you, only time has changed, not place.'

Still unsure of what the wizard meant, Kira's eyes scanned over the countless rooftops spreading out before them. In every direction she looked, she saw people gathering on the roofs and pointing at them. But no matter what direction she looked, she had no idea where the Rogue's Mountain was. If this was where Paradon's castle once stood, it still gave her no clue as to the direction in which they should now fly.

'I still don't know how to find the mountain from here,' she said desperately. She looked pleadingly over to Dane and Shanks. 'Which direction should we go?'

Both her brother and Shanks shrugged as they too watched the gathering crowds.

Finally Paradon spoke. 'I'm using the Eye and can see you. Trust me, I can lead you here. But you must get your dragons into the air before it's too late.'

Suddenly from behind them, the doors to the roof burst open and soldiers charged out. Kira had never seen anything like them before. They were dressed in strange, shiny black armour that completely covered them from head to foot. Without eye slits, she wondered how they could see through their black helmets. In their hands, they didn't carry swords or even bows. Instead they clutched strange things she'd never seen before.

'They've got guns!' Paradon shouted. 'Everyone, put your hands in the air. Show them you surrender.'

'Surrender?' Shanks cried as he drew his sword and took a defensive stance. 'I never surrender.'

'You do now,' Paradon warned. 'Shanks, drop your weapon. You don't know this world. They don't need to be close to you to kill you. Trust me, please. Your sword and your armour are useless against their weapons. For the protection of everyone, do as I say and you'll get out of this alive!'

Kira watched Shanks hesitantly lower his sword down to the ground and raise his hands in the air.

Soon more soldiers filed out on to the roof. Standing still and holding her own arms up high, she couldn't see their faces to know where they were looking. But from the angle of their heads, they had to be looking at the dragons.

As the soldiers drew closer, Kira heard Jinx start with a low rumbling growl. Stealing a glance back to him, she saw his twin tails start to whip the air as he took a threatening step forward.

'Calm down, Jinx,' Kira called. Then she turned back to the men. 'Stay back. He doesn't like strangers.'

'They can't understand you,' Paradon called. 'Kira, you don't speak the same language any more.'

'Then you tell them!' Kira snapped. 'Jinx looks like he's getting ready to attack. You've got to warn them.'

A moment later, Kira heard strange words coming from her pendant. For the first time since they'd arrived, the men turned and concentrated on her. When Paradon finished translating the warning to the soldiers, they raised their weapons and pointed them at

Kira. Soon one stepped forward and shouted strange angry words at her.

Immediately Paradon started to speak again. But from the look of the soldier's raised weapons, Kira saw it was making the situation worse. 'Paradon, it's not working! Warn them again. Tell them to stop!'

Before Paradon could speak another word, Jinx let out a ferocious angry roar. Looking back, Kira watched him rear up on his hind legs and open his large blue wings. Beside him, Rexor did the same, though the armour restricting his mouth kept him from roaring.

Torn between looking at Jinx and turning back to the soldiers, Kira screamed as they raised their strange weapons to the dragons. As she watched, loud steady popping sounds filled the air and sparks of fire came out of the end of the weapons.

'Everyone, get down!' Paradon cried. 'They're shooting at the dragons. If they hit you, you'll die!'

Before everyone made it to the ground, both Jinx and Rexor lunged forward. Carefully racing around them, the dragons had only one target in mind. The soldiers.

As the dragons attacked the armed men, Kira heard terrified cries coming from their black helmets, reminding her of what she'd heard when she and Elspeth were at Lasser Commons and Elspeth had used Jinx to attack the guards.

Trapped on the rooftop, the men's weapons were useless against the two rampaging dragons. As they scattered and tried to get away, Kira saw Jinx's two whipping tails knock several men over the side of the building.

Kira quickly pulled Kahrin's head to her chest so she wouldn't see the awful sight of the dragons killing the soldiers. Lying behind her, Dane and Shanks spoke in shocked disbelief as both Jinx and Rexor came to their defence.

'Dragons don't do that,' Dane cried. 'They don't care who they attack! They should have gone for us as well. Why didn't they?'

'You still don't understand, do you?' Kira challenged, turning back to her brother. 'Jinx would never attack us. Nor would he let Rexor. But you saw Rexor. He didn't want to hurt us. Shadow says he likes you, Dane. Why can't you believe it?'

'Because they're dragons!' Shanks cried.

As the last soldier fell beneath the vicious claws of Rexor, Kira sat up and looked at the terrible sight around her. All the soldiers were dead. Some were still on the roof, while others had been knocked or thrown off the side.

'Keep your eyes closed,' Kira said gently to her delicate sister. 'Don't look.'

'I'm all right,' Kahrin said reaching to pull Kira's hand from her eyes. 'I want to see.'

Kira hesitated for a moment before releasing Kahrin. Climbing to her feet she watched her sister closely as she too stood up. After looking around, Kahrin calmly stepped over to Jinx.

'Careful, Kahrin,' Dane warned as he eyed the blue dragon warily.

At her approach, Jinx turned and faced Kahrin. A moment ago he had been a ferocious monster killing anyone he could find. But as Kahrin approached he lowered his head to her, inviting her to scratch behind his ears.

'Thank you, Jinx,' Kahrin said lightly and she put her arms around his thick neck.

Kira watched her sister embracing Jinx with fascination. She realized this was the first time since she'd been rescued from Lasser that she had shown any emotion towards the dragon. Actually, it was one of the few times she had showed any emotion at all.

As for Jinx, despite what Paradon said about twin-tailed dragons only liking their riders, her beloved blue dragon seemed to like Kahrin just fine.

'This isn't over yet!' Paradon's voice warned from the pendant. 'The choppers are almost there. All of you get off that roof now!'

Realizing the danger, Dane cautiously stepped up to Rexor. The tall black dragon calmly looked at him, showing no signs of hostility. Carefully reaching for the reins, he climbed into the saddle. Shanks was quick to follow and climbed on behind him.

Stepping up to Jinx, Kira kissed him lightly on the snout before helping Kahrin climb back into the saddlebox.

Once they were all seated, Kira looked around at the dead soldiers on the rooftop a final time. She regretted that they had died so needlessly. But she knew she had done all she could to stop it. They just wouldn't listen.

'Kira, you lead and we'll follow,' Dane called as he directed Rexor over to the edge of the building.

Nodding, Kira turned back to Kahrin to make sure she was strapped in. Then she gave the reins a light tug and ordered Jinx to fly off the building.

CHAPTER
~2~

Elspeth felt very close to panic as she looked around at the unfamiliar world beneath her. Seated on Harmony with the fox, Onnie, still in his pouch on her back, she desperately searched the skies looking for her sisters, brother and Shanks. But wherever she looked she could see no traces of them.

'Where are they?' she cried to Onnie as he too looked around searching for the others. 'What's happened?'

Soaring through the clear, blue, cloudless sky, Elspeth looked down and couldn't see Paradon's castle either. All they passed over was lush green forest. Everything she knew was gone.

'Where is everyone?' she cried. 'We were right behind them.'

As well as her own fear, Elspeth could feel tension coming from the fox. Finally Onnie threw back his head and howled mournfully.

'What do you mean Paradon messed up again? How?'

After a few short yips from Onnie, Elspeth stole a look over her shoulder. 'I don't understand. We were right behind them. How could we get separated? Where are we?'

With so much fear and confusion crashing down on her, Elspeth felt tears rush to her eyes. 'Onnie, tell me what's happened.'

Instead of a clear answer, Onnie instructed Elspeth to turn Harmony around and head in the opposite direction.

'We can't leave!' Elspeth cried, as she was quickly overwhelmed in panic. 'We have to stay here. Kira will find us, I know she will!'

Elspeth's ear was filled with more yips as Onnie insisted they leave the area. He had an idea and needed to be sure. If Kira and the others suddenly appeared, he knew they would have the same idea and would follow them to their destination.

Elspeth could no longer see clearly as her tears blurred her vision. 'Where do you want to go?'

When he answered she looked at him again. 'Rogue's Mountain? Onnie, we can't. The Rogue is still there, he'll get us!'

When he suggested it was the only solution, Elspeth

shook her head. 'You're wrong. Paradon's castle is here somewhere. We just have to find it.'

Onnie refused to say more and kept insisting that Elspeth direct Harmony back to the Rogue's Mountain. Knowing there was no changing his mind once it was set on something, Elspeth searched the sky a final time before surrendering. Turning Harmony around, she saw the mountain rising in the far distance.

'Kira will find us, won't she?' Elspeth asked as tears continued to flow down her cheeks.

Leaning forward, Onnie gently licked them away. He then made several soft yips, promising that he would protect her and that somehow Paradon would find them.

Falling silent, Elspeth reached up and stroked Onnie's head as it rested on her shoulder. But even though he promised everything would be all right, as she scanned the empty skies around her, she didn't share his confidence. They were alone, and they were lost.

CHAPTER
~3~

'Don't go higher than the rooftops,' Paradon's voice warned from Kira's pendant. 'The choppers can't follow if you stay between the buildings. With luck you can still get away.'

Kira followed Paradon's instructions and directed Jinx down almost to ground level. Beneath them, the strange carts with no horses stopped as people poured out to point and stare up at them. The people walking on the road threw themselves down to the ground and cried out in terror at the sight of the two dragons soaring just over their heads.

'Go left at the next road,' Paradon called.

Kira turned in her seat and told Kahrin to pass along the message to Dane as he had Rexor following closely behind them.

As Kahrin started to call back to Dane, Kira looked forward again and tried to ignore the strange sights and sounds of what Paradon called the city. At the next crossroads, she pulled on the reins and directed Jinx to change directions and veer to the left.

'Keep going straight until I tell you,' Paradon called.

'How far?' Kira asked. 'I still can't see the mountain.'

'You will come upon it rather quickly,' Paradon said. 'The city is huge and comes all the way to the base of the mountain. There are no trees and no wildlife left except for what's on this mountain. It's all been used up.'

'What happened?' Kira cried realizing the world she once knew was truly gone.

'I'll tell you when you get there. Now, I want you to count roads. When you reach the fourth on your right, I want you to fly down it.'

Once again, Kira told Kahrin to pass along the message.

As she concentrated on counting roads, Kira became aware of strange, loud thwumping sounds filling the air around them. Looking up, she felt her heart skipping beats. Just above the rooftops, she saw several of the black flying machines that Paradon had mentioned. They didn't have any beating wings and nothing on them seemed to move except for something spinning on the top of their bodies. But however they stayed in the air, they were somehow keeping pace with Jinx and Rexor.

'It's the choppers,' Paradon warned. 'Kira, tell Kahrin to warn the others. Don't go any higher in the air until I tell you to. They carry terrible weapons. But more than that, the rotors that keep them flying could be deadly if the dragons were struck by them. Just keep low and I'm sure you'll be fine.'

'Can't you stop them like you did the dragon knights at your castle?' While she spoke, Kira tried to count roads and keep an eye on the choppers overhead.

'I will when the time is right. For now, just concentrate on following my instructions. You are almost at the fourth road. Prepare to turn right.'

As Kira turned Jinx down the fourth road, she screamed. They were heading straight for a tall red horseless cart!

'Up, Jinx!' she shouted, drawing back on the reins. As Jinx responded to the command, he roared in fear and rage. Skimming over the top of the tall vehicle, Kira cringed at the sound of the dragon's sharp claws raking along its roof.

'What was that?' she cried as she turned back to see the red vehicle stopping and people pouring out.

'A public transport vehicle,' Paradon explained. 'Be

careful, Kira, there are lots of them in the city. Take the dragons up a bit higher, but don't go near the choppers.'

In the excitement, Kira had nearly forgotten about their pursuers. Stealing a glance up, she inhaled sharply as one of the black flying machines started to descend between the tall buildings.

'He's coming down for us!' Kira cried.

'The fool!' Paradon shouted. 'He'll be killed.'

'So will we if he catches us!'

'I don't think they want to kill you,' Paradon said. 'They won't risk hurting the dragons.'

No sooner were the words out of the pendant than Kira heard similar popping sounds to the ones the soldiers' weapons made on the roof. But these sounds were louder and somehow bigger.

'They do want to kill us!' she cried.

Looking up, Kira saw the big black flying machine drawing closer as it came down between the buildings, trying to reach them.

'Go left on the next road!' Paradon ordered. 'Jinx and Rexor can outfly him, I know they can!'

Kira prayed Paradon was right as she quickly directed Jinx to turn left. At the approach of the next crossroads, she had him go right.

'Is Dane still with us?' she called back to Kahrin.

'Yes,' her sister answered. 'The chopper is further back, but it's still chasing us.'

Despite her fear, Kira was getting angry as well. Those machines were trying to hurt her family and dragons. Paradon said Jinx could outfly them. Well, she was going to give her blue dragon the chance.

As each road approached, Kira would direct Jinx to veer down it. It wasn't long before the dragon understood what she was doing. Without needing further direction, Jinx roared as he flew through the caverns of the tall city, easily evading the pursuing choppers.

Letting him have his head, Kira relaxed her grip on the reins and turned back to Dane. Rexor was flying confidently behind them, keeping up with Jinx as they manoeuvred along the city roads.

As they changed directions time and time again, the choppers lagged further behind. But when they rounded one sharp turn, they heard a terrible explosion behind them. Looking back quickly, Kira saw that the chopper that had flown down between the buildings hadn't quite made the turn and had smashed into the corner building.

There was no time to cheer or celebrate their success. As they neared yet another corner the choppers overhead suddenly opened fire.

Kira and Kahrin's screams mixed together as they heard the sickening sounds of the weapons and watched as Jinx's beautiful blue wings took the full impact. The skin was being cut to ribbons and blood flowed from his wounds. His roars turned to howls as he tried to stay in the air. Beneath them on the road, countless people were being struck down by the chopper's awful assault.

'They're trying to disable the dragons!' Paradon cried. 'Kira, get Jinx up in the air. We've got to get him to the mountain.'

'But the choppers are up there!'

'I didn't want to use my powers, but I will. Get the dragons higher in the air before they crash.'

Trusting Paradon, Kira tightened her grip on the reins. 'Up, Jinx,' she shouted. 'Just a bit longer, baby. Fly up for me!'

Stealing a glance behind her, Kira saw that Rexor had been shot even worse than Jinx. Huge tears in the skin between the bones of his wings flapped in the wind as he struggled to keep flying. Yet despite their awful wounds, both dragons did everything asked of them.

'That's it,' Paradon coached. 'Higher, get them higher. I'm going to cast a spell to stop the choppers!'

'Higher, baby!' Kira cried. 'Go higher.'

'Kira, look!' Kahrin called from behind her.

Stealing a glance up, Kira watched as, one by one, the choppers started to explode. Soon huge chunks of debris flew into the air and crashed down on the rooftops and roads around them in great plumes of smoke and fire.

'Keep climbing,' Paradon called. 'I don't want you hurt by falling debris.'

As Jinx finally made it to the level of the rooftops, Kira saw that there were no choppers left. Directing her wounded dragon through the rainy dark-grey skies, she finally saw their destination rising in the distance. 'There!' she cried as she turned in her seat and pointed. 'Dane, over there! The Rogue's Mountain!'

Both Kira and Kahrin watched Dane give the signal that he understood. But it was brief as he fought to keep Rexor moving. Looking at the black dragon, Kira could see that he was suffering greatly and struggling to keep flying.

'Paradon,' she called into her pendant, 'Rexor is badly wounded. Can you help him?'

'Not without risking hurting your brother and Shanks,' he replied. 'Just keep going, it's not far now.'

Keeping her attention split between staying on

course for the mountain and watching Rexor behind them, Kira feared they weren't going to make it. Rexor was losing a lot of blood and flying erratically in the sky. She could see Jinx too was bleeding from all the holes shot through his wings. But as bad as Jinx was hurt, Rexor was much worse.

Yet despite their wounds, both dragons kept flying.

Checking the sky, Kira couldn't see any more choppers coming after them. Instead she saw other noisy flying machines rising into the air from the base of the Rogue's Mountain.

'Paradon, there are things flying up from the mountain.'

Kira could hear Paradon cursing. Finally he said, 'They're jet fighters. There's a military base at the bottom of the mountain. They've been trying to get in here for ages, but I cast a spell that put a shield over the mountain to keep them out.'

'What about us? Will it let us in?'

'Of course, that's the reason I cast the spell in the first place. I knew I would find you eventually and when I did, I wanted you to have some place safe to land. Mind you, those fighters are not making this any easier.'

Kira stole another quick glance back to Rexor. Despite Dane's best efforts, the dragon was losing height.

Turning forward again, she could see the mountain wasn't far now.

'They're coming!' Kahrin cried from the seat behind her.

Kira already knew the fighters were coming. She was facing them. Turning in her seat, she tried to reassure her sister. 'It will be all right, I promise. Paradon won't let them hurt us.'

As she watched, Kira saw the fighters racing towards them. They were moving faster than anything she could imagine. Before she could count the fingers on one hand, they had zoomed right over their heads, so low she could almost touch their silver undersides.

The sounds of the passing jet fighters and whoosh of the wind they made caused both dragons to falter in the sky.

'It's all right, Jinx,' Kira called. 'Just keep flying to the mountain.'

'Kira!' Dane shouted.

Turning back, both Kira and her sister screamed as they saw Rexor thrashing in the sky. The dragon was struggling to flap his wings, but the tears in the skin and open wounds were proving too much. He wasn't going to make it.

CHAPTER
~ 4 ~

Back when Elspeth and Kira first left the Rogue's Mountain and met Paradon, the journey to his castle had taken several days. But they had been on foot. With Harmony, the journey was much quicker.

As they approached the mountain, Elspeth looked around and could see no sign of the Rogue or his offspring.

'Maybe after Blue died, they left the mountain,' she suggested.

Directing Harmony to fly up the side, she immediately noticed a big change in the mountain. Soaring over the highest peak, she looked down and couldn't find the meadow where they had once lived. All she could see was the sharp rocky top.

'This is the Rogue's Mountain, isn't it?' she asked Onnie, looking around for another mountain range.

In answer, the fox threw back his head and howled mournfully.

'What do you mean?' she asked, looking back at him. 'How could it change?'

As she continued to look around, she finally saw something she recognized. Beneath them was the plateau where the Rogue and Blue had first fought the three dragon knights. Directing Harmony down, they landed on the rocky shelf.

'I just don't understand,' Elspeth said as she carefully climbed down from Harmony's saddle. Helping Onnie out of the pouch on her back, they started to look around. 'This is where the Rogue fought the other dragons, right?'

When Onnie agreed it was, Elspeth looked around and then pointed. 'And over there is the trail we took up when we collected everything from the dead knights and dragons.'

Once again, Onnie agreed.

Telling Harmony to stay and rest, Elspeth and Onnie crossed over to the trail. 'It still looks the same,' she said as she started to climb. When she reached the top, she was on the same path they had taken leading to the large crack in the wall that led to their secret meadow. Over to her left, she saw the cluster of trees the Rogue had clipped his wing on. But as she walked further along, there was no crack leading to the meadow.

'It's gone,' said Elspeth as her hand trailed along the cold rocky wall where the crack should be. 'What could have happened?'

At her feet, Onnie howled and then suddenly dashed further along the trail. He was soon disappearing around a sharp bend.

'Onnie, wait!' Elspeth cried. 'What's wrong? Where are you going?'

Running to keep up with him, Elspeth rounded the bend and saw the fox standing at the edge and looking into the far distance. As she approached, he started howling again.

'What is it?'

After a few short yips, Onnie stared up at her. He leaped up into her open arms and together they continued to look out from the top of the mountain. Beneath them, Elspeth saw the thick, dense forest. In the distance, she saw the smoke rising from several small fires. She looked back down on Onnie. 'I don't understand. What are we looking at?'

When the fox yipped again, Elspeth frowned. 'That can't be a village. Our village was the closest to the Rogue's Mountain, and it's in the other direction. Besides, with the war on, Paradon said King Arden has gathered all the people from the villages to work at the palace. Those are just small fires.'

In her arms, Onnie not only insisted it was a village, but added that if it was the one he thought it was, he knew it very well.

'How can that be?' Elspeth asked. 'I don't remember anyone living on this side of the mountain. We'd have seen them when we lived here.'

In an answer Elspeth didn't understand, Onnie explained that the village he once knew had been destroyed long before she was born. And if this was the same, there was a wizard called Elan living there who they needed to see immediately.

Elspeth frowned and looked down on Onnie in confusion and despair. 'Please, Onnie, I don't understand. How can that be the same village?'

Elspeth listened carefully as Onnie tried to explain what he believed happened. Many times he had to repeat himself to make her understand. Finally she held him closely to her chest. 'So, Paradon's spell went wrong?'

Onnie yipped.

'And you're sure we didn't go three seasons in the future?' When Onnie yipped again Elspeth looked at the smoke rising from the village. 'You think that is a village from long ago?' After a long pause, Elspeth looked at him. 'But Onnie, if that's true, where is everyone else?'

The answer to that question Onnie didn't know. All he could tell her was they had to go to the village so he could be certain.

When Elspeth heard this, she shook her head violently. 'No, we can't! If you are wrong and they see us with Harmony, Lord Dorcon will find out and catch us.'

In her arms, Onnie yipped again.

'How can we hide her? She's not a small dragon I can keep in my pocket.'

The argument continued for some time until Elspeth finally surrendered to the will of the fox. 'All right, we'll go down there and try to find Elan,' she said. 'But if I get in trouble, it will be your fault!'

With the decision made, Elspeth carried Onnie back down the trail to Harmony. As they approached, the red dragon lowered her head and started to whine.

Stepping up to her, Elspeth stroked her armoured snout. 'I would never leave you, Harmony,' she soothed. 'We just had to go and see where we are.'

Immediately the dragon calmed under Elspeth's touch.

'Good girl,' Elspeth said. Then she helped Onnie get

back into the pouch on her back before she climbed up to the dragon's saddle.

'All right, Harmony,' Elspeth called. 'Let's fly down to the village.'

Soon they were leaping off the plateau and heading higher in the sky. Coming around the side of the mountain, they flew closer to where the smoke was rising from the trees. Beneath them, Elspeth saw the tops of cottages and signs of a small village.

'It is a village,' she said, as she reached up to scratch Onnie's head. 'I'm sorry I doubted you.'

With Onnie resting his paws on her shoulder, he licked her hand. Then he instructed her to have Harmony skirt around the village to avoid being seen.

As they soared in the sky, Elspeth finally saw a clearing on the far side of the village. 'Down there,' she called to Harmony, not needing to use the reins. 'Let's land in that clearing.'

When Harmony lightly touched down on the ground, Elspeth climbed from the saddle. 'I hope you're right,' she said to Onnie.

The three walked together through the clearing until they reached the outskirts of the village. Onnie ordered everyone to stop, and after a few short yips he darted into the trees and disappeared.

'Onnie wants us to wait here for a bit,' Elspeth explained to Harmony as she scratched the dragon's ears. 'He says he wants to see if it is the same village he remembers.' She paused before adding, 'If it is the same, I think we're in big trouble.'

Elspeth waited patiently with the dragon. Before long, Onnie reappeared and called her forward.

'You have to stay here, Harmony,' she said. 'Onnie and I are going to the village and we don't want the people to see you. Will you stay here and wait for me?'

In answer to her request, Elspeth watched Harmony settle down in the soft pine needles of the forest floor. As she started to walk away with Onnie, she called back to the dragon, 'We won't be long.'

Walking in silence, Elspeth cradled Onnie in her arms. Soon the trees thinned and she could see the village spreading out before them. Thatched cottages lined the main, muddy path running through it. Outside some of the homes, villagers sold their vegetables and wares on rough trestle tables.

As they walked further into the village and passed a gathering of people, Elspeth noticed them stop talking and stand and stare at the strange newcomers. Clutching Onnie to her chest, she heard him growl softly at the people who pointed and stared. She looked down at him and saw the skin drawn back from his teeth and the angry expression on his face.

'I thought you liked it here?' she said softly.

Onnie's growls increased in response.

'What do you mean, you have bad memories? Of what?'

The fox refused to explain as he continued to growl at the people they passed. Instead he instructed Elspeth to continue walking until they came to the very last cottage at the far end of the village.

As they drew near the final cottage, Elspeth noticed that it was on its own, set very far apart from the others. Outside the cottage, many herbs and plants hung upside down to dry in the open air. The cottage itself looked terribly out of place and unused as heavy dark curtains blocked the windows and old thick cobwebs covered the outside.

'Are you sure this is the right place?' Elspeth asked nervously as she stared at the odd-looking structure.

When Onnie agreed, she stepped closer to the door. Directly above the threshold, a large raven was sitting in a huge nest that had twigs and straw hanging down. As they approached, the raven started to caw and flap its wings threateningly.

'Stop that,' Elspeth said. 'There's no need to be nasty.'

Immediately the raven looked at Elspeth and stopped. It cocked its black head to the side as if trying to figure her out. Then it flew out of its nest and landed neatly on her shoulder.

As Elspeth looked up and concentrated on the raven, the door to the cottage burst open. 'What's going on out here? What's all this noise?'

Startled, Elspeth found herself facing a very tall man with short light hair and a stern expression on his face.

'I'm sorry. I was just talking to your bird.'

The man looked at Elspeth curiously. Then he looked at the raven sitting contentedly on her shoulder and the fox being held in her arms.

'Corvellis, what are you doing there?' he demanded, though his tone was softening. The bird cawed again, then flew on to his outstretched arm as he looked at Elspeth. 'I'm sorry, did she hurt you?'

Elspeth shook her head. 'No, she was very sweet after I spoke to her. She's lovely. You said her name was Corvellis?'

'Indeed it is, though I'm rather surprised by her behaviour. Usually she attacks visitors to our door.' The man then lifted his arm so the raven could return to her nest. When she was settled, he looked back to Elspeth. 'But by the looks of your red friend there, I would think you have a special charm with animals.'

Elspeth shrugged and smiled. 'I just like them. That's all.'

'Who is it, Father?'

From behind the tall man came a boy. He might have been her age or maybe a bit older. He had dark hair and bright shining eyes.

'I'm not sure,' said the tall man. Then he looked back to Elspeth. 'Who might you be?'

'I'm Elspeth, and this is Onnie.'

The moment Elspeth said Onnie's name, the man's eyes darted to the fox. He took a step back, and warned his son away from the door.

'Onnie-Astra!' he said angrily. Then he started to shout, 'Get that evil monster away from my home!'

CHAPTER
~5~

'Dane, Shanks, hold on!' Kira cried. Then she called into her pendant, 'Paradon, please help them: Rexor is falling!'

From her pendant, Kira could hear Paradon casting spell after spell. But nothing was working. Rexor started to spin in the sky as he fell.

In the distance, Kira could also see the jet fighters banking and coming back for them. Rexor was already going down. One more pass from those monster machines and she knew Jinx would follow.

'Please, Paradon!' Kira cried. 'They're coming!'

When she heard the final words from the last spell spoken, Kira felt the air around them change. The rain stopped falling on her face and the wind stopped whipping her hair. Looking back to Rexor, she saw he had stopped falling and was being cradled in unseen hands. Soon the black dragon was lifted higher in the air and brought closer to Jinx.

No longer needing to flap his tired and wounded wings, Jinx let them hang down at his sides as they were drawn towards the top of the mountain.

'Paradon, it's working!' Kira cheered.

Behind them, the jet fighters approached. But as they buzzed past the two stricken dragons, nothing happened. The winds in their wakes did not touch them nor move them in the sky.

'Keep going!' Kira called as the unseen hands continued to carry them up the side of the mountain. Soon they were passing over the top rim. Sucking in her breath, Kira saw the first familiar sight she'd seen since arriving in this mad world. Her meadow.

It was lush and green, spreading out beneath them. As they drew near, she saw the same fruit trees that she and Elspeth had picked so long ago. The small pond was still there as water gently trickled down the side of the rocky wall. Across from the pond she saw the vegetable garden. It was as though time had not touched this place at all. Nothing had changed.

Standing in the centre of the meadow was Paradon. Sitting on a tall plinth before him was the large grey boulder he called his 'Eye to the World', which he used to cast stronger spells and see events that were happening all around him. Still in the same tattered cloak, his hood was drawn up over his head and his hands were raised in the air.

Drawing her eyes back to Rexor, Kira could see the dragon's body was limp and his eyes were closed. Fear clutched her heart. Was he dead?

A moment later, both dragons lightly touched down on the soft grass of the meadow. Quickly undoing her harness, Kira ignored the searing pain in her side as she climbed out of the saddlebox and jumped down to the ground.

'Paradon!' she cried as she ran over to the cloaked figure. When she drew near and was about to embrace the wizard, she immediately noticed a great change in him. He was badly hunched over and now much shorter than her. He was leaning heavily on his staff, as though he would fall without it.

'Paradon?' Kira asked. 'It is you, isn't it?'

An impossibly old and gnarled hand reached up to push back the hood of the cloak. 'It's me, child,' Paradon said gently.

When the wizard's face was revealed, Kira sucked in her breath. There were so many wrinkles she couldn't see his nose. He had no hair on his head, and no beard. His eyebrows were long and hanging down the sides of his face. The only thing she recognized about the wizard were his sparkling blue eyes.

'Paradon, what happened to you?' Kira cried as she drew closer and embraced him.

Paradon chuckled, and it was the same sound Kira knew and loved. 'Time, my dear child. Time has happened to me. But don't worry about me; your dragons are in trouble.'

Releasing him, she turned back to Jinx. He was whining as Kahrin stroked his blue head where it lay on the ground. His wings were stretched out either side of him. As she approached, she could see the terrible damage caused by the chopper's awful weapons.

'It's all right, baby,' she said gently as she bent down and kissed him on the snout. Scratching behind his ears, she leaned closer. 'We'll make you feel much better very soon.'

Beside Jinx, Kira saw that Dane and Shanks were on the ground and looking at Rexor. Like Jinx, his wounded wings were stretched out, but unlike Jinx, Rexor didn't move or make a sound.

'Is he alive?' Kira asked, as she left Jinx and stepped over to her brother.

'Barely,' Dane said. 'I don't know how he managed

as long as he did. But now, I don't think there is a lot we can do for him.'

Beside him, Shanks stumbled and struggled to stay on his feet. 'I don't think there's a lot you can do for either of us,' he said as his voice started to fade. He held up his hands to show they were covered in blood. 'We're both in a bit of a mess.'

Shanks staggered forward as his eyes rolled back in his head. Finally he collapsed to the ground.

CHAPTER
~ 6 ~

'Shanks!' Dane cried and he knelt down beside his friend. 'Shanks!'

'He's been shot,' Paradon said as he quickly inspected the knight. 'Quickly, Dane, get his armour and top off. We've got to stop that bleeding.'

He then turned to Kira. 'I'm living in your old cave. Please take Kahrin with you and get my medicine chest. It's in the kitchen area. Also look around; you'll find some mixing bowls. Oh, and there is a jug of water on the table; bring that as well. Go now and be quick!'

Without pause, Kira called Kahrin forward. Running towards her old cave, she instinctively looked up the rocky wall, as though checking for the Rogue. But the dragon wasn't there. He was from another age. A time long passed. Even the waste pile was gone. Now the green grass of the meadow went right up to the entrance of the cave.

'It's down here,' she said to Kahrin. 'This is where Shadow and I lived when we were here on the mountain. It's where I found Jinx.'

Racing down the trail to the upper level of the cave, memories came flooding back to Kira. Despite living with the threat from the Rogue and Blue, she and Elspeth had been happy here.

Passing down into the lower level, Kira was immediately struck by the changes in her old home. It was no longer wild and raw. This cave had comforts she never imagined possible, including several of Paradon's favourite things from his castle as well as many items she didn't recognize at all.

'It's over here,' Kahrin called.

Snapped out of her thoughts, Kira followed Kahrin over to Paradon's kitchen area and found his herb chest lying on the same oak table that had been in the castle's kitchen. Kira then found several large mixing bowls. Gathering everything together, they left the cave and rushed back to where Paradon was helping Dane remove Shanks' jerkin.

At their approach, Paradon nodded. 'Very good, bring it here.'

Soon the wizard was mixing the healing medicines together into a thick paste while speaking soft magic

44

words. With Dane's help, Shanks was rolled over on to his stomach.

Kira sucked in her breath when she saw the two large holes in the smooth skin of his back. He was losing so much blood she didn't think he could survive it.

'I've worked with the doctors at the battlefront,' Dane said as he inspected the holes in his friend's back, 'and I thought I'd seen every kind of wound there is. But I've never seen anything like this before.'

'I had prayed you never would,' Paradon said. 'Those machines are capable of doing much worse. Now, Dane, listen to me very carefully. I am going to use magic to remove the bullets that are still in him and repair the damage on the inside. When I do, I need you to pack his wounds with this paste and then put the bandages on him. The rest will be up to Shanks.'

'What can I do?' Kira softly asked as she looked down on Shanks' limp form. Fear clutched her heart when she saw how pale he had become.

Paradon watched her for a moment before saying, 'Shanks is a strong lad. I'm sure he'll be fine. The best thing you can do right now is see to Jinx and Rexor. They need you. Dane and I will take good care of our friend here. You and Kahrin take some of this medicine and spread it on the dragons' wounds.'

Kira felt torn. She knew Jinx needed her. So did Rexor. But she couldn't draw herself away from Shanks.

'It's all right, Kira,' Dane said. 'I know he won't die. He's too stubborn to. Please help the dragons.'

'Come on, Kira,' Kahrin said softly, as she reached down to scoop the medicinal paste into two other bowls. 'Jinx needs us.'

Kira looked at her sister's face and saw concern for the dragon in her eyes. She nodded and reluctantly drew herself away from Shanks. Crossing over to Jinx, Kira saw that his head was still down on the ground but his eyes were clear and sharp. As she approached, he lifted his head to her and started to whine.

'I know it hurts, baby,' she said softly as she stroked his snout. 'We'll make you better.'

'What about Rexor?' Kahrin asked. 'He looks dead.'

Kira's eyes left Jinx and concentrated on the black dragon. Rexor was down. His head was flat on the ground and his eyes were shut. As she watched his side, she saw that his breathing was dangerously shallow. She realized he needed her now even more than Jinx.

She turned back to Kahrin. 'Do you think you could work on Jinx while I see to Rexor?'

Kahrin's eyes drifted over to the black dragon. Finally she nodded.

Taking her own bowl of medicine, Kira crossed to Rexor. He was a mess. She didn't know where to start. Both his wings had been ripped to shreds. But it was the big holes cutting right through the heavy armour on his sides that worried her most.

'It's all right, Rexor,' she said softly, realizing the dragon probably couldn't hear her. 'Just hold on, we'll help you.'

As her eyes drew up to the saddle, she saw more blood. But it wasn't dragon's blood. This was from Shanks. He had been shot while they were flying, but hadn't told Dane.

Stealing a glance back to Paradon and her brother, she saw the old wizard holding his hands over Shanks' open wounds. A moment later, she saw two pieces of metal rise out of the wounds. Immediately after, Dane packed the holes with the medicine and started wrapping bandages around him.

When they finished, Paradon sat back on his heels. 'That's all we can do for the moment. We just have to wait for the medicine to work its own magic.'

With Shanks sorted, Kira called to the wizard. 'Paradon, I need your help. I can't get to Rexor's wounds because of his armour.'

Paradon nodded and, patting Dane lightly on the

shoulder, he climbed unsteadily to his feet. As he moved, Kira realized that time had taken a terrible toll on the wizard. He looked as though he was in a lot of pain.

'Now let's see to this dragon,' Paradon said as he leaned heavily on his staff to walk over to Rexor.

'Those things cut right through his armour,' Kira said as she pointed to several large holes.

'They're called bullets,' Paradon said. 'And they are nasty. Stand back, I'm going to try to take off his armour.'

Taking several steps back, Kira watched Paradon close his eyes and speak softly. At first nothing happened. But when he repeated the spell, all the armour, the saddle and covers on the dragon disappeared. It reappeared several paces away.

'You did it!' Kira cheered. But as she looked at the wizard, it seemed as though using his magic had hurt him. She put her arm around his waist for support. 'Are you all right?'

When Paradon looked at her, he smiled. But it never reached his eyes. 'I just need a moment. It's been a long time since I've used this much magic. I'm a little out of practice.'

'Maybe you're out of practice,' Kira said softly, 'but,

Paradon, do you realize every spell has worked? You saved us when those choppers were after us, and you brought us safely here.'

'I just hope I have enough left in me to save Shanks and Rexor.'

'You will,' she said confidently.

When he smiled again, it did reach his eyes. 'You have always had faith in me, haven't you?'

Kira nodded. 'Of course. You're the best!'

Tears welled in the old wizard's eyes as he drew his arm around her. 'Then come and help me try to save this poor creature.'

With the armour and saddle off Rexor, Kira got her first full look at the kind of treatment palace dragons received. Where the many buckles sealed the saddle and pieces of armour in place, heavy calluses and scars had formed in place of the smooth black scales. She also saw where Rexor's spinal plates had been roughly sawn off to allow the saddle to be put on. The plates had tried to grow back, but were now bent and badly misshapen.

Lightly stroking his side, Kira understood why the king's dragons were so mean and dangerous. They had to be in terrible pain all the time.

'Can we save him?' she asked as she worked with the

wizard. As he had done with Shanks, Paradon held his hands over the open wounds to draw out the bullets. When they were gone, Kira packed the wounds with medicine.

'I don't know,' Paradon admitted. 'His wounds go very deep. It may be more than my magic and the medicine can heal. All we can do now is make him comfortable and hope for the best.'

When they finished with Rexor's larger wounds, they set to work on his ripped wings. 'Even if Rexor survives, it will be some time before he's able to fly,' Paradon said. 'That's if he can fly again. I have never seen this kind of damage done to a dragon before. In the old days, all knights had to use against them were lances, bows, swords and sometimes fire. Dragons were killed, but they were never wounded like this.'

'You said there weren't any more dragons,' Kira said as she smoothed more paste into a large torn part of Rexor's wing. 'What happened to them?'

'Like so many things from the past, they too are gone. Dragons died out a very long time ago. I can hardly remember why. I just know when the last dragon died, it was a great loss.'

Kira wanted to ask more, but a deep moan from Rexor stopped her.

'Step back,' Paradon warned, 'I think he's waking. He might be dangerous.'

Moving away from the black dragon's wing, Kira watched Rexor's golden eyes flutter open. He lifted his head a bit and then started to moan. Letting his head fall back down to the ground, his pitiful whines filled the air.

'Poor baby,' Kira called as her heart went out to the suffering dragon. Heedless of the danger, she walked over to the dragon's head and reached up to scratch behind his ears.

'Kira, don't be a fool,' Dane warned when he saw what she was doing. Leaving Shanks, he quickly crossed to Paradon. 'Rexor isn't Jinx; he could kill you!'

'I know he's not like Jinx,' Kira defended. 'But, Dane, he's suffering. When Jinx is hurt, this is the only thing we can do to calm him down. Why should Rexor be any different?'

'Because Rexor is a palace dragon. You can't trust him!'

As if in answer, Rexor lifted his head again. He turned to Kira and seemed startled to find her there.

'It's all right, Rexor,' Kira said softly, 'I won't hurt you.'

'Get away from him!' Dane ordered. 'He'll kill you!'

'But he's hurt,' Kira argued.

'That's what makes him so dangerous!' Dane then turned to Paradon. 'Will you tell her? Palace dragons are deadly.'

Just as Paradon was about to speak, Rexor's head moved closer to Kira. He closed his eyes, let out a long moan and settled down again.

'See,' Kira challenged. 'He didn't want to hurt me. Dane, dragons aren't evil. It's what we do to them that makes them so. And if Rexor lets me scratch behind his ears, I'm going to do it and you can't stop me.'

Dane threw up his arms in frustration. 'You and your dragons!'

CHAPTER
~7~

'Get away from my door!' Elan cried.

Elspeth could hardly believe the startling change in the man. He was pointing an accusing finger at Onnie and ordering them away.

'Wait, please,' she begged. 'His name isn't Onnie-Astra, he's just Onnie. And he's my friend.' Then she looked down on the fox in her arms. 'Aren't you?'

Seated in her arms, the fox squinted threateningly. Then he pulled back the skin from his teeth and started to snarl viciously at the tall man.

'Onnie, that's not nice. Stop it,' Elspeth ordered.

Immediately Onnie stopped. But he continued to growl softly.

Elspeth then looked at the man. 'Please don't send us away. I'm really sorry. He's not usually like this. I don't know who Onnie-Astra is. This is just my Onnie. And he says I need to find a powerful wizard called Elan to help us. Is that you?'

The man nodded hesitantly, but wouldn't take his wary eyes off the fox. 'I am Elan,' he said cautiously. 'What do you want here?'

'I'm not sure,' Elspeth admitted. 'We're lost and Onnie says you're the only one who can help us get back to where we belong.'

Elan remained motionless and looked at both Elspeth and Onnie for a long time. Then his eyes went up to Corvellis sitting calmly in her nest above the door. She was watching Elspeth and showed no hostility and gave no warning. The raven had always been a good judge of character. If she accepted Elspeth, he must too. Finally he opened the door and invited them in.

When she entered, Elspeth was surprised to find herself in a very neat and comfortable cottage. It didn't look anything like the outside of the building. There was a huge hearth with a warm fire burning and a cauldron with stew cooking inside it. If anything, it reminded her of her own home before Lord Dorcon arrived to destroy it.

'Please sit by the fire and warm yourself,' Elan said. Then he turned to the boy. 'Jib, go out and find your mother. She's shopping in the village. Tell her we have guests.'

The boy nodded and quietly left the cottage to find his mother.

'You must forgive my first reaction,' Elan said softly. 'I'm not normally so rude. But I was shocked to hear your friend's name. Long ago, I knew of someone called Onnie-Astra. Believe me, he was an evil piece of work. Then one day he vanished. Some say he left the area, but others suggested he was turned into an animal and fled. I myself don't know what happened to him but was glad when he was gone. So when I heard your fox's name—'

'You thought he was Onnie-Astra,' Elspeth finished. 'But he isn't because this Onnie is very nice.' She bent her head down and kissed the top of the fox's red head.

In response, Onnie looked up and excitedly licked Elspeth's chin, casting her into fits of giggles. 'I love Onnie, and he loves me. So they can't be the same.'

When she looked back at Elan, he was still staring at Onnie and didn't look completely convinced. Changing the subject, Elan asked, 'So, you say you need my help?'

Elspeth nodded. Then with Onnie's help, she began telling the story of her life so far: starting on the family farm, right through to living on the Rogue's Mountain, the sacking of Lasser Commons and finally flying on Harmony through Paradon's Eye.

While he listened, Elan nodded his head and looked very interested. But when Elspeth finished, he started to laugh. 'My dear child, you do have a vivid imagination. I especially liked the part about flying with your dragon through the great Eye in the sky!'

In her arms, Onnie started to yip. Elspeth looked down on him and then back to Elan. 'Onnie says you don't believe us. But I swear it's true. We've come through the Eye and now we're lost. Please, you've got to help us!'

It seemed the harder Elspeth tried to convince him, the more Elan laughed. 'Of course I believe you,' he said lightly, trying to regain his composure.

Soon the door to the cottage opened and Jib entered followed by a beautiful woman. She stepped up to Elan and put her arm around him as she faced Elspeth. 'And who do we have here?'

Still laughing, Elan said, 'Gwen, I should like to introduce you to a very special young girl. This is Elspeth.' Then he pointed to the fox. 'And that is her friend Onnie.'

Suddenly frightened, the woman backed away. 'Onnie-Astra?'

Elspeth had been growing angry at Elan's laughter. But when his wife called Onnie that name again, it was all too much. Standing abruptly, she poured Onnie to the floor and started for the door.

Turning back, she shouted angrily, 'If you won't help us, fine! We'll find our own way home. But I won't stay here and have you calling Onnie that name. He's not Onnie-Astra!'

Throwing open the latch, Elspeth stormed from the wizard's cottage. Above the door, Corvellis took to the air and started after her, cawing as she went.

Racing down the main trail, tears filled Elspeth's eyes as she tried to ignore the curious glances of the people watching her. Before she reached the other end of the village, she heard Harmony starting to roar. Moments later, the villagers screamed in terror as the large red dragon burst through the trees and ran towards her.

Racing up to the dragon, Elspeth threw her arms around Harmony's thick armoured neck and started to cry. 'He won't believe us! I hate it here, I want to go home!'

At her feet, Onnie started to yip and race in circles.

'No, I won't go back,' she cried. 'He laughed at us.

We don't need his help. We'll find our own way home.'

Releasing Harmony, Elspeth stepped up to her side. Before she started to climb the ladder leading up to the saddle, she called down to the fox, 'Come on, Onnie. Let's go to the Rogue's Mountain. We'll find something else to do.'

But the fox refused to move. Instead he turned and dashed back in the direction of Elan's cottage.

'No, Onnie, come back!' Elspeth cried. 'He won't help us!'

Suddenly Corvellis swooped down from the sky and landed on Elspeth's shoulder. She started to caw loudly.

'No, I won't go back!' Elspeth cried. 'He's mean. Just go home to your master, Corvellis, I don't want you here!'

As she tried to drive the raven away, Elspeth became aware of the villagers gathering to stare at her.

'What are you all looking at?' she challenged angrily. 'Haven't you ever seen a dragon before?'

'Not this close,' came a voice from the crowd.

Looking up, Elspeth saw Elan walking towards her as the frightened people parted to let him pass.

Angrily catching hold of Harmony's reins, Elspeth started to turn the large dragon around. 'Come on, Harmony, let's get out of here.'

'Elspeth, wait!' Elan called. 'Please, I'm sorry. I didn't mean to laugh at you.'

'Leave me alone,' Elspeth cried. 'We don't need you.'

'Yes you do,' Elan insisted.

Onnie had been walking at Elan's side to bring him back to her. But as Elspeth started to lead Harmony away, he raced forward and blocked her path.

'No, Onnie, I won't. If you like Elan so much, you can stay with him. But I'm going!'

From behind her, Elspeth heard Elan calling strange words. Moments later, she couldn't move. It was as thought she'd been frozen in place. All she could move were her eyes.

'I'm sorry, Elspeth,' Elan said as he approached. 'But you can't leave just yet. If what you say is true, and seeing this dragon here I now believe it is, then you do need my help.'

Elspeth wanted to yell at the wizard, but she couldn't move her mouth. Beside her, she could hear Harmony starting to whine and realized the dragon was as frozen as she was.

When Elan moved to stand before her, he said, 'I will release you if you promise to come back to my cottage and speak to me. If you agree, blink your eyes twice.'

Elspeth was angry, very angry. The last thing she

wanted to do was speak to the wizard again. Instead of blinking her eyes, she shut them.

'Very well,' Elan said casually. 'I can wait here all day.'

Opening her eyes again, she saw the tall wizard waving his hand in the air. Suddenly a chair appeared. Taking a seat, he casually crossed his legs and sat there staring at her.

'As you can see, I'm quite comfortable right here. Just let me know when you are ready to cooperate.'

After living with Paradon for so long, Elspeth was used to seeing magic. But in all her time with the wizard, he had never used his powers against anyone. Being trapped by Elan, her temper grew. She would rather stand there frozen than give in to him.

'Well,' Elan said some time later. 'Are you ready to let me help you yet? All you have to do is blink your eyes twice.'

At her feet, Elspeth heard Onnie yipping, begging her to blink her eyes so that Elan would release the spell and help them. But she was still mad at the fox, and wasn't listening. Closing her eyes again, she wished someone would come forward to help her.

Not long after, Elspeth heard a woman's terrified scream. This was followed by another scream and then another. Soon the gathered crowd started to disperse and run back to their homes. When they had gone, Elspeth and Elan were able to see what had caused the panic.

Moving together down the muddy trail, several wolves walked side by side with three large stags. Behind them, more forest animals were walking peacefully together, coming to Elspeth's aid.

Elan jumped to his feet. As they drew closer, the wolves started to growl at Elan while the stags lowered their antlers threateningly.

'All of you, calm down,' the wizard said, holding his hands up. 'Just calm down and go back to the forest.'

Ignoring his words, the animals continued to advance. Elan's eyes darted to Elspeth and then back to the approaching animals. 'I don't know how you are doing this, Elspeth, but, please, you must stop; for their protection as well as your own. These villagers are very superstitious. If they see you can control animals, I may not be able to protect you.'

Finally as the wolves came up to the end of Harmony's tail, Elan turned back to Elspeth. 'All right, you win. I'll remove the spell. Just tell them to go!'

A moment later, the spell was removed and Elspeth could move again. But so could Harmony. Rearing on her hind legs, she prepared to attack Elan.

'No!' Elspeth shouted. 'Harmony, sit down!' Then she looked at the approaching animals. 'All of you, stop right there!'

Harmony immediately stopped, as did all the other animals. Standing and staring at Elspeth, the wolves started to howl mournfully.

'It's all right,' Elspeth said gently as she fearlessly approached the wild animals. Standing before her, the wolves started to whine and the stags dropped their heads.

'Thank you all for coming,' she continued as she petted and fussed over the animals. 'I'm fine, I promise. You can all go home now.'

Behind the larger animals, Elspeth saw badgers, foxes and rabbits. Natural forest enemies had drawn together to help her. Smiling at them, she felt deeply grateful.

'Really, he didn't hurt me. Please, you must go home.'

Hesitantly at first, the animals slowly turned and started to drift away. Finally when they were all gone, Elspeth turned back to Elan. 'That wasn't a very nice thing to do to me.'

Elan stepped forward and looked at her. 'I'm sorry, Elspeth. But you were angry and going to leave. You know you need my help. I had to make you see sense.'

'So you froze me?'

'Yes,' Elan admitted. 'But it was you who defeated me; you with your animals.'

Elspeth frowned. 'I didn't do anything. They just came, that's all.'

Around them the people who had fled to their homes opened their doors and started to come back out. They were chatting amongst themselves and pointing at Elspeth again.

'They came because you called them,' Elan said. Then he looked at the gathering crowd before turning back to her. 'I'm truly sorry I laughed at you. Please come back to my cottage. We have much to discuss.'

Elspeth hesitated, unsure of what she should do. On the ground Onnie yipped and insisted they go back to Elan's cottage. Finally she asked, 'What about Harmony?'

Elan looked at the large red dragon and then back to the frightened villagers. 'It's too dangerous to leave her here,' he said, motioning to the villagers. 'We'll bring her back to the cottage with us. The people won't do anything against her if she's with me.'

CHAPTER
~ 8 ~

The first night back on the Rogue's Mountain, everyone stayed outside in the meadow. Kira and Dane carried Paradon's bed up from the cave and put Shanks in it. Then they made a large fire to keep the wounded dragons warm and set up camp.

Kira split her time between checking on Shanks, and then over to Jinx and Rexor. Despite Dane's constant protests, she continued to scratch Rexor's ears and stroke his head just as she did Jinx. The only compromise came when she asked Paradon to remove the armour restricting Rexor's mouth. In this case, Paradon sided with Dane and refused.

Still unsure of the black dragon, Kahrin remained with Jinx and took over the roll of caring for him and giving him all the attention he craved.

As they settled around the fire, they stared up at the many choppers hovering high over their heads. Their searchlights lit the meadow and were shining on the wounded dragons. But as they tried to move lower into the meadow, they found they couldn't.

'You're sure they can't get in?' Dane asked nervously.

As Paradon fed more logs into the fire, he nodded his head. 'They've been trying to get on this mountain for more winters than I can remember. But of all the spells I've cast, this one seems to be holding and protecting the mountain. This is the only place left that still has trees and wildlife. If the shield fails, all will be lost.'

'What happened?' Kira asked. 'I still don't understand. What happened to your castle? And how can there be no more trees or animals? What kind of place is this?'

Paradon lowered his head. 'It is a sad world ruled by the greedy descendents of King Arden. A long time ago there was another war as people tried to fight against their unjust rulers. It was a very bad one. My magic wasn't enough to protect the castle and it was destroyed early in the battle. With no place left to live, I fled up here where I had once lived as a child.'

Kira's eyes lit up with realization. 'You lived on the Rogue's Mountain? Elspeth and I always thought someone had lived here before us. It was you!'

65

When Paradon nodded, she continued, 'When? Why were you up here?'

Paradon closed his eyes. 'It was a very, very long time ago. I was just a little boy.' He opened his eyes and looked at the group again. 'But my powers came early. The trouble was I couldn't control them. We were living at the palace where my father served King Arden's grandfather. One day, I was playing in the courtyard when my powers got away from me. I accidentally destroyed the castle entrance and portcullis and knocked down half the outer wall. The king was so furious he wanted me executed. Instead, my parents hid me up here and made me stay until I could learn to control myself.'

'So your father created this place for you?' Dane asked.

Paradon shook his head. 'No, the meadow and everything you see were here long before then. We don't know who created it. But it was here that I first met Onnie. That red fox and I lived here for many, many winters.' Pausing for a moment, Paradon chuckled. 'I think I would have gone mad with loneliness if Onnie hadn't been with me. And how funny that now, so many winters later, I should end up back here where I started.'

Sitting beside her sister and leaning against Jinx, Kahrin asked, 'What happened to all the trees and animals?'

Dropping his head, Paradon picked at the fire. 'They're all gone. Ages ago a few brave people tried to fight for nature and what was left of the forests. But those making profit from its destruction quickly and violently silenced their voices. Now, only this mountain remains to stand as a reminder of what they've lost.'

'This world is so ugly,' Kahrin softly said.

'It is,' Paradon agreed. 'And the people of this world have even less freedom than the people of your time.'

'How can that be?' Kira asked. 'What about the prophecy? You said King Arden would fall and a new and better world would be created.'

Dane looked over to Kira. 'What prophecy? What are you talking about?'

As Kira looked to her brother and then Paradon, she realized that only she and the wizard knew the prophecy. 'We should tell him,' she said.

Agreeing, Paradon picked at the fire as he started to explain. 'Long ago, my great, great grandfather, Elan, was the court wizard to King Arden's ancestor, King Lacarian. Using the Eye, Elan had seen the destruction of the corrupt monarchy by a young, unmarried girl who had two long braids of red hair. This very special girl would dress as a boy, fight like a boy and ride a twin-tailed dragon who loved her. Elan saw that she would destroy the king and return peace to the suffering land.'

Kira then took over speaking for Paradon. 'After Elan told King Lacarian what he'd seen, the king had him killed so he couldn't tell anyone else. But it was too late. Elan had told his wife and son and the prophecy has been passed down through Paradon's family. But to keep it from coming true, King Lacarian started First Law against girls.'

Dane snapped his fingers. 'So that's why girls aren't allowed to do anything! I could never understand why First Law was only about girls. But now I know. The kings are afraid of you. And what a dirty dog that King Lacarian was!'

'All the kings are bad,' Kira agreed.

Then Dane looked at Kira as if seeing her for the very first time. 'Wait, it's you, isn't it?' he cried. 'Kira, you're the girl from the prophecy. You've got red hair in long braids, you dress like I do and you've got a twin-tailed dragon. Jinx loves you. He'd do anything for you.'

Kira shrugged. 'I'm not really sure.'

'I am,' Paradon said. 'Kira, if it wasn't you, then when you and the others flew into the Eye and disappeared from that time period, another girl would have risen up to challenge First Law. But it never happened. With you gone, King Arden's reign continued unchallenged. After him, it was his son and his son after that. Right up to this day. What you see around you, this filth, the ugliness of the city and the destruction of the beautiful forests of this world, is all a direct result of the prophecy being unfulfilled.'

'But is it too late?' said Dane.

Paradon stared into the fire. 'Not at all. Once Shanks and the dragons are well enough to travel, I shall cast another spell. It will send you back to where Elspeth is. Then you will find my great, great grandfather Elan and he will help you get back to where you really belong. After that, you can finally stop King Arden.'

'Elan?' Kira asked. 'Are you telling me that Shadow is actually back in the time of Elan and King Lacarian; the very same King Lacarian who started First Law against girls?'

Without speaking, the old wizard nodded.

'What?' Dane cried. He stood and angrily faced the wizard. 'You lied to us! You said Elspeth was safe! Now you're telling us that she's lost somewhere in the time of King Lacarian with only a crazy fox and palace dragon to protect her?'

'Dane, she is safe,' Paradon insisted weakly.

'How far back is she?' Dane demanded as fear for his little sister rose on his face. 'Tell us. How far back did she go?'

Paradon dropped his head and sighed heavily. 'From the point where you all started at my castle, you four came forward three thousand seasons into the future. Somehow, Elspeth travelled almost the same distance. Only instead of coming forward she went back in time.'

Kira could hardly believe what she was hearing. 'So you're saying that right now, Elspeth is six thousand seasons away from us?'

The old wizard nodded. 'I don't know how it happened. You were all together, yet somehow you split. Now she is back in the time of Elan and you are here in this world.'

'You keep insisting she's in the time of Elan, but is she with him?' Kira asked anxiously.

'I'm afraid I really don't know,' Paradon admitted sadly. He then pointed to the Eye sitting on its plinth beside him. It was still covered in vicious brambles. 'I

70

saw it happen on the day you left. Not long after you all entered the Eye. But I still don't know how or why. All I do know is that if she does manage to find Elan, he will protect her.'

'Can you see her now?' Kira asked as she stood and crossed over to the Eye. As she peered into the cold grey stone, the brambles shivered and filled in where she was trying to look. Moving around it, the brambles moved too. Giving up, Kira added, 'I really do hate this thing.'

Paradon nodded at her frustration. 'When I saw what happened to Elspeth, I was still living in our time; back in the tower of the castle. I've kept looking, but haven't been able to see her for a very, very long time.'

'Then how do you know she's safe?' Dane challenged.

'To be truthful, I don't,' admitted Paradon. 'I can only pray. Though we do know that Onnie is with her and that he'll do everything he can to protect her.'

'Don't forget Harmony,' Kahrin added. 'She really likes Elspeth.'

Paradon nodded. 'Indeed she does.'

Dane frowned and sat down again. 'I still don't understand how it all went wrong. We all entered the Eye together. How could we separate?'

'I just don't know,' Paradon admitted. 'I should never have cast that spell. I knew I wasn't up to the task. Now look what's happened.' He stopped speaking as tears rose in his tired old eyes and trailed down through the many wrinkles on his face.

Kira moved over to the old wizard and sat down close beside him. Putting her arms around him, she tried to offer comfort. 'It's not your fault, Paradon,' she said gently. 'We told you to do it. It was our decision, not yours. You tried to warn us, but none of us had a choice. Lord Dorcon and his legion were at the castle. If you hadn't done it, we'd all be dead now.'

'I promise you, I tried to help,' Paradon pleaded as his voice broke.

Kira felt her heart break for the old wizard. 'You did help us, Paradon. You saved our lives. I know it didn't work out the way we planned. But we're alive. Shanks won't die, I know it. And when we are ready, we can all go back and find Elspeth.'

Paradon looked at Kira and smiled, but it was so pain-filled she felt tears stinging her own eyes.

'I can't go back with you,' he said sadly. 'This is my time. I have lived thousands of seasons to get here. This is where I must remain.'

Kira shook here head violently. 'We're not leaving

you here at the mercy of those things!' She angrily pointed up to the sky and the choppers hovering over the top of the Rogue's Mountain.

'Kira's right,' Dane added. 'This is a terrible place. We won't let you stay.'

'I must,' Paradon said. 'It's the only way.' He turned to Kira and took her hand in his own thin bony hands. 'Don't you see? Me, a much younger me, is still back at that castle waiting for your return. I'm there, Kira. Watching through the Eye and praying that you will come home. That Paradon is still *me*, and he misses you more than you will ever know. But there can't be two of us there at the same time. I must remain here.'

'But you'll be all alone.'

'Not for long,' Paradon said curiously.

'What do you mean?'

'Look at me, child. I'm impossibly old. I'm tired and in so much pain. I have lived longer than anyone has a right to and it's unnatural. But I've done it for you. I have cast spell upon spell to keep myself going this long so I could protect you when you arrived. Now that you are here, my last act as a wizard will be to cast a final spell that will send you all safely back to Elspeth. After that, I shall finally rest.'

'But you can rest with us in our own time,' Kira

argued. 'We'll find a way for it to work—'

'Kira,' Dane interrupted softly. 'Paradon isn't really talking about rest.' He looked over to the old wizard. 'Are you?'

When Paradon shook his head, Dane continued. 'After you cast your final spell, you're going to die.'

'Paradon, no!' Kira cried. 'You've got to come back with us. We can help you.'

A pain-filled smile lit the old wizard's face. 'No, I belong here and this is where I am going to stay.'

'But I don't want you to die!' she said as tears flowed down her cheeks.

'My dear, dear child,' Paradon said gently, 'we all die. Even wizards. I have lived a very long and mostly happy life. I want to rest. It's my time.'

Leaning over, Paradon gave Kira a weak hug. 'Let me send you back where you belong. I promise you, I'm there.' When he finished speaking, he kissed her lightly on the forehead. 'Now enough talk of death. Our job right now is to help Shanks and the dragons live. After that, time will take care of itself.'

CHAPTER
~9~

Elspeth sat at the dining table with Elan, his wife Gwen and their son, Jib. Onnie was in Elspeth's lap eating the pieces of meat from the stew that she handed to him. Harmony's head was lying in the doorway of the cottage while the rest of her large body took up the whole front garden.

'How did you do that with the animals?' Jib asked, looking at Elspeth as though she were his hero.

'I didn't do anything,' Elspeth admitted. 'They just came.'

Elan raised a light eyebrow. 'You truly believe that?'

When Elspeth nodded, Elan continued. 'Trust me, you summoned them. When you couldn't move, they heard your distress and had to come to you.'

'How?' Elspeth asked.

'The same way I cast spells. Magic.'

Elspeth shook her head. 'I can't do magic. Only

you and Paradon can do it.'

Elan laughed lightly and his blue eyes sparkled. 'Of course you can. There are many types of magic in this world. I have one type, you another.'

Elspeth considered this for a moment and then looked down on the fox. 'Onnie says Paradon is your great, great grandson. But I don't understand how it can be true. Paradon is old. But you are so young.'

Elan raised an eyebrow. 'Thank you. But I'm older than you think.'

'Really?' Elspeth asked. 'So Paradon is your great, great grandson?"

'I don't really know,' Elan admitted. 'But there is one way to find out.' Rising from the table, Elan disappeared down the short hall to another room. When he returned, he was carrying something in his arms that was covered with a black cloth. Setting on the table, he removed the cloth.

The moment the cover was removed, Elspeth gasped. 'That looks just like Paradon's Eye!'

'It does?' Elan asked.

'Yes, only Paradon's Eye is much, much bigger. But it has the same swirling colours in it.'

Elan looked at Elspeth a moment before asking, 'You can see the colours?'

Elspeth nodded. 'Kira couldn't. But I can. They're so pretty. Just like this . . .' She reached into her leather top and pulled out her pendant. 'Paradon gave this to me. He says it is the child of the Eye. I used to be able to speak to him with it, but now I don't hear anything.'

Elan leaned forward and inspected the dark, round piece of stone clasped in the gold dragon's claw. 'May I borrow that for a moment?'

Elspeth shook her head. 'Paradon said that once I put it on, it couldn't be taken off or stolen from me. He said with this, he would always be able to reach me.' She then lowered her head. 'But he was wrong.'

Clutching the pendant, Elan moved it around in his hand. 'I can feel the spell protecting it. It is very powerful magic.'

'Where did it come from?' Gwen asked.

Elan looked over to her. 'Somehow, this shard has been taken from my stone globe.'

'That can't be the same Eye,' Elspeth said looking at the colour-filled stone on the table. 'It's too small.'

Elan considered for a long moment. 'If your pendant came from what you call Paradon's Eye, then they are one and the same. I have a feeling that this globe here is a lot younger than the one you know. My father once told me that as the stone ages, its power and size grows.

So if the Eye you saw is bigger, then it is definitely much older.'

Elspeth frowned. 'I don't understand.'

'Me either,' Jib added.

Falling silent, Elan pulled his globe closer and gazed into the swirling colours. After a time, he looked over to Elspeth and nodded. 'Now I understand.'

'Understand what? Could you see Paradon and his castle?'

'No. What I saw wasn't very clear. But it was enough to show me what has happened to you. I'm just not sure I can explain it in a way that you will understand.'

Gwen had remained silent for most of the meal. But now she rose from the table and crossed the cottage. Going to Elan's desk, she pulled out a clean scroll and then a quill and ink bottle. Bringing it back to her husband, she set it up before him. 'I think it might be easier if you show us.'

Smiling up to his wife, Elan reached for her hand and kissed it lightly. 'What would I do without you?'

Gwen also smiled. 'You'll never have to.'

Opening the rolled scroll, Elan reached for the quill. Dipping it in the ink, he drew a long single line. At one end of the line, he drew the picture of a castle with a large ball beside it. At the other end, he drew a small cottage with a much smaller ball. Then he drew dots all along the line.

'Now, Elspeth,' he said, inviting her to stand beside him as he worked. 'This picture here represents Paradon's castle where you lived with your sisters and brother and this is the Eye that you know. And here at the other end of the line is our cottage with my stone globe. As I understand it, you and your family were at Paradon's castle when Lord Dorcon and his men arrived to get you. Correct?'

Elspeth looked down on the picture and nodded.

'Very well,' Elan said. 'So, you all asked Paradon to cast a spell that would send you three seasons into the future.'

Again Elspeth nodded.

Elan quickly drew men on horses outside the castle. He then drew a line extending from the other side of Paradon's castle. Along that line, he drew three more dots. 'Each dot represents one season. So when you entered the Eye in the sky, you were supposed to come out here, just three dots away.' Elan paused to draw a picture of three dragons representing Jinx, Harmony and Rexor.

Elspeth looked at the line, and understood what Elan meant. 'Yes,' she agreed. 'So Lord Dorcon and

79

his men would have left the castle and we would be safe.'

Elan considered. 'It was a very good plan. It should have worked.'

'But what went wrong?' Elspeth asked as she looked at the scroll. 'Where are we now?'

Elan rubbed his chin exactly the same way Paradon always did. 'I'm not sure how it went wrong,' he said. 'But what I am sure of is this.' Taking the quill, Elan drew a second line running beside the first line with all the dots and added a single dragon flying above the line. 'Instead of going three seasons into the future, you appear to have travelled many seasons into the past.'

'How many?' Elspeth asked, almost in a whisper.

Elan shrugged. 'I don't know.' He then looked at Onnie. 'Your friend insists that Paradon is my great-great-grandson. As Jib is my only child and he doesn't have any children of his own, I would say it is at least five to six hundred seasons.'

Standing on Elspeth's chair, Onnie howled.

'Onnie says it's much more than that,' Elspeth explained.

Elan's eyes darkened as he studied the fox. 'And how would you know that?'

'Yes,' Elspeth agreed, frowning at Onnie. 'How

did you know that Elan was Paradon's great-great-grandfather?'

Onnie refused to answer. Instead he yipped and dashed away from the table. Running down the hall, he disappeared into one of the bedrooms.

'He always does that when he doesn't want to tell me something,' Elspeth explained. 'He'll be back.'

With the fox out of the room, Elan quietly asked Elspeth, 'Tell me, how long have you known Onnie?'

'A long time,' Elspeth explained. 'He lived with Paradon until Lord Dorcon attacked our farm. Then Paradon sent him to help us. He took us to the Rogue's Mountain and led us to our home up at the top.'

Seated beside Elan, Gwen leaned forward and whispered, 'So you don't really know who he is or where he comes from?'

Elspeth shrugged. 'Paradon didn't know where he came from either; just that he'd been with him since he was a little boy. But now he stays with me.'

'And you can actually talk to him?' Elan asked.

Elspeth nodded. 'Paradon said he could understand how Onnie felt, but I'm the first person who could ever understand him.'

Elan considered. 'And what has he told you of himself?'

'Nothing,' Elspeth said. 'Onnie says I'm too young to understand. But one day he'll tell me.'

Elspeth watched as Elan and Gwen looked at each other. Their expressions were very suspicious.

'Wait,' Elspeth said, starting to get angry again. 'You still don't think he's Onnie-Astra, do you? Because he's not! You said Onnie-Astra was evil. But my Onnie is good. He loves me and has helped my family and me many times.'

Elan reached out and patted Elspeth's hand. 'Of course they're not the same,' he said reassuringly. 'Onnie-Astra could not have lived as long as that. No, they just have similar names. That's all.'

Elspeth stared into Elan's eyes and then looked over to Gwen. Once again she had the feeling that they didn't believe their own words. Finally she looked down at the scroll again and pointed at Elan's cottage. 'So if we have come here, where are Kira and the others?'

Elan also concentrated on the scroll. 'I'm afraid I just don't know. The globe couldn't show me. Something must have gone wrong with Paradon's spell. Perhaps they made it there.' He pointed at the third dot beyond Paradon's castle. 'I don't know. All I do know is that you are here.'

'Onnie says you are a powerful wizard. Can you send us home?'

Taking in a deep breath, Elan let it out slowly. 'Please sit down, Elspeth.' When she was seated, he continued. 'I am powerful. But travelling in time is something I've never heard of before and really wouldn't know how to do. I know Paradon had a very good reason for doing it, and I know you must go back. But unless I know exactly where you came from and what kind of spell was required, I just can't send you home.'

CHAPTER
~10~

'What!' Elspeth cried. 'What do you mean you can't send us home? You have to! Onnie said you would. Please, we can't stay here.'

A sudden scurrying on the floor caught their attention as Onnie returned and leaped into Elspeth's lap. Seeing her upset, Onnie looked at Elan and scowled viciously, before turning back to her.

'Please,' Elspeth begged, 'we want to go home,'

'I know you do,' Gwen said softly as she rose and moved over to Elspeth. Wary of the fox, she put her arms around her. 'But I don't see how we can do it.'

'You've got to try! We just can't stay. I've got to get back to my family!'

'Elspeth, listen to me,' Elan said gently. 'Without knowing exactly where you came from or the spell that is required to send you back, attempting to do it could make things worse. If I were to miss your time, you would be left alone with no one there to help you.'

'But I can't stay here,' Elspeth whined.

'You may not have to,' Elan offered. 'If Paradon cast the travel spell, then using the Eye, he should be able to see where you went. He might be casting another spell right now to bring you home. I'm so sorry, but you've got to stay here until Paradon comes for you.'

'How long will that be?' Tears were filling her eyes as Elan's words started to sink in.

Elan shook his head. 'I just don't know.'

Gwen leaned down and kissed the top of Elspeth's head. 'You are welcome to stay here with us for as long as it takes.'

Elspeth looked up into the woman's lovely face. Then she looked over to Elan and finally Jib.

'Please stay with us,' Jib said. 'You can teach me how to talk to animals.'

Elspeth's eyes trailed over to Harmony's head where it lay in the doorway. The red dragon was watching her. 'What about Harmony?' she asked. 'Would I be able to keep her here?'

Elan sighed and shook his head. 'I'm afraid not. Firstly, the villagers would never allow it. I'm sure they weren't too happy with the animal display this morning. I hardly think they'll tolerate a dragon living amongst them. Besides, King Lacarian won't allow anyone but his knights to keep dragons. If he learns of Harmony, he'll have his men come here and take her back to the palace.'

'You mean because of First Law?' Elspeth said miserably.

'What is First Law?' Elan asked.

'You know, the First Law. Where girls can't do anything and especially can't go near dragons.'

Gwen was the one who spoke first. 'We've never heard of it.'

'Really?' Elspeth said. 'But everyone knows it. It's, it's the First Law. The only real law of the kingdom.'

'We don't,' Elan said as his voice filled with concern. 'Tell us about it.'

Elspeth sniffed back her tears as she closed her eyes and started to repeat the six points of First Law.

'First Law,' she said. '*One*: Girls are not allowed to leave their homes unless escorted by their father, brothers or husbands and may never travel any further than their neighbouring village. *Two*: Girls are never to be educated. *Three*: Girls are not allowed to hunt, fight or engage in any activities that are considered boyish. They may not dress as boys and must never carry weapons of any sort. *Four*: Unmarried girls are never allowed to visit the palace or approach the king. *Five*: Girls must be matched to the boy or man they are to marry by the age of twelve. They must be married before the age of thirteen. The day after the marriage ceremony, their husbands must send confirmation to the king. *Six*: Under no circumstances are girls ever to be allowed anywhere near dragons.'

When she finished, Elspeth looked over to Gwen. 'The punishment for breaking any one of these points is execution. But with the last one, girls get tortured and then killed if they are caught near dragons.'

'How awful!' Gwen cried. 'Girls can't do anything in your time.' She looked over to Elan. 'How could such an evil law exist?'

Jib looked at Elspeth and frowned. 'Wait, you're dressed as a boy. You carry a dagger and have a dragon.'

Elspeth nodded. 'I know. That's why Lord Dorcon is trying to catch us. When he does, he's going to kill all of us.'

Elan shook his head. 'This is terrible, simply terrible. You have lived with this First Law all your life?'

Elspeth nodded. 'So did my mother, and my grandmother and her mother before her.'

'When did it all start?' Gwen asked.

Elspeth shrugged. 'I don't know. It's always been.'

'Not always,' Elan said. 'King Lacarian may not be a good king, but he would never allow anything like that. It must have come long after him. My only concern with Harmony is that the king won't let anyone but his knights keep dragons.'

'But you're the king's wizard,' Gwen said to Elan. 'Couldn't you ask him to let her keep her dragon?'

Once again, Elan shook his head. 'King Lacarian doesn't care for me, which is why we don't live at the palace. I doubt he would ever grant my request.'

Elspeth was starting to feel very overwhelmed by everything. It was all becoming too much. 'If I can't keep Harmony, I'm not staying here. She needs me and I won't hurt her like that.'

'But child,' Gwen said. 'There is nowhere you can go where you can keep her.'

'We'll go into the forest to live,' Elspeth suggested. 'The animals won't hurt us.'

Elan shook his head. 'We can't let you do that. You're right about the animals; they won't hurt you. But there are very dangerous bandits living in the forest that would. They often surround the village and attack anyone who tries to enter. It would be far too dangerous for you out there.'

'Well, there's got to be somewhere we can go,' Elspeth said.

In her lap, Onnie started to yip. Elspeth looked down on him and then back to Elan. 'Onnie says there is a place we can go and still keep Harmony.'

'Where's that?'

'The Rogue's Mountain.' Elspeth pointed out the door towards the tall mountain.

'The mountain?' Elan repeated. 'You can't live up there alone. How would you survive?'

'We did before,' Elspeth explained. 'Kira and I lived up there a long time. There were fruit trees and a vegetable garden and a small pond for fresh water. Onnie used to hunt rabbits for us too. We had everything we needed.'

Elan frowned. 'All of that is at the top of the mountain?'

'Not right now,' Elspeth admitted in confusion. 'We were just there and somehow it's gone. But Onnie says you can make it for us. He thinks maybe it was you who made the meadow in the first place.'

Gwen turned to her husband and started to shake her head. 'Elan, we can't let her stay up there alone. It's far too dangerous and she's too young to stay on her own.'

Elan remained silent for a long time, just stroking his chin. Finally he looked over to Gwen. 'I think Onnie is right. The mountain is the safest place for them.'

'How can you say that?' Gwen challenged. 'She's just a child. She can't live up there alone!'

'I won't be alone,' Elspeth insisted. 'I have Onnie and Harmony.'

'But they're just animals,' Gwen argued. 'Elspeth, you need to be with people.'

'She'll also have us.' Elan offered. 'I'll go up there every day to check on her. We can all go for visits and, on occasion, Elspeth can come back down to us.' Then he reached out and took his wife's hand. 'Gwen, this is the best possible solution. Elspeth, Onnie and Harmony don't belong in this time. She has family who'll be looking for her. If I were Paradon, the mountain would be the first place I would look. Besides, I think it's safest for everyone if she sees as few people here as possible.'

'But the mountain,' Gwen said, wringing her hands. 'It's so wild up there.'

'Not for long,' Elan said. 'Onnie is right. I can go up with them and make it as comfortable as possible.'

Elspeth looked at Gwen. 'I'll be all right. We lived there before, didn't we, Onnie?' When the fox yipped in agreement, Elspeth squared her shoulders. 'I won't let them take Harmony away. She belongs with me.'

After the decision was made, Gwen went through the cottage. She gathered together some of Jib's extra clothing, a few blankets and bed covers, dried meat and fresh vegetables with some cooking utensils. Packing them all up in a large sack, she handed them over. 'Are you sure you don't want me to come up with you?'

Elspeth gratefully received the sack and shook her head. 'I'm sorry, but there isn't room on Harmony for all of us.'

Elan crossed to his wife and kissed her on the cheek. 'I'll get her set up, and then we can all go up for a visit.'

'I just don't know about this,' Gwen said, wringing her hands. 'The mountain is awfully high.'

'She'll be fine,' Elan assured her. Then he looked at Elspeth. 'Are you ready?'

Elspeth nodded. Then, helping Onnie get back into the pouch on her back, she gave Gwen a farewell hug. 'Thank you for everything.'

'Please stay safe,' Gwen said, hugging her back. 'Come down if you need anything at all. We are here for you.'

Thanking her a final time, Elspeth followed Elan

and Jib out of the cottage. Harmony was standing in the yard, waiting for her. When she saw the two extra people approaching, she started to growl.

'No, Harmony,' Elspeth chastised. 'Elan and Jib are our friends. They are going to make a home for us. Be nice.'

Instantly the dragon calmed and allowed everyone to climb up on to her back.

'This is the first time I've seen a dragon this close,' Jib said excitedly. 'She's really beautiful.'

Elspeth nodded. 'She sure is. But you should see our baby dragon, Jinx. He's bright blue and has two tails.'

'That must be quite a sight,' Elan said as he settled on the cramped saddle behind his son. 'I've never heard of a twin-tailed dragon before.'

'Paradon says they're very rare.' Then she looked back at Jib and Elan. 'Are you ready to go?'

When they agreed, Elspeth waved a final time to Gwen and caught hold of the reins. With a light tug, she directed Harmony out of the cottage's front garden and on to the main trail. Around them, the villagers had come out of their homes once again and were staring in fear at the dragon walking calmly through the village.

When they reached the end of the long row

of cottages and the area opened enough for Harmony to spread her large wings, Elspeth ordered her into the sky.

The journey was brief as they flew up to the top of the mountain. Passing over the peak, Elspeth pointed down. 'Somehow, there was a big meadow right there. The Rogue and Blue lived up on that side of the wall while we entered through a crack on this side.'

Elan stared down on the snow-covered peak of the mountain and couldn't believe that there had ever been an enchanted meadow there. He realized then that it must have been him who had created it for Elspeth.

'Can you take us down so I can get started,' Elan called.

Directing Harmony around the mountain, Elspeth had the red dragon land once again on the rocky plateau. As she climbed down from the saddle, she explained the story of how she and Kira had seen the dragon fight, as well as how Onnie had taken them to the crack in the wall.

Directing them up the rough trail, they were soon walking along the same rocky shelf leading to the crack in the wall. 'You see that cluster of trees,' Elspeth said as she pointed to the grouping of tall pine trees, 'that's where the Rogue hit his wing and fell down. It was just passed here that we found the crack.'

Leaping down from the pack on Elspeth's back, Onnie ran to the exact spot where the crack had been.

'Right there, where Onnie is standing,' Elspeth said.

'How are you going to do this, Father?' Jib asked.

Elan rubbed his chin again. 'As with all magic, first you must imagine what you want to happen. See it clearly in your mind. Then you say a combination of words that will achieve it.'

When Elspeth looked at them curiously, Elan explained. 'Jib is also a wizard, though he's only now learning to use his powers. Once I build the meadow, he can help me plant the trees. Now, stand back and let's get started.'

Elspeth picked up Onnie and stepped away from the wall. Standing before her, Elan closed his eyes and raised his hands in the air. As when Paradon cast a spell, he muttered words under his breath. But unlike Paradon, when he finished speaking, the spell worked immediately.

Beneath them, they heard a heavy rumbling starting from deep inside the mountain. The ground began to tremble and shake as small pebbles fell down the side of the tall rocky wall. Soon Elspeth heard a loud cracking sound.

'There, Father!' Jib cried. 'It's starting!'

As she stared at the solid wall, Elspeth saw a tiny crack starting to form at the base. A moment later the crack broadened.

'Tell me when it is as wide as you remember it,' Elan said.

Nodding her head, Elspeth watched the crack growing larger. Finally when it reached the width she remembered, she called, 'stop.'

Striding forward, Elan confidently entered the crack. 'Let's see what this meadow of yours looks like.'

Elspeth didn't move for a moment. She couldn't believe that it had been so easy for the wizard.

'Are you coming?' Elan called back.

'Yes,' Elspeth said as she ran forward to follow Elan and Jib through the crack. Clutching Onnie in one hand, her other hand trailed along the wall. 'This is just how I remember it!'

'Good,' Elan agreed. 'Let's hope the rest of it is as you remember it.'

Soon they were rounding the bend in the crack and saw light shining in the distance. 'There should be a cave just on the other side,' Elspeth explained. 'Kira and I lived there until we found Jinx. Then we moved to a different one.'

No sooner had she spoken the words than they were emerging into the same cave. Ahead of them, she saw the entrance to the meadow. Pouring Onnie to the floor, Elspeth dashed forward on to the green grass of the meadow. 'Onnie, look, it's exactly the same!'

'Not quite yet,' Elan said as she joined her. 'We just have a few more things to sort out.'

Working with Elspeth and Onnie, Elan and Jib finished the details of the meadow as Elspeth remembered them, including the second cave where they had lived and found Jinx, the waterfall and pond, fruit trees and vegetable garden.

When they finished and were inspecting the new cave, Elspeth returned to Elan's side. 'You're much better than Paradon with magic. His spells always went wrong. He tried his best, but nothing ever worked the first time.'

Elan rubbed his chin. 'I don't understand how my great-great-grandson would have such trouble.'

Elspeth shrugged. 'He said his master tried to teach him, but the words never came out right. The same happened when Paradon tried to learn to read. He just couldn't.'

'Paradon couldn't read either?' Elan said.

When Elspeth nodded, Elan continued. 'Now I

understand. My mother had the same problem. No matter how hard she tried to learn to read, the words never made sense to her. She didn't have any magic, but if she'd had, I'm sure her spells would have been the same as Paradon's.'

'Your mother was allowed to read?' Elspeth asked in awe.

'Of course. Everyone is taught.'

Elspeth shook her head. 'First Law forbids girls from learning.'

'That really doesn't sound like a very nice place,' Jib said.

Elan rested his arm on Elspeth's shoulder. 'While you are waiting for Paradon to arrive, I think we should teach you to read.'

'Really!' Elspeth squealed. 'You'd do that for me?'

'Of course,' Elan said. 'Everyone should be allowed to read.'

CHAPTER
~ 11 ~

Shanks slowly recovered. He was very weak, but before long he was able to eat some broth that Paradon prepared and was sitting up in bed. Jinx was also up and moving around again. Though his beautiful blue wings were still very tender, he was healing quickly.

But as he healed, Jinx insisted on following Kira everywhere she went while she tried to care for Shanks and Rexor. As for the black dragon, it took most of the medicine and Paradon's spells to keep him alive. The wounds he suffered had been the worst of all and unlike Jinx, the dragon didn't have much will to live. It was Kira's constant attention and care that finally drew him back to life.

'I really wish you wouldn't get so close,' Dane complained as he stood back watching Kira feed tiny pieces of meat to Rexor through the armour restricting his mouth. 'Have you forgotten what happened to Father with his dragon?'

'Of course not!' Kira snapped. 'Ariel attacked him and ate his leg. But Dane, Rexor has got to eat. With that armour on his snout, how else are we going to get food into him? This is the only way. I didn't think you'd want to do it. Would you?'

Dane shook his head. 'Not really. You're the one who likes these beasts, not me.' Finally giving up the argument, he started to walk back to Shanks. Before he got there, he called back over his shoulder to her. 'Just be careful and don't turn your back on him.'

'Would you please stop worrying about me and take care of Shanks!'

When he was gone, Kira stroked Rexor's armoured snout. 'Don't you listen to him. He doesn't know what he's talking about.' She then fed another tiny piece of meat to the dragon. Beside him, Jinx was pressing in close, trying to get Kira's attention.

'I don't think he likes you caring for Rexor,' Kahrin said softly as she stood beside Jinx.

'Oh, I see you there, baby,' Kira laughed and held out a piece of meat to him. Then she said to Kahrin, 'I think you're right. Jinx is jealous.'

* * *

'That sister of yours really does love her dragons, doesn't she?' Shanks said as he sat up in bed watching Kira split her attention between Jinx and Rexor.

'It's driving me mad,' Dane responded. 'I keep warning her, but she refuses to listen. Rexor isn't a pet. But you can bet that's what she's trying to turn him into.'

'A pet dragon. Who'd have thought it?' Shanks chuckled.

Dane nodded, then added, 'I'm really not crazy about Jinx, but I don't think he'd harm her on purpose. Rexor is different. If she's not careful, he'll kill her.'

'I'm not so sure about that,' Paradon said as he slowly stepped up to the bed to check on Shanks. 'Elspeth has a very special way with all animals, that much is true. But Kira has her own magic when it comes to dragons. Look at the way Rexor is holding his head and accepting food from her. There is no malice. He welcomes her attention. Even craves it. You've seen it for yourself; he likes it when she scratches his ears. I have no doubt that he'd be the same with you if you let him.'

'Me stroke Rexor?' Dane said. 'That will never happen!'

Paradon turned to Dane and shook his head tiredly. 'Then the loss is yours, I'm afraid. Kira was right about one thing. If palace dragons were treated better, they would certainly serve better. You saw what they did to

Rexor's spinal plates. Until I removed his saddle and armour they were causing him constant pain. Can you blame any animal for reacting violently when they are in pain?'

'But what will happen when you put it all back on him again? He will become as dangerous as he was before.' Dane said.

Paradon sighed tiredly as he sat on the edge of Shanks' bed. 'I'm not putting it back on him. When Rexor is well enough, he'll have a saddlebox just like Jinx, one that won't touch his healing spinal plates.'

Dane threw his hands in the air. 'You've all gone dragon mad!' he said in frustration. 'What's next? Keeping dragons in our chambers at night? Sleeping with them?'

Paradon chuckled. 'You didn't spend enough time at the castle to see for yourself, but that's exactly what has happened. Jinx spent every moment with the girls. Day and night.'

'Well, don't expect me to do the same!'

Paradon and Shanks watched Dane storming away. 'Ignore him,' Shanks said. 'The truth is, Dane is terrified of dragons. I remember when his father assigned Rexor and Harmony to us. Dane told him how he felt and his father nearly hit him. Dane doesn't really hate dragons. Because of what happened with Ariel, he just can't trust them.'

'His fear is well founded,' Paradon said. 'But what Dane can't see is that dragons are intelligent beasts. They have likes and dislikes, just like people do. If Dane is judging all dragons because of what happened with Ariel and his father, he is wrong. Those two were never a match. Just like you and Harmony. She will never accept you. But Rexor does.'

'It reminds me of Marcus and his dragon, Beauty,' Shanks said thoughtfully. He then told Paradon the story of the old knight who had helped him and Dane escape the palace. 'Marcus swore that the ghost of Beauty was helping him and telling him he had a job to do before he died.'

'I don't doubt it,' Paradon said. 'Who are we to say dragons don't have souls and care for their riders? Look how Rexor fought to save you on the roof and how he kept flying long after he was hurt.'

'But to think they care for their riders?' Shanks mused.

'Care for what riders?' Kira asked as she stepped up to the bed.

Shanks smiled at Kira when he saw her. Then Jinx arrived, trailing right behind her. 'Does he really follow you everywhere?'

When Kira nodded, he shook his head. 'I don't think your husband is going to like that very much.'

'I don't have a husband and I don't plan to have one,' Kira said, 'no matter what First Law says. No one, not even King Arden, is going to tell me who to marry and when!' Then her cheeks turned pink as she added, 'Unless I can choose him for myself, I'll never get married!'

Shanks smiled his brightest smile at her. Then he winked at Paradon. 'Well, whoever the poor unfortunate fellow is, he'd better like dragons!'

Shocked by his response, Kira stepped forward and punched him on the arm. 'Well, whoever he is, Shanks-Spar, he'll be much nicer than you!' She turned angrily to Jinx. 'Come on, boy. Let's see how Rexor is doing!'

Shanks watched Kira storm off and started to chuckle. 'I think I hit a sore spot.'

The old wizard watched Shanks' gaze follow Kira. He smiled. Finally he said, 'Well, whoever the lucky fellow is who catches her heart, he'd better watch himself. Our Kira has a rather large blue friend who will do anything to protect her.'

'He's not the only one,' Shanks added as he settled back down to rest.

CHAPTER
~12~

Elspeth was soon settled in the meadow with Onnie and Harmony. True to his word, using magic, Elan and his family often appeared at the top of the mountain for visits and to bring supplies. During these times, Elspeth was taught how to read.

When the lessons finished, Gwen would lay out a picnic while Elspeth played in the grassy meadow with Onnie, Jib and Harmony, chasing each other around.

Over time, Elspeth convinced Elan to remove all the uncomfortable armour from Harmony. Hesitant at first, he finally surrendered to her plea and cast a spell removing the painful pieces of metal mounted to the dragon, including the restraints keeping the dragon's mouth shut. All that were left were the reins, which Elspeth was sure didn't cause Harmony any problems.

'I certainly hope I don't live to regret this,' Elan

said when he finished and Harmony was free of the painful armour.

'You won't,' Elspeth stated confidently as she stroked Harmony's uncovered snout. 'It was all hurting her. Especially that saddle on her back.'

When Elspeth pointed out the brutal cuts to the dragon's spinal plates to allow the saddle to sit flat, Elan nodded. 'That does indeed look very painful.'

'It is, but in time, Harmony will heal. Won't you?' she said, still stroking the dragon. In response, the dragon lowered her head and gently nudged Elspeth.

'I still wish I could do that,' Jib said as he enviously watched Elspeth with her dragon.

'Well, I wish I could do your magic,' Elspeth said. 'Then I could make Lord Dorcon disappear for ever.'

Elan shook his head. 'We never use our powers to hurt people.'

'But what if they're very bad, like Lord Dorcon and King Arden?'

Elan sighed. 'We may want to. But we can't. That would be an abuse of power. Only evil wizards use their powers to harm people.'

Elspeth looked at Elan and frowned. 'There really are evil wizards? Paradon never told us.'

'There are,' Elan agreed. 'Onnie-Astra was actually

the worst of all. He was the most evil wizard there has ever been.'

Elspeth shivered at the sound of that name again. She immediately looked over to Onnie. Opening her arms, the fox leaped up and licked her chin. 'What did he do?'

Elan looked at the fox in Elspeth's arms and hesitated. Finally he said, 'Many, many bad things. He hurt and killed a lot of people, just for the pleasure of it. But he wasn't alone. Onnie-Astra had twin brothers who were almost as bad.'

'That whole family was evil,' Gwen added, joining the conversation. 'My grandparents were killed by their father. He wanted my family's estate for his own so he killed my grandparents and stole it. He built a castle on their land. I believe the twins are still there and never leave it.'

Elspeth shivered and hugged the fox tighter. 'If they are still alive, does that mean Onnie-Astra is alive too?'

Elan shrugged. 'After he disappeared, no one heard from him again. Maybe the twins killed him or maybe he just ran away. I don't know.'

'You think the twins would kill their own brother?'

Gwen nodded. 'It wouldn't surprise me. They always hated each other.'

'My father once told me,' added Elan, 'when Onnie-Astra was very young, the twins used to fight with him all the time. They used to attack their younger brother because he had more power than they did. In fact, the twins had to combine their powers just to be equal to Onnie-Astra.'

All this talk of evil wizards was making Elspeth shiver. 'Well, I hope I never meet Onnie-Astra or the twins. They sound really scary.'

In her arms, Onnie lowered his head and licked her hands. Then he yipped.

'What did he say?' Jib asked.

Elspeth smiled. 'Onnie said I shouldn't be frightened because he would protect me.'

Once again, Elan and Gwen looked at the fox with an odd expression. 'Indeed,' Elan finally said. Then he deepened his voice as he stared at Onnie. 'As would we all.'

CHAPTER
~13~

While Elspeth waited patiently for Paradon to come for her, three long winters came and went without notice. Living on the mountain, she was hardly aware of time's passing. Falling into a comfortable routine, each night she and Onnie would climb on Harmony's back and fly up to the ridge area where the Rogue and Blue had nested.

They would sit together on the edge of the mountain for half the night gazing into the star-filled sky, hoping and praying that this would be the night the Eye opened and she could finally go home.

But as more seasons flew by without any signs of Paradon or her family, Elspeth started to lose hope. 'We've just got to face it, Onnie,' she sighed late one evening, 'they're never coming back for us. We're stuck here.'

The fox threw back his head and howled mournfully.

'How can I keep hope when it's been so long?' Elspeth said sadly. 'I'm sure if they were coming, it would have been before now.'

Standing up, Elspeth helped Onnie climb back into his pouch. 'I'm tired of waiting. We've simply got to accept that we'll never get home.'

Seated in his pouch, Onnie rested his paws on Elspeth's shoulder and asked her what else there was to do but wait.

'I don't really know,' she admitted. 'I guess we'll stay here on the mountain. This is the only place we can live and still be together. I wouldn't want to live anywhere else. Would you?'

When Onnie yipped in agreement, Elspeth looked over to the dragon waiting patiently behind her. 'We haven't taken Harmony out for some exercise in a very long time. I think we should go for a quick flight. Then maybe we can go down to the village to see Gwen and Elan. I know it's a bit late, but they've been asking us to visit more often.'

Elspeth stepped up to the red dragon, climbed up her wing and settled on her bare back. 'Harmony, I know you don't like to fly at night, but you need your exercise. This really is the only time to do it so the king's men don't see you.'

Without hesitation, Harmony leaped gracefully off the ridge. Elspeth directed her to fly around the top of the mountain for a bit and then further out over the dark forests. After a time, she pulled on the reins and directed the dragon to fly down to the clearing on the outskirts of the village.

When they landed, Elspeth stepped up to the dragon's head. 'Now, Harmony, I want you to stay here for a bit and rest. Onnie and I are going into the village, but we won't be long.'

Elspeth smiled as the large red dragon settled down in the soft pine needles. She tucked her front claws under herself and wrapped her long tail comfortably around her body.

'You look just like a cat,' Elspeth teased as she stroked the dragon's snout. 'Stay here and we'll be back soon.'

As Elspeth started to walk away, she became aware of hushed movement in the trees surrounding them. Onnie heard it also and leaped down from his pouch. Standing erect, his full tail lashed back and forth as he sniffed the air.

'What is it, Onnie?' Elspeth whispered, straining her eyes to see into the darkened trees. 'I'm sure it's not animals.'

Moments later, Onnie started to growl. Behind his growls came the deeper, more threatening sounds of Harmony's warning growls as the dragon unwrapped her tail and stood up in anticipation.

'Who's out there?' Elspeth demanded as she drew her dagger. 'Show yourselves.'

Instead of an answer, the sounds of movement increased. Suddenly there was a single shout as a large group of bandits burst out of the trees.

'Get the dragon!' the bandit leader ordered. 'We'll take care of the girl!'

Elspeth looked around quickly and saw that they were surrounded. Several huge men charged towards her as the rest concentrated on capturing Harmony.

Acting on instinct alone, Elspeth called out to the animals of the forest for help. She also called to Harmony. But she needn't have. The dragon was already charging the bandits and scattering them as she ran towards Elspeth.

As the first bandit neared Elspeth, Onnie raced forward and sank his teeth into the man's ankles. When he fell, the fox attacked his head. Before the second man could touch her, Elspeth saw flashes of black and white as two large badgers raced forward. Snarling and growling, they too attacked the bandit's legs.

Soon Harmony was at Elspeth's side and viciously attacking anyone who came too close. Looking around quickly, Elspeth could see that most of bandits carried heavy ropes and were trying to get them around Harmony's head. It was then she realized that Harmony was their target. The bandits wanted to steal her dragon.

'Help us!' Elspeth shouted into the darkness. 'Come forward and help us!'

The forest erupted in sound as more animals arrived and attacked the bandits. But with so much activity going on around her, Elspeth failed to see a lone bandit creeping up from behind. Suddenly she felt an arm catching hold of her as a knife went up to her throat.

'Drop your dagger!' the bandit threatened. 'Do it now!'

Elspeth could smell his stinking, filthy body. Following his orders she dropped her dagger. 'You can't have my dragon!' she cried.

'We'll take anything we want!' the bandit responded, breathing his foul breath into her face. 'No slip of a girl is going to stop us. Now stop the animals or you're dead!'

Elspeth was about to call to the animals when Onnie saw what was happening to her. Yipping and barking in rage, the small red fox launched himself at the man.

'Onnie, stop!' Elspeth warned when she felt the bandit tighten his grip.

'You've got a tamed fox?' he demanded. Then he called to the others. 'Everyone, look, she's got a fox!'

'A fox,' the other bandits muttered. 'She's got a fox!'

Before Elspeth could speak another word, or call out for more animals, there was a warning shout from one of the bandits. He was pointing a shaking finger behind Elspeth and the man holding her. 'Bear!'

Suddenly a huge black bear stood on his hind legs and growled ferociously. His large black paw lashed out, knocking both Elspeth and the bandit to the ground. Falling together, Elspeth felt the bandit loosening his grip on her.

Using the opportunity, Elspeth kicked and fought her way free of the bandit just as the bear moved in to attack him.

Onnie quickly joined the attack as he ordered Elspeth to move to a safe distance.

'Stop this madness!' a loud voice suddenly boomed. Around them the woods were flooded with peals of thunder and flashing light.

Looking over to the new voice, Elspeth saw Elan. He was standing with his hands raised in the air as lightning bolts flew from his fingertips. The lightning struck the bandits still fighting to capture Harmony, driving them away from the dragon.

'The wizard!' several cried. 'Run!' They immediately stopped their attack and disappeared into the safety of the woods.

'Elspeth!' Elan cried as he ran over to where she was lying.

Elspeth sat up and gratefully hugged the wizard.

'Are you all right?' he demanded as his eyes went up and down her body, searching for wounds. 'Did they hurt you?'

Elspeth shook her head. 'No. The animals saved me.'

Onnie immediately rushed to her side while she looked around the area. Most of the animals had survived the fight and were looking to her for their next command. Further away, the black bear left the bandit he had attacked and came lumbering forward.

When Elan helped Elspeth climb unsteadily to her feet, she turned to the bear. She stroked his large head. 'Thank you for saving me.' Elspeth then looked at all the animals around her and repeated her thanks. Finally she told them all to return to the forest.

As they started to drift slowly away, Elspeth looked at Elan and thanked him also. Then she asked, 'How did you know we were in trouble?'

Elan went down on one knee and hugged her again. The strength of his embrace told her just how frightened he'd been.

'I woke up and heard Harmony roaring. I knew then something was up. Lucky for both of us, Gwen can sleep through anything and didn't stir. I wouldn't have wanted her to see this.'

His voice then became stern as his grip on her arms tightened. 'Elspeth, what in the stars are you doing out here this late at night? Haven't I warned you time and time again that there are dangerous bandits living in this forest? Do you realize what could have happened to you? Those bandits were only interested in Harmony. They'd have killed you and Onnie to get her.'

Elspeth stole a glance at Harmony and saw the many ropes hanging from her neck, around her wings and tied to her legs. She looked back to Elan and dropped her head.

Elan then looked at Onnie and continued. 'And you, Onnie. You should have known better than to let Elspeth come down here at night. What were you thinking?'

Onnie also dropped his head in shame.

'When I think of what could have happened to you,' Elan said as he shivered. Then his eyes went from her to search the area. 'Elspeth, where is your bow? You're an excellent shot. Why didn't you bring it with you?'

'I couldn't. It's broken,' Elspeth explained. 'I went to practise with it, but when I pulled back too hard on the string it broke the bow.'

Elan took in a deep breath to calm himself. 'Paradon gave it to you when you were eight. You're almost thirteen now. No wonder it broke.' He paused and then made a decision. 'All right, first thing we do is get you back to the mountain and cleaned up. I don't want Gwen or Jib to ever hear of this. If they do, they'll never stop insisting you move in with us.'

'I can't. I won't leave Harmony,' Elspeth said.

'I know,' Elan agreed softly, 'which is why we'll never tell them. Then, in the morning I'm going to make sure you have a brand-new bow that will never break. I don't ever want you caught out again.'

As the excitement passed, Elspeth felt herself starting to shake. Elan was right. This could have turned out so much worse if the animals and he hadn't come. Finally she looked around at the bodies of the bandits and fallen animals. 'What about them?'

'I'll take care of them,' Elan said, 'after I get you all safely back to your mountain.'

CHAPTER
— 14 —

Elspeth and Elan never did tell Gwen and Jib what happened on the night she came down from the mountain. Instead, Elspeth filled her days practising with the new bow Elan made for her. She wasn't going to leave herself open to attack ever again.

As more winters flew by, her skills were sharpened to the point where she hit any target she wanted from every possible position, either on Harmony's back or while hanging upside down from a tree. No target was ever missed.

Throughout the passing seasons, the bandits seemed more determined than ever to get hold of Harmony. Elspeth reasoned that with only the king's knights allowed to keep dragons, should the bandits ever capture and harness Harmony, they would be unstoppable against any village they attacked.

So determined were the bandits that they even

climbed the mountain and entered the meadow through the crack in the wall. They had prepared themselves to find Elspeth, Onnie and the dragon there. What they hadn't counted on was the army of other animals Elspeth now kept around her at all times. The fight was brief but brutal as the surviving bandits were driven back down the mountainside by Elspeth with her deadly bow and all the other animals protecting her.

When it was over, Elspeth used Harmony and several large bears to help hide the evidence of the attack. She hated to lie to the family from below, but if they knew just how often the bandits came after her, she realized that even Elan would insist she give up Harmony and leave the mountain.

That she would never do.

So instead, when the family came for their regular and most welcome visits, they found no traces of the battles. What they did find was Elspeth living very contentedly with all the animals, her dragon and Onnie at the top of the mountain.

During these frequent visits, Elspeth would teach Jib how to use a bow. He was a quick student and anxious to learn all the skills she could teach him.

As Elan watched both Elspeth and Jib training, he

whistled in approval. 'Elspeth, I wouldn't be surprised if you could beat all of the king's best knights. But I think there is one skill you have been neglecting.'

'What's that?' Elspeth said, lowering her bow.

'Your power over animals,' Elan said. 'Elspeth, like any talent or power, it requires practice. Just like Jib with his powers, as you grow, yours are growing with you. But you don't have any control. Tell me, if you tried right now, could you summon just a wolf or a hawk? Or would all the animals in the area come?'

Elspeth looked at Elan and shook her head. 'I don't know. They'd probably all come along. But how do I learn?'

Elan rubbed his chin. 'I'm not sure. I've never encountered your kind of power before. All I can suggest is that you take some time each day to try to teach yourself how to use it. You never know when you're going to need it . . .' Making sure that Gwen and Jib didn't hear, he added softly, 'again.'

Elspeth let Elan know she understood what he meant – though she didn't let on that she'd already used her power countless times on all the other bandit attacks. So instead she nodded and lied. 'You're right. I really should learn how to use it properly.'

CHAPTER
~ 15 ~

'Why don't you let us spend more time down here?' Kira asked as she and Paradon worked in the kitchen area of the lower cave preparing food. They'd only been in the future world a short time, but while they had been there, Paradon kept them living out in the meadow and away from spending any time in the cave with his things.

'It's better if you don't become too comfortable with the trappings of this time,' Paradon said. 'There are things in here that are not dreamed of in your own world. Seeing them now, means you might miss them when you go back.'

'All I'll miss from this time is you,' Kira said softly. 'The rest of this stuff scares me too much. I especially don't like that thing you have on the wall that shows pictures of what's happening.'

'Television,' Paradon said. 'It's called a television.'

Kira was referring to the first time she saw herself on the news broadcasts. She had seen the recorded images of the choppers chasing them through the caverns of the city when they first arrived. The cameras had captured pictures of Jinx and Rexor being shot. If Paradon hadn't come to their aid, those pictures would have also recorded everyone being killed.

'Still,' she added, as she pulled fresh vegetables out of the big white box Paradon called the 'refrigerator'. 'There might be a few things I would miss.'

'Such as?' the wizard asked.

'Chocolate,' Kira answered quickly. 'I do like chocolate.'

'Anything else?'

'I also like the music and how it can be kept and replayed. I would love to be able to have that in your castle.'

Paradon laughed. 'Is that all? Of all the wonders here in this cave, all you would miss is chocolate and music?'

Kira considered for a moment then nodded. 'Yes, that's all. Everything else here is terrible. No dragons, no trees, nothing but smelly, dirty skies and sad lonely people. I just hope things are better for Elspeth where she is.'

'I'm sure they are,' Paradon said. 'At least she is in a time of dragons, when trees and nature are respected and cherished. I have no doubt she is fine and anxiously awaiting your arrival.'

'I just hope she found Elan,' Kira added. 'I'd hate to think of her all alone back there. She's strong, but she's still so very young. I worry about her all the time.'

'As do I,' Paradon agreed. 'But she does have Onnie and Harmony. If no one else is there to help, they would do anything to protect her.'

'I know,' Kira agreed. 'But still, we've been together for so long, I feel lost without her.'

'You'll be together again soon,' Paradon assured her. 'In fact, I'll be sending you all back to the very moment she arrived there. So you needn't worry about her being alone for long as she won't be.'

Kira said nothing. But she still couldn't understand how all this time travel stuff worked. All she could do was hope that Paradon had the power to do what he promised.

Not far from the kitchen area, Jinx sat watching her. He tilted his head to the side when she looked at him. Unable to resist, Kira crossed to him and scratched behind his ears. Her eyes were then drawn to the dark caves that lead deeper into the mountains. So long ago, those caves had been their only escape from the Rogue.

She turned back to the old wizard. 'Do those caves still lead through the mountain and come out at the lake?'

'They did,' Paradon answered. 'But I sealed them off long ago when the soldiers tried to enter. They are quite determined to discover the mountain's secret. They have no idea it's just one old wizard and a bit of magic. I think they believe it is some kind of super weapon.'

'What happened to all the magic?' Kira asked. 'Aren't there any other wizards?'

'No, sadly, I'm the last—'

Suddenly from above, Kira heard Kahrin shrieking in terror and Rexor's weak roar. Moments later, Kahrin breathlessly arrived at the entrance of the cave. 'Kira,' she called down. 'Choppers are coming down into the meadow!'

'Choppers?' Kira cried. She looked to Paradon. 'How?'

'I don't know,' the old wizard answered as he started moving up the entrance ramp. 'Maybe they've found a weakness or I didn't close the shield properly after you arrived.'

Panic for her family had Kira racing up the ramp

past Paradon. With Jinx following closely behind, the old wizard was knocked to the ground and sent tumbling back down the ramp.

Kira ran out of the cave and on to the grass. Her eyes grew wide with fear. Two choppers were lowering down into the meadow at the far end near their very first cave.

Though still badly wounded, Rexor had lifted his head and was doing his best to roar at the approaching choppers. He then tried to drag himself closer to attack.

Shanks was sitting up and struggling to climb out of bed while Dane had already drawn his sword and was running at the descending choppers.

When Jinx caught sight of the choppers, he threw back his head in a ferocious roar. He raced passed Kira. Opening his wings, he launched himself into the air after the flying machines.

'No, Jinx!' Kira cried, chasing after him. 'Stop!'

Unable to control the dragon, Kira watched him flying at the choppers. In response, both choppers opened fire on the approaching dragon. But this time, Jinx was too fast. He easily manoeuvred out of the path of the bullet streams as he flew at the closest chopper.

Before the deadly war machine could escape,

Jinx caught hold of the chopper's landing gear. Flapping his wings to bring it down, he started to shake his big blue head.

Unprepared for the added weight of the large dragon hanging from its underside, the chopper rocked back and forth in the sky. It started to lose height. Fighting for control, it veered too close to the upper wall of the meadow. Suddenly the chopper's spinning rotors clipped the stone wall and broke violently apart, firing twisted metal fragments into the air.

The second chopper tried to manoeuvre away from the lethal fragments, but failed as huge pieces of twisted rotors struck it multiple times. When one cut into the fuel supply, the chopper exploded, turning it into a huge fireball of burning debris that rained down from the sky.

The blast from the explosion knocked Dane and Kira to the ground. Shielding their heads, they both lay directly under the path of the falling debris.

Crouched in a ball, Kira heard the sound of chunks of burning metal hitting the ground all around her. But when she uncovered her head, she saw that both she and Dane remained unharmed.

She then looked back and saw Paradon standing at the entrance of the cave with his hands held high in the air. The air around him sparkled as he cast the spell of protection. Kira gratefully realized that the wizard had saved their lives yet again.

But there was no time to celebrate. As she sat up, she looked back to the first chopper and watched it coming down. Jinx was still clinging to the landing gear of the machine and tearing at it in a fury.

'Let go, Jinx!' Kira cried, fearful that her beloved dragon would be crushed under the weight of the crashing chopper. But just before it hit the ground Jinx released the landing gear and glided to safety.

When the chopper crashed down, there was no explosion, no fire. Instead the air was filled with the sickening, groaning sound of crunching metal and breaking glass.

Standing away from the stricken air machine, Jinx reared up on his hind legs, opened his healing wings and roared triumphantly.

'Kira!' Dane cried as he crawled over to her. 'Are you all right?'

Kira sat up and nodded. 'How about you?'

'I'm fine,' he laughed, hardly able to believe he was still alive. 'But we shouldn't be! We were right under that thing when it blew.'

Kira started laughing too. 'It was Paradon. He cast a

spell that worked! Dane, he protected us.'

Beside them, Jinx started to growl again. Looking over to him, Kira saw that all his attention was on the wrecked chopper. As she inspected the mangled machine, she thought she saw movement from within.

Quickly standing, Kira drew her dagger. 'There's someone alive in there!'

Dane also raised his sword. Together he and Kira stepped cautiously around the burning pieces of debris and crossed over to the fallen chopper. As they drew near, Kira wondered how anyone could have survived. The chopper looked nothing like it did before. The metal was bent and twisted and the glass was shattered and scattered all over the grass.

But when they approached its side and peered in, both Kira and Dane sucked in their breath as they saw two men struggling to get themselves free of the wreck. Kira couldn't see their faces because of the armour they wore. It was exactly the same as the armour worn by the men on the roof when they'd first arrived. But they were both alive and looking at them.

'Kira, Dane, stand back,' Paradon warned as he stepped up to the wreck.

Kira looked at the old wizard and saw him clinging to his staff for support. Crossing to him, she put her arm around his waist and helped him to stand.

'There are two men alive in there,' Dane said. Lifting his sword, he reluctantly moved closer.

'Dane, what are you doing?' Kira demanded.

'I have to finish this.'

'You're not going to kill them, are you?'

'We have to,' Dane said. 'They tried to kill us. They're dangerous.'

Kira shook her head. 'You can't do that. We're not like them, Dane. Look at them. They're just men. If we hurt them, that makes us no better than Lord Dorcon.'

'What if they have weapons?' Dane said. 'What if they try to attack us again?'

'But what if they don't?' Kira challenged.

'I think your sister is right,' Paradon said. 'Dane, you don't know this time. These men had no choice; they were ordered to come here. I have no doubt they have families who care for them. Think of their families if nothing else.'

Kira looked at her brother and saw the hesitation there. He didn't want to hurt the men either. He was just looking out for his family. Finally Dane nodded and lowered his sword. 'You're right.'

'Can you speak to them?' Kira asked Paradon.

'I can try,' the wizard said.

With his arm around Kira for support, Paradon approached the wreck and leaned in. In a language Kira and Dane couldn't understand, they heard the men's frightened response to Paradon. Then they took off their helmets.

Kira was shocked to see they were just young men. While they spoke, their eyes kept darting over to Jinx who was standing before the wreck and growling viciously.

'It's as I suspected,' Paradon said when he finished and looked over to Kira. 'They have no weapons on them. And believe me, they are a lot more frightened than you are.'

'So what do we do with them?' Dane asked.

Paradon rubbed his chin. 'Well, I think we should help them out of the wreckage and then get them settled in that cave over there.'

'You think they should stay in the meadow with us?' Dane asked.

'Not with us, Dane. But here in this small cave. It won't be for long. Shanks and Rexor are healing and you'll be leaving soon. After that, their men can come and collect them.'

'But in the meantime, they'll be here!' Dane said. 'What if they come after us again?'

Paradon chuckled. 'Look at them, Dane. They're terrified of Jinx. Do you really think they would try something with no weapons of their own, against two large dragons?'

'I guess not,' Dane admitted.

'Now, if you wouldn't mind helping me get those two out of there, we can settle them in their new home. After that, I think I need some rest. Today's excitement has left me a bit drained.'

Kira looked into Paradon's pale eyes and saw the exhaustion settling there. Saving them from the burning debris and resealing the hole in the shield over the meadow had taken a heavy toll of the old wizard.

'Paradon,' Kira softly said. 'Dane, Kahrin and I can help the men. All I want you to do is tell them what we are going to do and then rest.'

Paradon sighed heavily. 'I won't argue with that.'

Once again Kira looked at Paradon and felt fear rising. The old wizard was fading fast. What if he didn't have the strength to send them home? What if they never left this terrible world? What would happen to them then? And what about Elspeth? What would happen to her?

CHAPTER
~ 16 ~

Still more seasons came and more seasons went on the mountain. For Elspeth, spring had arrived and passed quietly into summer with no sign of Paradon or her family. Living on the mountain, she finally accepted the fact that no one was coming back for her and that she would spend the rest of her life here.

But she felt far from alone. There was a family down in the village that cared for her and whom she loved deeply. She had Onnie and Harmony as constant companions as well as all the animals living with them in the meadow.

Elspeth learned to control her powers tightly. And though she was never sure how it all worked, she could summon any number of different animals at any time to do whatever she asked of them.

As the time passed, she was completely unaware of the changes in herself. But somewhere along the way, she had grown from a child into a strong, independent young woman. Though she could never see the changes in herself, she did notice them in Jib.

He had shot up like a weed and standing next to his father, was almost as tall as Elan. Training long and hard, Jib had also become a very powerful wizard. He could now get himself up to the meadow without needing his father's help or powers.

Jib's nightly visits to the mountain always brightened Elspeth's spirits and kept away any loneliness she might have felt. When he arrived, they would often go up to the highest ridge and sit together counting stars.

'It will be my birthday soon,' Jib said staring up at the full moon. 'I'll be eighteen.'

Elspeth sat beside him clutching Onnie in her arms. She playfully shoved him. 'You're getting old.'

'Old enough to get married,' he said awkwardly. 'This is what I wanted to speak to you about.'

'What's that?' she asked, turning to look at him.

'Well, you're old enough to marry too. I know Mother always hoped that we'd get together.'

In her lap, Onnie started to growl softly as the fur on the back of his neck rose.

'Jib, wait, please,' she said holding up her hand. Elspeth felt her mouth go dry. She'd been dreading this moment for a long time. She was sixteen, the age when most girls in the village got married. Had she been back home, under First Law, she'd have been married for three years already. But it wasn't right for her.

'You know I care about you,' she said as she stroked Onnie's head and calmed the fox down, 'but you are like a brother to me. You're my best friend. I couldn't marry you. I belong up here on the mountain with Onnie.'

Jib looked at Elspeth in surprise and then burst out laughing. Soon he was rolling around on the ground. 'Marry you?' he struggled to say. 'Are you mad? I don't want to marry you!'

Suddenly annoyed by his laughter, Elspeth challenged, 'Why not? What's wrong with me?'

Regaining control, Jib sat up again and swept his arm in the air to include the whole area. 'There's nothing wrong with marrying you. That's if you don't mind a cottage full of animals!'

Elspeth looked around. Gathered behind them was an odd assortment of wildlife. These included Harmony, several badgers, a young wolf and multiple owls. Beneath them, the meadow was filled with wolves, bears and many other forest creatures that lived with her and kept the bandits away.

'All right, so I like animals,' she admitted.

'And they love you,' Jib said earnestly. 'So do I. But you're like a sister to me. Not a wife.' Jib paused and reached for Elspeth's hand. 'Elspeth, I want to marry Mariah.'

'The butcher's daughter?'

Jib nodded. 'I've been in love with her for ages. And I know she feels the same about me. She and her parents have been away visiting family and are coming back tomorrow evening. I want to ask her then. The trouble is, I don't think Mother likes her very much. Because she's been hoping you and I would get together, she won't accept anyone else.'

'But what can I do?' Elspeth asked.

'Please come down to the cottage and talk to her. Tell her what you just told me. That you see me as your brother and friend and that there is no hope for us getting together.'

Elspeth felt a strange sadness sweeping over her. She knew the day would come when their lives would change. But it all seemed so sudden.

Finally she nodded. 'All right. Tomorrow evening, before you speak to Mariah, I'll come down for a visit. Don't tell anyone I'm coming. We'll just behave as we normally do. Then I'll figure out some way to tell her.'

Jib grinned and playfully shoved her over. 'You're the best!'

Standing, he reached for her hand and drew her up. 'I hope some day you find someone special too. You deserve it.'

Elspeth smiled. 'I hope so.'

'I'd better get back.' Grinning like a child with a favourite toy, Jib stepped away from Elspeth. 'See you tomorrow night!' Raising his hands in the air, he cast the spell that would take him from the mountain back down to the cottage.

When he was gone, Elspeth sat down again. Soon the animals around her started to creep forward, seeking her attention. Staring into the night sky, she sighed sadly. 'I don't think I'll ever find someone who'll love me like Jib does Mariah.' Picking up the fox, Elspeth hugged him tightly. 'It's going to be you and me for ever, Onnie.'

CHAPTER
~ 17 ~

After Kira and Jinx arrived back at the campfire from taking food to their prisoners in the far cave, they settled down to eat.

'How are they?' Paradon asked, handing a bowl of stew to her.

'Hungry,' Kira answered, also reaching for bread. 'And they're still completely terrified of Jinx.'

'Good,' Dane said. 'That will keep them from trying anything against us.'

'I don't think they would anyway,' Kira said. 'Looking at them, it doesn't seem like they want to try anything at all. They're just lying around doing nothing.'

'They won't try anything,' Paradon said. 'This is most likely the first break those two men have ever had in their lives. In this world, work never stops. It is long and hard with no rewards and no time off.'

'Like those choppers overhead?' Kira asked. 'They

never seem to stop. I had hoped that after what happened with the first two, they wouldn't come back.'

'They won't leave,' Paradon warned. 'Not as long as we're here.'

'And not as long as we hold their men,' Dane added.

'I'm afraid they don't care about their men,' Paradon said. 'All they are interested in is capturing the dragons. No doubt they are searching for more holes in the shield.'

'How long do you think it will be before we can go?' Shanks asked. He was out of bed and sitting beside Dane at the fire.

'A while yet,' Paradon responded. 'You still aren't fit to travel. And, though he is healing, Rexor is far too weak to fly.'

Jinx was beside Kira as she and Kahrin sat leaning against his thick neck. 'Jinx is much better,' Kira added. 'I actually think attacking that chopper did him some good. He's found that he can fly again. He'll be ready the moment Shanks and Rexor are.'

Dane looked over to Paradon. 'But how are you feeling? Are you strong enough to cast the spell to get us home?'

Paradon considered for a moment and then nodded. 'I have to be. We've got no choice.'

Kira heard something in his voice. 'What's wrong, Paradon?'

Poking at the fire, Paradon wouldn't look at her. 'I was looking in the Eye today and saw something that none of us expected.'

'Did you see Shadow?' Kira demanded. 'Has something happened to her?'

'Sadly, no, I couldn't see Elspeth. But what I did see was very disturbing indeed.'

'What was it?' Dane asked.

'Well, it seems that when I opened the shield to let you all come in, in my fear and worry for you, I didn't close it properly.'

'We know. The choppers got in,' Kira said. 'But you've closed it again.'

Paradon nodded. 'But not before several groups of soldiers got in at the base of the mountain. They are on foot, but they are making their way up the side of the mountain right now.'

'What?' everyone cried. 'Soldiers are coming up the mountain?'

When Paradon nodded, Dane continued. 'Where are they? How long do we have until they get here?'

'Quite a while yet,' Paradon said. Then he actually chuckled. 'This is the first time they have ever encountered any sort of wildlife. They are having great difficulties walking amongst trees. They're tripping over roots and stumbling on stones. Not to mention the animals they are encountering. All of this is new to them and it's slowing them right down.'

'Slow or not, we've got to prepare,' Shanks said.

'Indeed we do,' Paradon agreed. 'If we're lucky, you'll all be gone before they arrive. But if we're not, then we are going to have to fight.'

'Have you seen which way they are coming?' Kira asked. 'Will they use the crack in the wall?'

Paradon shook his head. 'Actually, I've already sealed the crack. I didn't want our two new friends to try climbing down the mountain. It was too dangerous for them. No, when the soldiers arrive, they will have to climb to the upper rim.' Paradon paused and pointed to the rim surrounding the meadow. 'If they use their weapons against us, I'm afraid it will be like shooting fish in a barrel.'

'Well, we'll use our bows to fire back,' Kira said.

'But I can't use a bow,' Kahrin said softly.

'Not yet,' Paradon said. 'Before they arrive I think we should use this precious time to practise your fighting skills. I hate to suggest it, but I think it might be a good idea for Dane and Shanks to teach you girls how to fight. Hand-to-hand as well as with swords.'

'Swords?' Kira repeated in shock. 'Paradon, you always said you didn't want me to learn sword fighting because it was ugly and brutal. You said I should use a bow.'

'Sword fighting is brutal,' Paradon answered. 'That wound you received at Lasser should be proof enough. But it also proved that you have no experience with fighting up close. If you are going to protect this mountain and then go back to fulfil the prophecy, you've got to learn all you can.'

'He's right,' Dane agreed. 'If we want to fulfil the prophecy and end King Arden's reign, we are going to have to fight. Knowing all you can about it will help. We can teach you everything you need to know.'

The next morning, while Paradon used the Eye to follow the slow progress of the soldiers up the mountain, Dane and Shanks started to teach the girls how to fight.

Still recovering from his wounds, Shanks spent time with Kahrin teaching her how to use a bow while Dane gave Kira instruction on how to hold and use a sword.

'Kira, hold your sword a bit lower,' Shanks called as he watched Dane and Kira with their wooden swords.

'If you don't, Dane can come in at you from below.'

'Like this,' Dane said. Moving quickly, he slashed under Kira's wooden sword and struck her in the side. Just getting over her own sword wound, the blow knocked her to the ground and drove the wind from her lungs.

'Kira!' Shanks cried. He crossed over and put his arm around her. 'Are you all right?' He then looked over to Dane. 'You're supposed to teach her, not kill her!'

'It's all right, I'm fine,' Kira said, gasping for breath.

'Kira, I'm so sorry!' Dane said as he kneeled beside his sister. 'I forgot all about your wound.'

Behind them, Jinx moved closer and started growling lightly at Dane and Shanks as they crowded next to her. Further away, the recovering Rexor also took several curious steps forward.

Gritting her teeth against the throbbing pain, Kira looked at the dragons. 'Stop it, Jinx,' she said. 'I'm all right.'

With the help of her brother and Shanks, Kira climbed painfully to her feet. She looked at Dane. 'Really, I'm fine. We've got to keep training. I don't think those soldiers coming up the mountain will care that I was already hurt.'

'Sadly, Kira is right,' Paradon added as he and

Kahrin slowly crossed to her. 'However, I would suggest that you take it a bit slower. With the two of you still recovering from your wounds, it wouldn't be wise to overdo it.'

'I really am sorry, Kira,' Dane said softly, feeling awful for hurting her. 'Why don't we take a break?'

'Good idea,' Kira agreed as she rubbed her aching side. She then looked at the two large dragons hovering protectively behind her. 'And as for you two,' she said stepping back to Jinx. 'I'm fine and I don't ever want to hear either of you growling at Dane or Shanks again. Do you understand me?'

'I don't think they do,' Shanks said as he warily watched the two dragons pressing closer to Kira. 'One more mistake like that and we'll be their next meal.'

'No you won't,' Kira said to Shanks as she reached up to scratch behind Jinx's ear. When she finished with him, she turned to Rexor and did the same. 'They're just protective of me and don't understand that we are training.'

'Then I wouldn't worry about the soldiers coming up the mountain, or Lord Dorcon for that matter,' Shanks added as he stood back watching her with the dragons. 'Not with those two protecting you.'

'They'll protect all of us,' Kira said.

'Yes, of course!' Shanks teased. 'Just like those choppers up there want to protect us and the soldiers on the mountain are coming to invite us to a party.'

After several more days, Shanks was feeling well enough to actually join in the training. Working with Dane, they slowly demonstrated the moves the girls had to learn.

It was then the girls' turn to try. After many mistakes and several more blows to Kira's wound, both Kira and Kahrin started to learn the principles of sword fighting.

'I still prefer using a bow,' Kira said tiredly as they sat around the campfire late that evening.

'I really like using the bow,' Kahrin added. 'It's fun.'

'So do I,' Shanks agreed. 'But sometimes we have to fight in situations where a bow isn't possible. That's why you've got to learn sword and hand-to-hand combat.'

Kira looked at Shanks. 'Have you ever had to fight hand-to-hand?'

Shanks nodded. 'Not too long ago. It was after they took Dane back to the palace to face punishment for your father trying to kill Lord Dorcon. I was with several other knights in territory we'd just claimed. We were on the ground looking for survivors when knights from King Casey's legion attacked us. There was no time to get back to our dragons, so we fought.'

'Did you kill anybody?' Kahrin asked softly.

Shanks lowered his head.

As Kira watched him, she was sure he wasn't going to say anything. Finally he looked back up at Kahrin. Kira could see the pain in his eyes.

'I did,' he answered. 'I don't think I'll ever forget the knight's face. He was just a boy.' Shanks then looked over to Dane. 'Do you remember Little Toby from our class?'

'I do,' Dane said.

'Well, this boy looked just like him. He was so scared. When it was over, right before he died, he started to cry. I remember holding him in my arms. He gave me his mother's name and begged me to find her and tell her that he loved her.' Shanks lowered his head and started to shake. 'I felt so guilty and sick. I realized then that the war was senseless. We weren't fighting enemies for a good cause. We were fighting boys who were trying to protect their families.'

Dane looked at Shanks. 'You never told me any of this.'

'I've never told anyone,' Shanks admitted. 'I knew then if we hadn't been called back to the palace to come after Paradon and the girls, I would have deserted. I just couldn't fight any more.'

Finally Kira spoke. 'Shanks, the fight isn't over. When we go back, we've got to do something to stop King Arden.'

When Shanks looked up at her again, there was determination shining in his eyes. 'I know,' he said. 'And this is one fight I won't shy away from. The prophecy may say that it's you who will bring down the monarchy. That's fine. But what it doesn't say is that you will have a lot of help.'

CHAPTER
~ 18 ~

The day after Jib's visit and the revelation that he wanted to get married, Elspeth didn't feel like practising her bow work. Instead, she wandered around the meadow. Surrounded by animals, she felt strangely alone.

She knew she should be happy for Jib. Part of her was. But another part of her was reminded of just how alone she truly was. Living on the mountain with only the animals for companionship, eight winters had somehow slipped past and her childhood had ended.

Elspeth had long ago surrendered hope of Paradon or her family ever coming for her. But looking around at the meadow, she realized how much she still missed them. Elan and Gwen had taken her into their hearts and treated her as family. She loved them dearly. But still, something was missing.

'What's wrong with me, Onnie?' she asked as she wandered aimlessly around. 'Why can't I be happy for

Jib? I don't want him for myself. Why shouldn't he marry the girl he loves?'

With no answers to be found, Elspeth waited for sunset. When it was almost dark, she helped Onnie into the pack on her back and climbed up on Harmony's wing.

'Why don't we go for a quick flight before we head down to the village? I don't want to get there too early.'

Giving the order to Harmony to take off, they were soon leaving the meadow and flying down the mountainside. The moon was full again and starting to rise on the distant horizon. Directing Harmony forward, they made their way back to the area where Paradon's castle would one day stand.

Along the way, several owls joined them in their silent journey in the sky. Their presence would normally make Elspeth smile. This evening however, having them flying alongside only served to remind her of how different she truly was.

'All of you go home!' she ordered. But her calls were ignored. Nothing she could do or say would drive the birds away.

With his paws resting on her shoulder, Onnie started to yip. She stole a quick glance at him and sighed. 'I know Paradon's castle won't be here for many, many winters yet to come. But I just needed to see it.'

When she had searched the whole area and found only trees, Elspeth turned Harmony around. 'I guess we can go back now,' she said. 'It's time to tell Gwen the truth.'

Flying back towards the village, Elspeth looked down and saw multiple torches moving swiftly along the road that cut through the forest.

'They're going awfully fast,' she said to Onnie. 'Let's go down and see what's happening.'

Elspeth directed the dragon down, and started to follow the line of the road. Ahead of them they saw several men on horseback shouting and chasing a carriage that was racing to get away.

As the dragon passed unseen overhead, Elspeth looked back and watched one of the mounted men leap off his horse and attack the driver of the carriage.

'Harmony, takes us back there,' Elspeth ordered urgently. 'It's the bandits again. They're going after that carriage!'

Following her orders, the dragon banked and then turned in the sky. As Harmony started back towards the carriage, Elspeth heard the sound of women's cries. Just ahead, she saw the carriage had been stopped. One man held the torches while three others dragged two women from the carriage. A man was lying motionless on the road, while the driver was lying several paces behind the stricken carriage.

'They'll kill those women if we don't stop them!' Elspeth cried. She then leaned forward on the dragon. 'Harmony, roar as loud as you can. Let them know we're coming!'

Harmony let out a roar that set Elspeth's nerves on edge. When it stopped, the dragon tucked her wings in tightly to her body and landed with a hard jarring thump on the narrow road.

Reaching for her bow and quiver, Elspeth climbed down from the dragon. Onnie leaped down from his pouch as she raced forward. Fixing an arrow in her bow, she walked past the driver and saw that his throat had been cut and he was dead.

Further ahead, she saw the stunned expressions on the bandit's faces as they watched her coming. It had been ages since they'd tried anything against Harmony. The last thing they ever expected was Elspeth, Onnie and Harmony trying something against them!

'Get away from those women!' Elspeth shouted as she drew back her arrow. 'Do it now, or you'll regret it!'

'Look who's here!' the leader of the bandits said

excitedly. He then pointed down to Onnie. 'And she's brought our fox with her.'

Elspeth ignored the taunts and raised her bow higher. 'I said, let them go!'

The leader smiled, showing all his broken teeth. He took a threatening step forward. 'And I say give us the fox. We don't want your dragon any more. Just the fox. Hand him over and you're all free to go.'

'What do you want with Onnie?' Elspeth demanded.

'None of your business,' the leaders challenged. 'Just hand him over.'

Elspeth shook her head. 'Onnie stays with me! Now release these people before I lose my temper.'

Suddenly one of the other bandits lunged forward and caught hold of Onnie. Wrestling with him, he wrapped his hand around Onnie's mouth and held it shut to keep from being bitten. 'I got him!' he cheered. 'I got the fox!'

'Onnie!' Elspeth howled as she raced forward. 'Let him go or I swear you'll regret it!'

The other bandits pulled their daggers. Forgetting the women from the carriage, they all charged Elspeth. 'Get her!'

Madness erupted as more bandits emerged from the forest and ran at her. The one closest to Elspeth was quickly felled by an arrow, as were the second and third bandits. But before she could reload again, she was knocked to the ground. As Elspeth struggled to fight them off, Harmony roared ferociously and raced forward. Tearing through the men, she was able to free Elspeth.

Catching hold of two bandits, Harmony hauled them away. Lifting them in the air, she threw back her large head and bit down.

Not waiting to see what more the dragon did, Elspeth climbed quickly to her feet and faced down the other charging men. With no time to use her bow, she drew her dagger. Before she could use it, the owls swooped down out of the sky to attack them. But it wasn't only owls coming to her defence. Several wolves burst from the forest and were joining in the fight.

With the bandits now fighting for their lives against the owls, wolves and outraged Harmony, Elspeth searched amongst the men for Onnie. To her right, she heard movement in the trees. When she looked, she saw the outline of the man holding Onnie, running deeper into the dark forest. Panic filled Elspeth as she saw Onnie being taken away from her.

'Wolves,' she ordered, as she pointed after the running bandit. 'Stop that man! Bring me back my Onnie!'

Several wolves immediately stopped attacking the bandits and ran to follow Elspeth's command. As she waited at the edge of the road, she soon heard the terrible screams of the bandit and the howling of the wolves.

Moments later, Onnie reappeared. Racing out of the trees, he ran back to Elspeth and leaped up into her arms.

'Onnie!' Elspeth cried as she hugged him fiercely. It terrified her to realize how close she'd come to losing him. But soon her terror turned to rage as she looked over to what was left of the bandits.

With the owls, wolves and Harmony having taken care of most of the men, Elspeth saw the leader of the bandits standing with his back against the carriage. He was holding a knife to the throat of one of the woman victims.

Pausing to release Onnie and collect her bow, Elspeth fixed an arrow and drew it back. Stepping closer to the bandit holding the woman, she sucked in her breath when she realized it was Mariah's mother. Mariah was several paces away, standing and crying while her father was lying wounded and unconscious on the road.

'Stay back or I'll cut her throat!' the bandit viciously warned.

Beside her, Mariah cried out in terror, 'Mother!'

'Mariah, be quiet!' Elspeth harshly ordered. Then she concentrated on the bandit as she took several threatening steps forward. 'After what you just did to my Onnie, I'm not feeling particularly generous tonight. So I will give you only one chance to survive this. Release the woman and you will live. Otherwise you're a dead man.'

'You witch! Call 'em off!' he yelled, indicating all the attacking animals. 'Call 'em all off or I'll cut her!'

'Then do it,' Elspeth said angrily. 'She means nothing to me. But know this. The moment you do, I'll release my arrow.'

'No!' Mariah howled.

'I said, be quiet!' Elspeth snapped at Mariah. Then to the lead bandit she said, 'Last warning. Let her go and you will live. Hurt her and you'll die.'

The bandit's knife quivered at the woman's throat. Then he became aware of the huge red dragon standing beside him. Harmony's eyes were wild with rage as deep growls came from her throat.

'You'll shoot me, or have your dragon kill me the moment I do,' the bandit challenged.

'No I won't. I give you my word,' Elspeth said, 'which is more than you deserve. Now, let her go and you can leave here.'

The bandit glanced from Elspeth back to the angry dragon. Finally he looked back at Elspeth. 'All right, I'll do it. But call off your beast first.'

Elspeth released the tension on her bow and crossed over to Harmony. 'Let him pass, Harmony,' she said softly. Then she said to the bandit, 'Get going before I change my mind.'

Not needing to be told twice, the bandit threw down the knife and fled into the trees. When he was gone, Elspeth ran over to the butcher's wife who collapsed to the ground.

'Are you all right,' she gently asked as she helped her up.

The woman's eyes were bright with terror as she looked over Elspeth's shoulder to the red dragon. 'I—'

'Harmony won't hurt you,' Elspeth promised. 'She's with me.'

Then the woman whispered, 'My husband. They stabbed him.'

Leaving her, Elspeth moved to the butcher. Turning him over, she could see the bloodstain spreading on his shirt.

'Mariah, get over here,' Elspeth ordered.

The girl hesitated for a moment before she crossed to Elspeth.

Kneeling beside the butcher, Elspeth directed Mariah's hands to cover her father's wounds. 'Put your hands here and press down hard. You've got to stop the bleeding.'

Doing as she was told, Mariah pressed both hands down on her father's bleeding wound. 'What about our driver?' she weakly asked.

Elspeth shook her head. 'When we landed, I saw what the bandits did to him. He's dead.'

Mariah nodded sadly. Then she looked at Elspeth again. 'You're the animal girl that lives up on the mountain, aren't you?'

Elspeth bristled at the name. 'My name is Elspeth,' she said sharply. 'Not Animal Girl. Don't ever call me that again!'

'Thank you, Elspeth,' Mariah's mother said as she weakly stepped up to her. 'You saved our lives.'

Lying on the ground, Mariah's father stirred.

'He's losing too much blood,' Elspeth said. 'We've got to get him back to Elan.'

Mariah's mother looked at the carriage. 'When the bandits attacked, they cut the tethers to our horses. They've run off.'

'We'll take Harmony,' Elspeth said.

'Your dragon?' Mariah said fearfully.

155

Elspeth nodded. 'Unless you'd rather stay here and wait for someone else to come along.'

Mariah's mother quickly shook her head. 'Please, if you can take us by dragon, we would be in your debt.'

Elspeth stood and called Harmony forward. 'Stand back,' she ordered the women. 'This may look frightening, but I've done it before. Harmony is going to carry him in her mouth. You two will ride with me on her back.'

Both Mariah and her mother watched in fear as Elspeth manoeuvred the wounded man into Harmony's large open mouth. 'Nice and gentle,' she instructed the dragon. 'You can do this.'

After the butcher was settled, Elspeth helped Mariah and her mother climb on the dragon's back.

When Onnie was safely settled in his pouch, Elspeth climbed on as well. 'Hold on tight. This is going to be difficult,' she warned. 'This is a very narrow road and Harmony can't open her wings. She is going to need to run before she can leap up into the sky to fly.'

Elspeth felt Mariah's arms going tighter around her waist as she ordered the dragon to move.

Once they were airborne, the journey to the village was brief. As it was early in the evening, there were still people moving around on the main path running through the village.

Landing the dragon in the open patch at the end, Elspeth shouted for the people to move out of the way as Harmony ran through the village. Their screams filled the air when they saw the limp form of the butcher hanging out of the dragon's mouth.

'Elan!' Elspeth shouted as Harmony raced up to the wizard's cottage.

Instantly Corvellis started to caw loudly and launch in the air to greet Elspeth.

Soon the cottage door opened and Elan stepped outside. 'What in the stars is going on—'

'Elan,' Elspeth cried. 'The butcher's been stabbed. He needs your help!' Climbing down from Harmony, Elspeth helped Mariah and her mother down as well.

'We were set upon by bandits,' Mariah's mother explained as she carefully stepped up to the dragon's mouth to help Elspeth free her husband. 'Elspeth saved our lives.'

'Not me,' Elspeth corrected. 'It was Harmony, wolves and the owls who did most of the work.'

'Wolves and owls?' Gwen asked, stepping out of the cottage.

'Yes,' the butcher's wife said. Then she pointed up to

the owls still circling overhead. 'I don't know why they did it, but they helped us too.'

'Mariah!' Jib cried, running from the cottage. 'What's happened?'

'Jib!' Throwing herself into his arms, Mariah hugged him tightly and started to cry.

'Quickly, Jib, help me with him,' Elan said as he inspected the butcher's wound. 'We've got to get him inside.'

With Jib's help, the butcher was carried into the cottage. Elspeth stood back with Harmony and watched as Mariah and her mother disappeared into the cottage behind them.

'Aren't you coming in?' Gwen asked as she approached Elspeth.

'No, it's a little crowded in there,' Elspeth said as she started to climb back up on Harmony. Looking around, the villagers had gathered to stare at her. Already she could hear their muttered remarks about the 'Animal Girl', and calling her a savage that dressed like a boy and smelled like a wild animal.

'If you don't mind, I think I'll go back to my mountain. It's been a bad night and I want to spend some time with Onnie. Besides, I know I'm not welcome here.'

Gwen fearlessly approached Harmony's side and lightly touched Elspeth's leg. 'Please don't let them get to you. They're ignorant people who can't see who you really are.'

Elspeth looked back at the villagers and felt her anger starting to resurface. 'I've never done anything to give them cause to hate me. But look at them. Standing there and muttering about me.'

Gwen smiled apologetically. 'You're different. To some people, that's enough. But you know Elan and I love you, just as you are. You and your animals are always welcome in our home.'

Elspeth patted the woman's hand. 'Thank you, Gwen. But I can't stay.' Just as Elspeth was starting to turn Harmony around, she smiled sadly and looked back to the woman. 'Gwen, you just saw for yourself. Jib and Mariah are in love. Please don't stand in the way of their marriage.'

'Marriage?' Gwen repeated, suddenly shocked by the strange comment. 'Jib and Mariah?'

Elspeth nodded. 'Marriage.'

With one quick word, she directed Harmony to run through the village and take off into the air to return to the mountain.

CHAPTER
~ 19 ~

With the memory of the villagers' cruel comments still ringing in her ears, Elspeth vowed never to return to the village.

Jib's eighteenth birthday came and although there was a large combined celebration of his birthday and engagement to Mariah, Elspeth refused to go. Instead she and Jib had their own private celebration the day after. Seated together on the highest ridge, Jib held on to Elspeth's hand.

'The wedding is next season,' he said. 'Please tell me you'll come.'

Elspeth inhaled deeply and shook her head. 'I can't. Jib, I just can't face those people again and listen to the awful things they say about me. They hate me.'

'No they don't,' he said. 'They're just frightened of you. It was like that when my family first moved into the village. They thought all wizards were evil.

So they treated us the same way.'

'Why did you stay?'

'Where else could we go? It was always the same everywhere we went. But after a while, the villagers began to see that we were like everyone else.'

Elspeth lowered her head. 'Jib, I've been here over eight winters and it hasn't changed. They won't accept me. And the truth is? I don't care.'

'But I care,' Jib said gently. 'I won't get married if you're not there.'

'That's not fair,' Elspeth shot back. 'Besides, Mariah doesn't want me there either. She calls me Animal Girl too.'

Jib shook his head. 'Not any more. You saved her family. She cares, Elspeth. Believe me, she wants you to come. So do her parents.'

Elspeth sighed and looked out over the forests. 'I just don't know—'

'Elspeth, how could I get married if I knew you were up here all alone?'

'I'm not alone. I've got Onnie.'

Jib's eyes rested on the fox. 'Of course you do. We want him to come too. Please, Elspeth, Mother and Father said they would make you a dress fit for a princess. You will look beautiful. Please tell me you'll come.'

In her lap, Onnie started to yip. Elspeth looked down on him. 'Not you too?' Then she looked over to Jib. 'Onnie wants to see you get married.'

'Then it's settled,' Jib said. 'If Onnie wants to go, you've got to bring him.'

Elspeth shook her head, then started to chuckle. 'What am I going to do with you two?'

As summer gave way to autumn and the leaves changed from green to gold and red, preparations for Jib's upcoming wedding reached fever pitch. Against her better judgement, Elspeth finally agreed to go to the wedding.

Days before the event, Elan and Gwen visited the mountain to get Elspeth's final measurements. When Elspeth asked what kind of gown Gwen was making, Gwen would smile and say no more than, 'You'll see.'

Soon the day of the wedding arrived and Elan appeared in the meadow to collect Elspeth and Onnie. It was decided that for the good of everyone, Harmony, the owls, hawks, wolves and all the other animals that lived with Elspeth, should remain on the mountain.

'I don't feel right about leaving her up here,' Elspeth said as she stood with the large red dragon. 'What if the bandits come back?'

'If they do, they're in for a terrible surprise as they won't be able to get in here.' Waving his hand in the air, a large boulder suddenly appeared and blocked the entrance to the meadow. 'I'll remove that after the wedding. In the meantime, Harmony and all the animals will be safe while you're gone.'

Nodding her head in approval, Elspeth stepped up to her dragon and patted her thick neck. 'I've got to go for a while, Harmony. But I'll be back later. Please stay here on the mountain until I get back.'

The dragon lowered her head and started to whine.

Feeling guilty, Elspeth promised to return as quickly as possible. After that, she and Onnie travelled back to the cottage with Elan.

'You're here!' Jib cried when he saw her. 'Thank the stars!' Wrapping his arms around her, he gave Elspeth a hug that nearly squeezed the air from her chest.

'He's a bit nervous,' Gwen said as she laughed and put her arm around Elspeth. 'Now, let's get a look at you.'

Elspeth said nothing as Gwen gave her a thorough going over. 'All right, first thing, a bath, and then we'll do something with your hair.'

'What's wrong with my hair?' Elspeth said.

Gwen smiled. 'Your hair is lovely. But you keep it in

braids all the time. Just this once, I would like to see you let it loose.'

Biting back her protests, Elspeth let Gwen fuss over her. Before long she'd bathed, washed her hair and was now sitting as Gwen started to set it for the ceremony.

'Once Jib gets a look at you, I'm sure he'll regret not asking you to marry him.'

'Gwen,' Elspeth warned. Beside her, Onnie sat and appeared to be enjoying the struggle between the two women.

'I know, I know,' Gwen said. 'But a mother can dream.'

She then left the bedchamber for a moment. When she returned she was carrying a gown of the richest autumn-gold satin. It had fine stitching and pearls sewn throughout the form-fitting bodice.

Elspeth had never seen anything so beautiful in all her life. Rising from her chair, she reached for the gown and felt the smooth fabric. 'It's so beautiful!' she cried.

With Gwen's help, Elspeth was soon dressed in the gown. Instead of her stag-skin boots, Gwen produced a pair of fine gold slippers, the very same colour as the gown. After that, she fastened a garland of golden flowers and autumn leaves in Elspeth's red hair, which hung long and full down her back.

When she finished, Gwen stood back and admired her handiwork. 'You are by far the most beautiful young woman I've ever seen,' she said as tears filled her eyes. Then she embraced Elspeth. 'I know I'm not your mother, but I couldn't be more proud of you if I were.'

Elspeth felt tears stinging her own eyes. 'You have been as much a mother to me as my own was. Thank you for everything.'

On the floor, Onnie started to yip and howl. When Elspeth looked down on the fox, her cheeks blushed bright red.

'What's he saying?' Gwen asked.

After a moment, Elspeth looked back to Gwen, unable to repeat what Onnie had just said to her. Instead she smiled. 'Not much, just that he likes the gown.'

Elan and Jib were waiting in the main room of the cottage. When Gwen and Elspeth appeared, Elan whistled approvingly. 'My word!' he cried. 'Two shining stars plucked straight from the sky!'

When he saw Elspeth, Jib was struck silent. Finally he said, 'I knew mother was making you a gown. But I never imagined you would look so lovely in it.' Stepping forward, Jib embraced Elspeth and kissed her cheek. 'Thank you so much for being here for me.'

Teasing him, Elspeth pushed Jib away. 'Hey, watch the gown! I didn't just sit through all that torture to have you ruin it!' Then she looked back to Gwen. 'I think I should have brought my bow.'

'You may need it,' Elan said as he offered his arm to Gwen to escort her to the door. 'When those young men at the ceremony see you, you'll need more than your dragon to keep them away.'

Stepping out of the cottage, Elspeth looked around nervously. It had been some time since she'd been to the village and she was unsure how the people would react to seeing her with Elan and the family.

'Hey, I'm the one who's supposed to be nervous,' teased Jib as they walked arm in arm to the chapel.

'Yes, but they don't call you Animal Girl, do they?'

'True,' Jib agreed. 'But after today, I don't think anyone in the village will ever call you that again.'

Onnie was at her side and yipped up at her.

'Thank you, Onnie,' Elspeth said gratefully.

'What'd he say?' Jib asked.

Elspeth grinned. 'He said he'd bite anyone who calls me Animal Girl.'

Jib stopped and looked down on the fox. 'You bite

them and I'll hit them. Together we'll show everyone they can't hurt our Elspeth.'

The marriage ceremony was brief but beautiful. Seated with Elan and Gwen and clutching Onnie in her arms, Elspeth had tears streaming down her cheek as she watched Jib making his vows with Mariah.

After the ceremony, all the guests went to the village hall for the party. Pipers played cheery tunes while everyone danced. Standing at the back and clutching Onnie in her arms, Elspeth watched enviously as the men swirled the women around the floor. In the centre of the group, Jib danced joyfully with his new bride.

When the tune ended, Jib and Mariah laughed and crossed over to Elspeth.

'Thank you for coming,' Mariah said brightly as she leaned forward and kissed Elspeth on the cheek. 'And thank you again for saving our lives.' She turned to Jib, 'Would you excuse us? I'd like to take Elspeth to meet my father.'

Elspeth was drawn away from Jib and swallowed by the crowd as Mariah escorted her over to her father. Around her, she saw women glaring angrily at her while the men gave her appreciative glances.

'You look so pretty in that gown,' Mariah said. 'It's

no wonder the women are jealous. They're frightened you're going to charm the men away from them.'

'Hardly,' Elspeth said shyly. 'They're just surprised to see me here.'

'Well, I'm really glad you came. So is my mother.'

When they reached the other side of the hall, Mariah pointed out her father. As they approached, Elspeth saw the butcher staring at her. He dropped his drink as his eyes went wide with shock at the sight of her with the fox in her arms.

Moving closer, Elspeth could smell the drink on his breath and see that it had already gone to his head.

'I'm told it was you who saved my life,' he slurred.

Elspeth nodded her head. 'I had a lot of help.'

'So I hear,' he said. 'I can see your fox. But where is that red dragon of yours?'

'We thought it best if she didn't come.'

'A good idea,' he said darkly as he started to waver on his feet. 'Dragons are nasty beasts. They'd eat my guests.'

Stunned by his comments, Elspeth shook her head. 'No she wouldn't. Harmony is a good dragon.'

'There are no good dragons,' he drunkenly retorted. 'Or dragon riders for that matter.'

'Father, please,' Mariah said. She turned

apologetically to Elspeth, 'I'm so sorry, he didn't mean it. Father has had too much to drink. Since the attack—'

'Don't apologize for me,' the butcher spat. 'I can speak for myself. And the attack has nothing to do with this.'

'Father, stop,' Mariah begged. 'Please not tonight, not at my wedding.'

'Why not?' he challenged. 'You think I can't fight? Can't defend my family from bandits? That it takes this, this, Animal Girl to save me?'

In her arms, Onnie started to growl threateningly.

Elspeth stood silently before the drunken man, wounded by his vicious words. Because of her feelings for Jib, she refused to defend herself and disrupt the party. But, looking around, she could hear giggles from the women and saw embarrassed smiles from the men who had been staring at her all night.

'I'm sorry you feel that way,' Elspeth finally said. Then she looked at Mariah, 'I shouldn't have come.'

'No, you shouldn't,' the butcher agreed, blowing his foul breath in her face. 'You can dress up in all the pretty gowns in the kingdom, it wouldn't change a thing. You're still a savage. You even smell like a dragon. Go back to your mountain, Animal Girl. You don't belong here with us decent folk.'

Tears stung Elspeth's eyes, but she refused to let them fall. Turning from the drunken man, she started to walk away. His raucous laughter filled the hall behind her.

'Elspeth, wait,' Mariah called as she ran to catch up with her. 'Please, don't go. My father has had too much to drink. Since the attack, he believes he's useless to the family. It's not you he's mad at but himself.'

Elspeth sniffed and squared her shoulders. 'Look around you, Mariah. Look at how they are staring at me. This gown Gwen made doesn't change a thing. These people hate me. Now the women hate me even more because of the way the men are staring. And deep inside, the men resent me too because they're scared of me. There is nothing I can do to change this. I just don't belong here.'

'But you're my family now. I want you here.'

Elspeth shook her head. 'Elan and Gwen took me in because I was lost and they are good people. But if I stay here any longer, the villagers will turn on them and you. Don't you see? I've got to go to protect you.'

Clutching Onnie in her arms, Elspeth pushed through the crowd, trying to ignore the people muttering about her and staring rudely. When she left the village hall, she took a deep breath and tried to hold back the tears. But they wouldn't be stopped.

'I want to go home, Onnie,' she wept.

In her arms, Onnie yipped softly and gently licked her tear-stained cheek.

'No, not the mountain. I mean our real home, back with Kira, Dane and Kahrin. I want to see Paradon again. That's where we belong. Not here.'

Deep sobs of pain and loss came from Elspeth as she carried Onnie along the trail to Elan's cottage. At her approach, Corvellis cawed and leaped off her nest to greet her.

But as Elspeth approached the cottage, she heard a voice call from the shadows.

'So where's your dragon now, Animal Girl?' When he held up his torch, Elspeth recognized the bandit from the attack on the butcher. 'What? No bow? No dagger? No animals? You're all alone,' he teased. 'Good, it'll make my job easier.' Then he called into the dark, 'Get her!'

From out of nowhere, a thick heavy net came crashing down on Elspeth and Onnie. Before she could call out for help, she saw the lead bandit raising a club high in the air. 'You don't know how long I've waited to do this!'

Elspeth heard his cruel laughter filling the air as she felt the first blow strike the back of her head. Exploding with pain, she felt herself starting to slip. In her arms, Onnie howled and tried to leap at their attackers. By the time the second brutal blow came, darkness arrived and she passed out.

CHAPTER
~20~

Rexor slowly healed. But as each day came to an end, the soldiers were that much closer to the top of the mountain.

'How long do you think we have?' Kira asked as she stood beside Paradon at the Eye.

'Not long,' Paradon answered. 'A few more days. Perhaps less. It's only their inexperience with wildlife that has helped us. But even so, their determination is growing. Nothing is going to stop them from getting in here.'

'What about magic?' Kahrin asked, joining them at the Eye. 'Can you cast a spell against them?'

Before Paradon could answer, Kira turned to her sister. 'No magic. Paradon has got to save all his strength for the spell to send us back to Elspeth. If the soldiers come, we'll just have to fight.'

'I'm ready if we have to,' Shanks said.

'So am I,' Dane agreed.

'Let's just hope you don't have to,' Paradon finished. He then looked over to the dragons. 'Jinx is ready to go. It's only a matter of time with Rexor.'

Turning back to the black dragon, Kira saw that Rexor had crawled up behind Jinx. His wings were still folded and very tender, but at least he was moving around again.

She crossed to him. 'You just concentrate on getting better, Rexor,' she said softly. Reaching out, Kira stroked his snout.

'Do you think he'll be ready in time?' Dane asked.

Startled to find her brother so close behind her, she turned and smiled at him. 'I think he'll try his best.'

As she watched him, Dane seemed to be fidgeting on his feet.

'What is it?' she asked.

'Do you think he would let me scratch him?'

Kira knew how frightened Dane was of dragons. But in the past few days, she had also noticed him watching her with Jinx and Rexor as though he was taking note of everything she was doing. Looking at the determination in his eyes, she knew he was trying to overcome his fear.

'I think he would actually like it,' Kira answered. 'He

really seems to like it when I rub his ears right here.'

Once Kira demonstrated how Rexor like to be scratched, she watched Dane carefully approaching the dragon.

'Good boy,' he said nervously. 'I'm not going to hurt you.'

Kira watched Rexor closely. She was almost certain the dragon wouldn't turn on her brother. But, as Dane was always so quick to point out, he wasn't Jinx. This was a palace dragon, not used to being touched.

As Dane took a step, Rexor moved his head so that he could approach. While she watched, Kira saw Dane reach out a trembling hand. Finally he made contact with one of Rexor's tall pointed ears. 'Easy boy,' he repeated over and over. 'I'm not going to hurt you.'

In response to her brother's touch, Rexor sighed heavily and closed his eyes.

'I did it!' Dane cheered, as he continued to scratch the dragon. 'Kira, do you see? I really did it!'

'I see,' Kira said as her emotions welled up. She then took a couple of steps back to let him spend time with his dragon. When he turned back to her, his face was beaming. 'I wish father could have seen this.'

'Me too,' Kira said. 'He'd be very proud of you.'

Shanks came up from behind and stood beside Kira.

He was also smiling at Dane's success. Then he nudged Kira playfully. 'He'd also say you were all mad for trusting dragons!'

Kira nudged him right back. 'No he wouldn't. Father liked dragons. It was Ariel who changed him. He'd have loved Jinx and Rexor.'

'Of course he would,' Shanks teased as he patted Kira on the head as though she were a silly child. 'You just keep telling yourself that if it helps.'

'I'll tell you something, Shanks-Spar,' Kira said as her temper suddenly flared. 'You don't know what you're talking about!'

Shanks laughed all the more and then winked at her. 'Hey, Dane,' he called as Dane stepped away from Rexor, 'Your sister's kind of cute when she's angry.'

Kira looked from Dane's shocked face back to Shanks. She felt her own face flushing. 'Do you see that pond over there?' she finally said, pointing a shaking finger at where she and Elspeth used to get their water. 'Why don't you go soak your head?'

With his fears finally behind him, Dane took over the care of Rexor. He fed the dragon and tended to his wounds. When he thought no one was looking, he fussed over the dragon.

During the times he wasn't caring for Rexor, he joined everyone else in preparing for the soldiers' imminent arrival. 'All right,' Shanks was saying, 'if they do come over the top ridge, we've got to be prepared down here.'

Working together, they built safe areas where they could shoot their arrows from, but were protected from shots from above. As well, traps were set at the base of the walls to catch the first soldiers down.

But as each day passed and the preparations were made, Kira noticed that Paradon seemed to be drifting away. He ate very little, and if he did sleep, she never saw it.

'Paradon, what's wrong,' she asked fearfully as they worked together preparing the evening meal in the cave. 'And please don't tell me it's nothing because I know you too well.'

The old wizard stopped chopping vegetables and looked thoughtfully over to her. 'The time has come for you to leave here,' he said softly. 'Whether Rexor is ready or not, you must go.'

'Why? Are the soldiers here?'

Paradon nodded. 'They'll be here by tomorrow.' He paused and lowered his head. 'I didn't tell you this before because there seemed no point. You have all worked so hard to try to protect this mountain. But you will fail. There are just too many of them. I've seen their weapons, Kira. They aren't coming here to capture you. They're—'

'They're coming to kill us, aren't they?' Kira finished.

Once again Paradon nodded. 'It's the dragons they want. Not you. You must be gone before they come.'

'We will be,' Kira said. 'And you're coming with us.'

Paradon shook his head. 'No, child, I won't. I've already told you, I must stay here and cast the spell that will see you safely away.'

'But that was before we knew about the soldiers!' Kira cried. 'They'll kill you if you stay!'

'Listen to me, child. It is all right.'

'No it's not!' Kira protested as tears rushed to her eyes.

The old wizard reached up and brushed the tears away. 'It's what I want and what I've waited for. Please don't cry for me, Kira. I'll finally be able to rest.'

'But you can't die,' she said miserably.

Paradon pulled her into a tight embrace. He chuckled lightly as he kissed her cheek. 'I don't think I have much choice. But you, my dear, dear child, you have a long life before you. You must leave here and go back to your own time. Stop King Arden and prevent this wretched world from ever existing.'

Kira sniffed as she clung to the old wizard. 'When do we go?'

'Tomorrow morning,' Paradon answered, 'before the sunrise.'

'But we haven't even tested Rexor to see if he can fly.'

'He'll fly,' said Paradon confidently. 'He has to. Besides, you and Dane have cared for him well. His wings are healed. We'll give him tonight to rest, and then get you all going before the soldiers arrive.'

'But—'

Paradon squeezed her again. 'No buts,' he said softly. 'The time has come. You must let me do this for you. Go back where you belong, Kira. I told you before. A much younger me is still there, waiting for you.'

Kira wanted to argue. She wanted to fight. But deep in her heart, she knew the old wizard was right. The soldiers were coming. Like it or not, she knew that the time to go had finally come.

No one felt like eating. Gathered around the fire, everyone discussed the plans for opening the Eye and how they had to get the dragons through it as quickly as possible.

'Now, remember, once you arrive in Elspeth's time, I want you to head to Elan's village. It's on the other side of the Rogue's Mountain. Go there and find Elan. If Elspeth isn't with him, I am sure he will help you find her.'

'We still need to saddle Rexor,' Dane said. 'And really, we should test him for flying.'

Paradon rose stiffly to his feet. 'I'm afraid we don't have time to test him, we are just going to have to trust in him. But as for the saddle . . .' Crossing to the black dragon, Paradon raised his hands in the air and cast another spell. As had happened with Jinx so long ago, one moment there was nothing; then, in the next, Rexor had a saddlebox identical to Jinx's, sitting neatly on his back.

With Dane at his head to reassure him, Rexor did not fight the new arrival on his back. Nor did he show any reaction when Dane and Shanks stepped over to the black dragon's healed wing and climbed up into the saddlebox.

As Dane settled in the lead seat and tried on the safety harness, he looked back to Shanks. 'This is much more comfortable than the old saddle.'

'Definitely,' Shanks agreed, as he settled in the rear seat. 'Maybe we should start making these things and selling them back to the palace. We could earn a fortune.'

'Good idea,' Dane agreed. Then to the old wizard he said, 'Thanks, Paradon, this is really great!'

Paradon smiled at the banter between the two knights. 'I'm glad you like it.'

'We sure do,' Shanks agreed.

When the old wizard nodded, Kira moved closer to support him. 'Are you all right? You look pale.'

Paradon nodded and patted her hand softly. 'Just a bit tired.' He then turned to face her. 'Now, Kira, I need to ask you to do something for me. But it may upset you.'

Kira was already very upset by their impending departure. There was little more Paradon could say or do to make it worse – until he made his request.

'No, Paradon, I can't!' she cried.

'Please, Kira, the Eye must not remain in this world. It contains too much power.'

'But I can't take it from you. It's yours, you should keep it!'

'The Eye will do me little good once you are gone. But leaving it on this mountain for the soldiers to find is far too dangerous.'

'It looks just like a rock. They'll never know what it is.'

'Indeed it does. But with the power that rock contains, I can't take that risk. Please, I'm asking this of you as a final request. Do this for me. Take the Eye with you when you go. Deliver it to Elan. He'll know what to do with it. It will also show him how and where to send you all home.'

Kira's eyes trailed over to the large grey bramble-covered boulder sitting on the plinth. As she looked, she noticed for the first time how the leaves on the brambles were starting to wilt. Her eyes immediately darted back to Paradon. Suddenly she realized just how tightly linked the two were; as Paradon failed, so did the brambles.

Finally she said, 'But if the Eye is with us, how can you use it to cast the spell?'

'Simple,' Paradon said lightly. 'I will use it to cast the spell and then when the Eye is open in the sky, I'll transfer it to Jinx's saddlebox. It will all happen very quickly.' Paradon paused, before taking hold of her hands. 'Kira, I will rest easy knowing you are taking it back where it belongs. This world has no room for magic. Please tell me you'll do this one thing for me?'

Kira felt her throat tighten. Finally she nodded. 'Of course. If you want me to take it back, I will.

But Paradon, if we can take it back, please come back with it.'

The old wizard shook his head. 'No, my place is here to make sure you get away safely.'

Kira didn't argue or fight. Paradon's mind was set, though it didn't keep the tears from welling in her eyes and trailing silently down her cheeks.

'Now, everyone,' Paradon said. 'Let's gather around the fire as we have done every night. We can't let our friends up there think we are planning something. If they do, they may tell their friends on the mountain to hurry up.'

Everyone's eyes went up to the choppers hovering malevolently overhead. Their spotlights were now shining on the new saddlebox on Rexor's back.

'Unless they are complete idiots, they've already got to know we are planning something,' Shanks said. 'They just saw you use magic to create the saddlebox.'

'Indeed,' Paradon agreed as he tiredly sat down. 'But they won't know what we're planning or when. That is our advantage.'

Kira remained close at Paradon's side as the night slowly passed. To keep the choppers from becoming too suspicious, the others lay down in their bedrolls, but no one slept.

Staring absently into the fire, Paradon poked at the flames with a stick. 'This reminds me of the night you and I kept watch on the north tower, right before Lord Dorcon and his men arrived at the castle. My, my,' he chuckled softly, 'that was such a very long time ago . . .'

'Not so long for me,' Kira said.

'True,' Paradon agreed. 'But this time we shall not wait for dawn.'

Kira could not look at Paradon. If she did, she knew she would start crying again. Instead she stared up into the dark, starless sky and followed the progress of the choppers as they endlessly hovered over the meadow.

Some time before the long night ended, Jinx started to growl. Rexor lifted his head and sniffed the air.

'Dane? Shanks?' Kira said softly as she looked around.

'I know—' Dane answered.

'They're here!' Shanks finished for him

Everyone stood and strained their eyes to see the upper rim of the mountain. As they watched, small pebbles started to fall where unseen soldiers knocked them over the side.

'Everyone, get to your dragons,' Paradon warned. 'And remember, the moment the Eye is open, I want both dragons to fly through together. We can't risk you getting separated.'

'What about the choppers?' Shanks asked.

'I'll take care of them,' Paradon said. 'Just get moving!'

Kira was frozen in place as Dane, Shanks and Kahrin prepared the dragons to go. Clinging to Paradon's hand, she felt herself starting to shake, but the frail old wizard remained strangely calm.

'Go, Kira,' the old wizard said.

'I can't leave you here,' she cried. 'Please, Paradon, please, I'm begging you, come with me . . .'

Paradon's eyes misted as he embraced her. 'I can't. I belong here. You must be brave for me, Kira. Enter the Eye and find Elspeth. Then end King Arden's rein.'

Kira felt too weak to move. 'I love you, Paradon,' she cried as she buried herself in his old cloak.

'I love you too,' he said back to her. 'Now, please go, my beautiful, brave girl. Go—'

Suddenly the meadow was flooded with bright light from above as the soldiers pointed their spotlights at them. Soon a loud angry voice filled the air with unfamiliar words.

'They're ordering us to surrender,' Paradon shouted as he gently pushed Kira away. 'Get going before they set up their weapons.'

'Kira, come on!' Dane and Shanks cried from Rexor.

Kira ran from Paradon over to Jinx. Tears streamed down her cheek as she settled in the saddlebox. Lifting her eyes again, she watched the old, pain-filled wizard stepping up to the Eye.

'Get them in the air!' Paradon shouted. 'Go now, the Eye is starting to open!'

'Hold on,' Kira said over her shoulder to Kahrin as she drew back on the reins. 'Come on, Jinx, let's go flying!'

Immediately Jinx ran a few steps then leaped easily into the air. Kira looked to her left, and saw Dane doing the same with Rexor. Though his wings hadn't been tested, he flew confidently into the sky. Soon both dragons were flying side by side as they circled the meadow.

Above them, the hovering choppers suddenly opened fire. But before their awful weapons could do any damage, they were shoved away from the top of the mountain.

On the upper rim, the spotlights suddenly went out. Cast into darkness, the soldiers struggled to set up their weapons. The few that were already set up were pointed at the dragons and fired. But like the choppers, their bullets never reached their targets.

'Thank you, Paradon!' Kira cried. Glancing back down, she could barely see the wizard in the colourful glow from the Eye.

'Look, it's over there,' Kahrin said as she tapped Kira on the shoulder. Not far ahead they saw a ball of light starting to grow in the dark sky over the Rogue's Mountain.

The first time they had witnessed the power of the Eye, it had been in full daylight. But in the dark pre-dawn morning, the entire sky was glowing with the swirling colours of the opening Eye.

'Go now!' Paradon called from the ground. 'Enter the Eye together.'

As Kira and Dane brought their dragons around and saw the colourful tendrils come reaching for them, Kira heard Kahrin exclaiming, 'Kira, look there, it's Paradon's Eye!'

Turning back, Kira saw the old stone Eye sitting in the third seat behind Kahrin. As she stared at it, the bramble leaves started to curl and die. 'Paradon!' she howled.

Held within the safety of the colourful tendrils, Kira looked over the side desperately searching for Paradon. As the shining glow filled the meadow, she could no longer see the old wizard, only his dark silhouette against the brightness. But as she watched him, the popping sounds of the soldier's weapons increased.

Looking over to the rim, by the light of the Eye, she could see their weapons were no longer pointed at the dragons. They were shooting at the wizard.

When her eyes darted back to Paradon, the silhouette was struck by the soldier's bullets and knocked to the ground.

'No! Paradon!' Kira shouted. Pulling back on the reins, she tried to get Jinx to turn back. But the tendrils held them in place. Unable to see more, Kira's agonized cries filled the air as the two dragons were drawn into the heart of the Eye.

CHAPTER
~ 21 ~

Elspeth awoke feeling dizzy and sick. Her head felt three times bigger and four times heavier than usual. There was a weight on her chest, and the sound of Onnie growling furiously.

Weakly opening her eyes, she found that she was lying on a bed that smelled old and musty. She also discovered the weight on her chest was actually from Onnie. He was facing away from her as every hair on his body was raised in threat and his tail lashed out angrily.

'She wakes,' came the sound of a raspy voice.

'Then she will live,' another voice said. 'Pity.'

Fighting to lift her head, Elspeth looked past Onnie to the figure standing at the end of the bed. When her eyes started to clear, she nearly screamed at the horrible sight of two wizened old men standing closely together.

'Don't scream,' one of the men ordered.

'No, don't,' said the other. 'We hate it when girls scream.'

'Yes, we do,' the first one agreed.

'But he hates it more than me,' said the second man.

At this, the first turned and looked at the second. 'I do not. You hate it more than me.'

'No, I don't. You do!' the second challenged.

Confused and frightened, Elspeth watched the two men starting to argue with each other. Finally the second speaker looked back to Elspeth and reached out to touch her foot.

'Don't you listen to him. My brother does hate screaming more than me.'

Just as his hand was about to touch her, Onnie leaped forward and viciously sank his teeth into the man's finger. Pulling it back, blood ran from the bite. But instead of cursing, the old man cackled. It was a shrill sound that hurt Elspeth's ears.

'Onnie-Astra doesn't want big brother to touch his girl,' he said.

'Onnie-Astra is jealous,' teased the first man.

Despite the pounding in her head, Elspeth forced herself to sit up. When her eyes finally focused, she was shocked to discover that the two men were joined together at the side. They had a large cloak that covered most of their single body and their hair hung down in long greasy streaks. Their terrifying faces were distorted with age, filth and evil. But they were identical.

Raising her hand to her head, Elspeth tried to force back the headache that threatened to make her pass out again. 'Onnie?' she called weakly.

At the end of the bed, Onnie instantly came back to her. But as the twins moved again, he turned and snarled viciously.

'How sweet, Onnie-Astra is in love,' said the first twin.

'It pulls at my heart. Mother would be so proud,' the second twin added.

Hearing that name again, Elspeth's fear turned to anger. 'His name is Onnie. Not Onnie-Astra!' she corrected. Then she instantly regretted raising her voice as it made the pounding in her head worse.

'Onnie-Astra never told his girl who he really was,' said Twin One.

'That was very, very naughty,' Twin Two added.

'But then again, Onnie-Astra always was the most naughty,' said Twin One.

Twin Two frowned and turned to his brother. 'No, he wasn't. You were. You were always the worst.'

'No, I wasn't,' corrected Twin One.

'Yes, you were,' said Twin Two. 'Mother always said so.'

'No, she didn't!' Twin One said.

'What do you want from us?' Elspeth cut in, trying to ignore their bickering taunts. 'Why have you brought us here?'

'So many questions,' Twin One said, concentrating on her again.

'Many answers yet to come,' said Twin Two. 'But first, no more fox. We need Onnie-Astra as he was.'

'Yes, let's turn him back,' agreed Twin One anxiously.

Elspeth lunged forward and caught hold of the fox. Clutching him protectively, she faced down the twins. 'Don't you dare touch him!' Instantly her head exploded with throbbing pain and she squeezed her eyes closed against it.

'Silence!' ordered Twin One as he instantly cast a spell that shut Elspeth's mouth.

'Down and freeze!' Twin Two called.

Suddenly unseen hands shoved her back down on the bed. As she tried to move, Elspeth found she couldn't. It was just like the time Elan had frozen her many seasons ago. Only this time she couldn't even open her eyes.

Still standing on her chest, Onnie howled and

started yipping. Elspeth could hear him cursing the twins and threatening to kill them if they didn't release her. But if the twins understood him, they gave no clue.

'Onnie-Astra will be silent or we will make his girl stop breathing,' Twin One threatened.

'She will live no more,' said Twin Two.

'I want to kill her now,' Twin One said excitedly. 'Let me do it.'

'No, I get to kill her first,' argued Twin Two. 'You kill her second.'

'Me first,' shouted Twin One.

Unable to see or speak, all Elspeth could do was listen. And what she heard terrified her. But it was more than the threat of death. It was the way they kept insisting Onnie was Onnie-Astra. It couldn't be true! Onnie would have told her. He wasn't the evil wizard Elan had warned her about. He couldn't be.

'Wait!' said Twin One. 'Before we kill her, the twins will reverse their spell and make Onnie-Astra a man again.'

'Yes!' agreed Twin Two. 'Then if Onnie-Astra frees the twins from the prison he made for them, we won't kill her.'

At the base of the bed, Elspeth heard the twins start

speaking together as they cast a spell. She felt the weight of Onnie on her chest suddenly increase until he leaped off. But when he made it to the floor, there was a very heavy thump.

'A fox no more,' Twin One cried.

'A wizard again. Many powers. Much evil,' finished Twin Two.

Elspeth felt her pulse racing as she heard something stir on the floor beside the bed. Then she felt a weight pushing down on the edge of the bed as a hand was placed there to help steady a body unused to standing on just two feet.

'Onnie-Astra is still a young man!' cried Twin One.

'No age at all!' agreed Twin Two.

'Not fair!' screeched Twin One. 'I want to be like Onnie-Astra!'

'No, I want to be like him!' argued Twin Two.

From beside the bed, Elspeth suddenly heard a new voice.

'I can't say the same for you two,' Onnie-Astra said coldly. 'I didn't think it was possible, but you're even uglier than I remember you.'

Elspeth listened to his deep, smooth voice and wanted to cry. It was true! All their time together and Onnie had lied to her. He was Onnie-Astra! The most evil wizard in existence. Elan was right!

'Long time apart, dear brother,' Twin One said.

'Make peace between us. We can conquer and rule together,' suggested Twin Two.

'Yes,' agreed Twin One. 'We will rule together.'

'Boys, boys, boys,' Onnie-Astra chuckled, but there was no humour in the laugh. 'Why would I want to join with you? I have more power than your combined strength, and we all know it. And I have Father's Jewel of Power. I would have to be mad to consider joining forces with two crazy old men like you!'

Elspeth could hear the evil hatred pouring from Onnie-Astra. How could she have been fooled for so long?

'We cast the spell on your girl,' threatened Twin One. 'You can't break it.'

'We will kill her,' Twin Two finished. 'We know you care for her. We have seen it. You can't fool us.'

'So be nice to us, brother, or your girl will die,' said Twin One.

'Yes, and I get to kill her,' threatened Twin Two.

'No you don't,' challenged Twin One. 'I'm older so I get to do it.'

'No you're not,' fought Twin Two. 'I'm older than you.'

'Enough!' Onnie-Astra shouted. 'You're twins! Both equally old and ugly. Now stop your petty arguing and tell me what you want.'

'You will bring us father's Jewel of Power,' Twin One said.

Then Twin Two added. 'Yes, first the jewel. Then you will free us from our prison.'

'After that, you can take your pretty girl away,' teased Twin One.

'And live happily every after,' cackled Twin Two.

Elspeth could hear the heavy breathing coming from the man beside her bed. But she had no idea what Onnie-Astra was thinking. She thought he cared for her, but how could he? If he had, he would have told her about himself long ago. This was the cold and evil wizard Elan had described. Lying frozen, unable to see or speak, Elspeth felt her heart breaking. Her own sweet Onnie was gone.

'Agreed,' Onnie-Astra finally said.

Then she heard movement. A moment later, she felt a soft finger stroking her cheek as Onnie-Astra knelt beside the bed.

'My sweet Elspeth,' he whispered softly into her ear. 'No matter what they say to you or what you hear, please know that I love you. I always have, and I always will. I will come back for you. I promise.'

Elspeth then felt warm lips pressing to her cheek.

'How darling,' Twin One teased.

'He loves her,' whined Twin Two. 'It warms my stony heart to see our little brother caring for his girl.'

'But he'd better bring father's Jewel of Power back to us if he wants his girl to live another day,' threatened Twin One.

'Yes, or I will kill her,' said Twin Two.

'I keep telling you, I get to kill her!' argued Twin One.

'No, I do! It was my idea,' cried Twin Two.

'But I paid the bandits for her, so I get to do it,' shouted Twin One.

'Stop!' Onnie-Astra boomed. Then his voice dripped with hatred as he stepped away from the bed. 'No one is going to kill my Elspeth, do you hear me!'

He paused and took several more steps. 'I do care for her, very much. But do not mistake my feelings for weakness. I am still Onnie-Astra! Should you harm her or even dare touch her, there is nowhere in this world you can hide from my wrath.'

'Threats from our little brother?' Twin One asked.

'Since when have we feared you?' said Twin Two.

'We're not frightened of you,' challenged Twin One.

Elspeth heard Onnie-Astra start to chuckle. But the sound of it chilled her heart.

'Oh yes you are, my brothers, make no mistake. You have always been frightened of me; ever since we were children.' He dropped his voice even further. 'Only Mother protected you from me back then. She's gone now and my powers have grown. If you go near Elspeth, nothing will save you.'

Elspeth could hear the twin's sharp intake of breath and knew they were very frightened.

'You wouldn't hurt your brothers,' said Twin One weakly.

Twin Two then added, 'We're all the family you have left—'

'Elspeth is my only family!' Onnie-Astra cut in sharply. 'Not you. But I will give you father's Jewel of Power. I have no need of it any more. I have more than enough power of my own.'

'Then give it to me,' cried Twin One.

'No, give it to me!' said Twin Two. 'Too many winters have I waited.'

'I've waited too,' argued Twin One. 'He will give it to me.'

'I'll give it to no one if you don't shut up!' shouted Onnie-Astra. Then he started to laugh. 'You are both crazier than you look if you think I would be fool enough to hide it here on the estate.'

'Where is it?' demanded Twin One.

'Tell us!' ordered Twin Two.

'Before you turned me into the fox, I hid it far away from this place. I will leave Elspeth in your care and go to retrieve it.'

'Send for it,' Twin One suggested.

'Yes, Onnie-Astra, use your powers and send for it. You need not leave your precious Elspeth here,' finished Twin Two.

'Are you telling me what to do?' Onnie-Astra shouted furiously. 'I should destroy you right now!'

'Wait!' Twin One called in a whining, pleading voice.

'No need to lose your temper, brother,' said Twin Two. 'We thought it would be faster to send for it.'

'Yes, faster,' agreed Twin One.

Elspeth heard Onnie soften his tone again. It was even more terrifying than when he shouted. 'I'm quite certain you remember the spell I put around you and this estate. No magic may enter, none may leave. I do not trust you, brothers – you will betray me. When I have the Jewel of Power, only then will I remove the spell and free you from your prison. But I must leave here to collect it.'

Elspeth heard his soft tread heading for the door. 'Do not attempt to cross me, brothers, or you will find yourselves regretting the moment you restored me.'

Then he was gone.

Shortly afterwards, Elspeth heard the twins drawing closer to the bed.

'He won't return,' Twin One warned. 'We should never have turned him back.'

'He will come,' said Twin Two. 'For her. We hold his prize right here in our hands. He would betray us, but not her. Onnie-Astra will return for his Elspeth.'

'Then he is in for a surprise,' Twin One cackled.

'Indeed, my brother,' said Twin Two. 'When he returns with the Jewel of Power and has freed us, he will watch his precious girl die.'

'Then we will kill him, too,' cried Twin One as they both started to laugh together.

CHAPTER
~22~

Kira felt no joy as they journeyed through the swirling colours of the Eye. Paradon was dead. She would never forget the horrible image of him being shot and collapsing to the ground.

Looking to the right, she saw Dane and Shanks flying closely at her side. The tip of Jinx's wing was actually touching Rexor's wing as they travelled. Everyone was doing their best to make sure they weren't separated this time.

As the blazing colours whooshed passed, Kira was sure they were in the Eye much longer than they'd been the first time. Looking around, she prayed that Paradon had got the spell right and they would find Elspeth.

Soon they all heard the familiar peal of thunder as they sailed through the other end of the Eye.

Looking around quickly, Kira was grateful to see her

brother and Shanks still on Rexor. Kahrin was seated behind her. Immediately she noticed the change in the air. Unlike the clogged foul air of the world they had just left, here they smelled the fresh welcoming aroma of a forest entering autumn.

'Kira,' Dane excitedly called. 'Look down there! It's Harmony!'

Sailing over the Rogue's Mountain, Kira looked down and saw their meadow. Standing in the middle of it was the red dragon. Like Rexor, Harmony no longer had any armour on her body. Unlike Rexor, her mouth was free of restriction.

When Harmony saw Jinx and Rexor soaring above the mountain, she started to roar.

'Where's Elspeth?' Kahrin asked.

'I can't see her,' Kira said. 'Maybe she's in the cave.'

As Kira watched, Harmony continued roaring, but didn't fly up into the sky. Then the red dragon turned. Following her eye, Kira saw two men come running out of the cave. When they saw them in the sky, both frantically waved their arms in the air, beckoning them to come down.

'Let's see who they are,' Kira called to Dane.

Kira directed Jinx down to land in the meadow. He growled at the two approaching men.

'Stop it, Jinx,' Kira ordered. Then she climbed down from the dragon and helped Kahrin down behind her.

'Are you Kira?' the older man called, cautiously approaching as close as Jinx would allow. Then he looked to the others and his eyes came to rest on the brand on Dane's face. 'You're Dane, aren't you? Elspeth told us what happened to you.'

Kira looked over to Dane, then back to the man. She nodded before asking, 'Where is our sister?'

'We don't know. She's vanished,' the younger man said.

When Kira heard this, she stepped away from Jinx and moved closer to the men. Only then did she notice just how tall they were. 'Who are you?'

'I'm Elan. This is my son, Jib.'

'Elan?' Kira repeated. 'Paradon's great-great-grandfather?'

Elan nodded. Then he looked at the blue dragon. 'And this must be the baby dragon Jinx,' he said. 'Elspeth was right, he does have twin tails.'

'He's not really a baby any more. He's getting bigger every day,' Kira said.

'Where is Elspeth?' Dane asked, speaking for the first time as he stepped up to Kira. 'You said she vanished?'

'We don't know,' Jib offered. 'She and Onnie were at

my wedding two days ago and disappeared. Some guests said rude things and upset her, so she left the party. But we haven't seen or heard from her since.'

'It's just not like her to leave Harmony,' Elan added. 'We know something has happened; we just don't know what. My raven is terribly upset, but can't tell me what's wrong. I've tried looking in my stone globe, but it won't show me anything either.'

Behind them, Harmony was still growling at Jinx and Rexor. Turning to them, Kira cautiously approached the red dragon. 'Easy, Harmony, this is your brother Rexor. You remember him. And Jinx. You're all friends.'

'I think they've been apart too long,' Elan offered. 'Harmony doesn't quite remember them.'

Dane frowned. 'It hasn't been that long.'

Kira watched Elan and Jib look at each other. Finally Elan came forward. 'I believe it's been a lot longer than you think. Perhaps you'd better come down to the village with us. We have a lot to discuss and need to find Elspeth. I also suggest you leave your dragons up here.'

Kira shook her head. 'We've never left Jinx alone. He'll try to follow us and if he can't find us, there is no telling what he'll do.'

'Father,' Jib said. 'We're wasting time. Let them bring their dragons. We've got to get moving.'

Everyone was seated around the dining table as Gwen served warm drinks. Jinx was at the door doing his best to squeeze in after Kira while Rexor sat behind him waiting patiently.

The villagers were never happy to see Harmony when Elspeth brought her down from the mountain. Now with two more dragons sitting outside the wizard's home, they barricaded themselves in their cottages and refused to come out.

When everyone was served and Gwen sat beside her husband, Elan looked at the group. He combed his fingers through his light hair. 'I don't know where to start.'

'We've got to find Elspeth. That's where we start,' Kira said. Then she looked over to Jib. 'What happened at your wedding?'

Elan started to shake his head. 'It's not as simple as that. A lot more has happened than you know. Tell me this first. Back when Lord Dorcon was at Paradon's castle and you all entered the Eye, where did you go?'

Kira frowned. 'You know about Lord Dorcon?'

Elan nodded. 'Elspeth has told us everything about

her life before she arrived here.' He looked over to Dane. 'And you wear the brand of the house of Dorcon on your face. They have large estates not too far from here. The style has changed a bit, but the mark is unmistakable. Perhaps while you are here you should cover it up so others don't think you're an escaped slave.'

'I'm not a slave!' Dane protested.

'I know you're not,' Elan said. 'But you wear the mark of one.'

'Can you fix Dane's face?' Kahrin asked. 'Make it better?'

'No!' Dane quickly said to his sister. 'I don't want it fixed. I want Lord Dorcon looking at his mark when I kill him!'

Shanks looked at his friend and chuckled before turning back to Elan. 'Dane's a bit sensitive about it. We tend not to talk about the brand and just let him get on with things.'

Dane gave Shanks a black look before concentrating on Elan. 'After we entered the Eye, we arrived in a terrible world, far, far into the future. The air was foul and dirty and they had all kinds of killing machines that flew in the sky like dragons, but they were nothing like real dragons. They were really strange. Then Jinx caught hold of one and pulled it out of the air. As it crashed, it sent pieces into another one. When they hit, it just sort of—'

'It exploded!' Shanks said excitedly, waving his hands in the air wildly while making a loud booming sound. 'The fire from it was so hot, it melted all the metal.'

'They were made of metal?' Jib asked.

Dane nodded. 'Paradon said there were no more real dragons so the people made the flying machines instead.'

'Paradon was there?' Elan asked.

Kira nodded, then her eyes misted as she recalled his terrible death. 'He was really, really old. He said he'd cast a lot of spells to keep himself alive to wait for us. But when we left, the soldiers killed him . . .' Kira broke off speaking as her tears resurfaced.

Dane took over and explained, 'Paradon said we'd travelled over three thousand seasons into the future.'

'Three thousand!' Elan exclaimed. 'My Lord, it's hard to believe . . .'

Shanks nodded. 'Paradon also said he didn't know how we got separated, but he knew Elspeth was back here. He'd hoped she would find you and that you would protect her until we came for her.'

'We've tried our best to keep her safe,' Gwen said softly. 'She's been like a daughter to us.'

Elan looked at his wife and then sighed loudly. 'Only now am I beginning to understand the scope of Paradon's failure; and how, even now, his spell has gone wrong yet again.'

'What do you mean?' Dane asked.

Elan looked at Kira. 'Tell me. Just how long were all of you in that future world?'

'How long?' Kira said as she started to frown. 'Less than a season. Why?'

He sighed again. 'Well, I'm afraid for Elspeth, Onnie and Harmony, the wait has been much, much longer. They've been here over eight winters.'

'What?' Kira cried. 'That's impossible! Paradon said he was sending us back to the moment she arrived here.'

Elan sadly shook his head. 'I'm sure he tried his best. But he missed his target. Elspeth is now almost seventeen.'

Kira shook her head. 'I don't understand. How could eight winters go by and yet we were gone only a short time?'

Elan rose from the table and crossed to his desk. He pulled out a clean parchment, quill and ink. 'Long ago, when we first figured out where Elspeth came from, she couldn't understand it either. So I drew for her a picture.'

Elan started to draw a diagram similar to the one he had done for Elspeth. Only this time, Paradon's castle was shown in the middle. He drew his cottage at one end, and two dragons at the other distant end. As he'd done before, he drew a long single line between all the places with lots of dots along it.

'All right,' he started as he gathered everyone together to watch. 'You all started right here at Paradon's castle. The plan was simple. To send you all here, just three seasons into the future.' Elan counted off three dots and put an X on the third.

'But during this first journey everything went wrong. You four ended up here, three thousand seasons into the future . . .' Elan drew a long sweeping line from Paradon's castle to the image of the two dragons. He then drew a separate line in the opposite direction showing Elspeth's journey into the past. 'For reasons we don't understand, Elspeth somehow went in the other direction and ended up here.'

Elan paused and combed his fingers through his thick hair. 'So now, you four were here with old Paradon,' he said indicating the future, 'and you needed to get here,' he pointed to his cottage at the other end of the line. 'The trouble is, you didn't arrive here at the cottage when Elspeth arrived.' He then put an X on several dots away from the cottage. 'You actually arrived here, eight winters after she got here. So although it was a short journey for you, it has been a very long wait for Elspeth.'

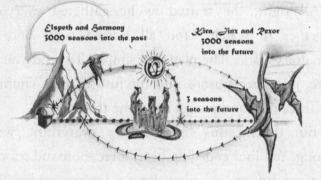

Elspeth and Harmony
3000 seasons into the past

Kira, Jinx and Rexor
3000 seasons
into the future

3 seasons
into the future

After Elan finished speaking, a heavy silence filled the room as everyone tried to take in and understand the depth of Paradon's failure.

Finally Shanks burst out laughing. 'So let me get this straight. Elspeth, the youngest member of the family, is now the oldest?'

Elan looked from Shanks to the other confused members of the family. He nodded. 'That's exactly right.'

Kahrin looked at the diagram and then returned to Elan. 'So where is Elspeth now?'

As Jib was starting to explain the events of the

wedding, they heard a deep and urgent voice coming from outside the cottage. 'Out of my way, Jinx, I need to get in there!'

Everyone turned as a figure wearing a black cloak pushed past Jinx's large head and entered the cottage. Throwing back his hood, he stepped forward. 'Kira, thank the heavens you're finally here!' He then turned to Elan, 'Elan, I desperately need your help—'

Gwen screamed.

Elan got to his feet and boomed, 'Onnie-Astra!' He raised his hands to cast an attacking spell at the evil wizard.

'Elan, no!' Onnie-Astra cried holding up his empty hands in surrender. 'Please, I'm begging you. Elspeth is in terrible danger!'

CHAPTER
~23~

The cottage erupted in madness as Elan stood before the cloaked figure preparing to cast a spell.

As Kira's eyes went from Elan to the cloaked figure, she couldn't understand what was happening. How did the stranger know her name? How could he get past Jinx when the dragon was so protective? Who was he?

Studying his sculpted features, his smooth blond hair and warm brown eyes, Kira suddenly realized he was by far the most handsome man she'd ever seen in her entire life.

'Elan, please,' Onnie-Astra continued. 'It's me, Onnie the fox.'

'Onnie?' Kira repeated. Shaking her head, she tried to break the powerful effect of the stranger's good looks. He wasn't much older than Jib or Shanks, but his face caused such a stir deep inside; she knew she would do absolutely anything he asked.

'Get out of my home, monster!' Elan threatened. 'You are not welcome here.'

'It's me, Elan, Onnie. Please you must listen to me.'

'Father?' Jib asked, confused by the stranger. 'Could it really be Onnie?'

'It is me!' Onnie-Astra said desperately to Jib. Then he turned to Elan. 'I'm not the same Onnie-Astra you once knew. I've changed. Now my brothers have Elspeth and they're going to kill her!'

'I don't believe you!' Elan spat. 'Get out now or I swear you'll regret it.'

'Elan, wait,' Gwen said as she put her hand on the wizard's arm. She looked back at Onnie-Astra with a charming smile. 'Let him stay as long as he likes.'

'No, Gwen. Turn around, don't look at him!' Elan warned as he forced Gwen to turn away from Onnie-Astra. 'You know the dangerous charms he has with that face.' He then called to Kira, 'You and Kahrin, turn away now. Don't look at him.'

Following the wizard's orders, Kira and Kahrin reluctantly turned away. Though Kira ached to look back into Onnie-Astra's handsome face.

'Please,' Onnie-Astra begged. 'I know I have a lot to answer for. And I know you have no cause to trust me, but Elan, think of Elspeth. She's alone with the twins.

Locked away so long, they've gone completely insane. They want me to hand over my father's Jewel of Power or they say they're going to kill her.'

Elan hesitated as he studied his long-time enemy and the most evil wizard in the kingdom. He then looked at Dane and the family. 'If we trust him, he could kill all of us.'

'But if he's telling the truth, they'll kill Elspeth,' Kira said. Unable to resist, she looked back at the enchanting face of the evil wizard. 'Are you really Onnie? Our Onnie – the fox?'

Onnie-Astra nodded. Then he squinted at her as the fox had done countless times. 'When we first met, you threw a pebble at me. Then you struck me.'

His eyes were the same! Kira thought. It really was Onnie. 'And you bit me,' she said as she smiled warmly.

'It was a nip,' Onnie-Astra said. 'If I really wanted to hurt you, I'd have broken the skin.'

'You're really Onnie the fox?' Kahrin said softly, also falling under the wizard's strange charms.

Onnie-Astra approached Kahrin. He went down on one knee and gently took both her hands and gave them a light squeeze. 'I was there when we freed you from Lasser. You carried me all the way back to Paradon's castle. You have always been very sweet to me, Kahrin.' Onnie-Astra then looked back to Kira. 'Unlike another member of your family . . .'

Kira felt her face going hot under Onnie-Astra's intense stare.

Elan carefully watched the exchange. He was waiting for the evil wizard to show his true self. But in all the time and stories he knew of Onnie-Astra, he'd never known him show any traces of tenderness; nothing like the man who had just spoken so gently to Kahrin.

Finally Elan lowered his hands. 'All right,' he cautiously said. 'Sit down and tell us what's happened.'

As Onnie-Astra took a seat at the table, he explained the events of the wedding and what happened after. 'It was the same bandit from the road. He and his men have been after us for some time. When he found us alone without Harmony, he hit Elspeth on the head to keep her from summoning animals to protect her. I tried to help, but they netted us. I couldn't move. Then they took us back to my family's estate to face my brothers.'

'How could they know it was you?' Elan asked, still not convinced it wasn't some kind of trick.

'The twins have been searching for me for a very, very long time. They've had hunters out gathering up foxes hoping to find me. But they never could. But when the bandits saw Elspeth with me and heard her calling my name, they knew I was the one the twins wanted. The twins paid the bandits a fortune to capture us.'

'Why?' Dane asked. 'What do they want from you?'

Onnie-Astra looked over to him. 'My brothers and I have been at war since we were children. Our father wanted it that way. He believed it would keep us strong if we were always using our powers against each other.'

'And against everybody else,' Elan added darkly.

'Elan,' Gwen warned as she touched his arm. 'Let him speak.'

Onnie-Astra dropped his eyes. Finally he said, 'No Gwen, Elan is right. I have done many terrible things. But that was the way of my family. When I was very young, my father saw that I had more power than my older twin brothers. So he cast a spell that joined them together and combined their powers.'

'They weren't born that way?' Gwen asked.

Onnie-Astra shook his head. 'No. My father realized that joined together, their strength almost matched mine. That way we could keep the fight fair.'

'Fair fighting?' Elan asked. 'Amongst evil wizards?'

'I know it all sounds mad,' Onnie-Astra admitted. 'It was. But in his own black-hearted way, our father cared

216

for us and didn't want us to kill each other.'

'What happened to you?' Elan asked. 'I was a young lad when you and your family simply vanished.'

Onnie-Astra nodded. 'When my father died, there was a struggle for his power. He'd put all his spells and powers in a jewel and wanted us to fight for it. So I cast a spell that imprisoned my brothers in the castle and kept their powers from working outside it. But before I could escape to claim the jewel, they turned me into a fox. As an animal, I had no powers.

'After a time,' Onnie-Astra continued, 'the twins realized only I could free them from their prison. But to do this, they needed to restore me back to a man. By then it was too late. I was long gone from the area.'

Onnie-Astra stood up and started to pace the confines of the cottage. 'Winter upon winter I wandered alone. Existing as a fox.' He paused and tapped his chest. 'But here, deep inside, I was still a man, feeling as any man felt. And what I felt was loneliness. I thought I would go mad with it. Until one day, I found a little boy wizard who was just as lonely as me. I stayed with him for many, many winters—'

'You're talking about Paradon,' Kira said as she gazed longingly at the evil wizard.

Onnie-Astra looked at her and nodded. 'Though he

couldn't understand me, his powers were enough that we could communicate on one level. It was wonderful. Suddenly I wasn't lonely any more. But then, a very long time later, Paradon sent me to help two girls who were struggling to stay alive.'

Gwen looked over to Kira. 'That was you and Elspeth.'

'Yes,' Onnie-Astra said. 'The very first moment I saw Elspeth, I felt something in me change. I didn't know what it was. But I knew I could never leave her. The greater thrill came when I discovered she could actually understand me. Hear my words and respond to me.'

'You cared for her,' Elan said.

Onnie-Astra nodded. 'Believe me, I couldn't understand it myself. You're right. I have lived my life caring only for myself. But suddenly there was this child I knew I would do anything for. That I would die for . . .'

'But she's not a child any more. She's almost a grown woman,' Gwen said.

Onnie-Astra nodded. 'And now I love her as a woman.'

Gwen nodded slowly and then asked, 'Has she seen you? Seen your face and felt its power?'

'No,' Onnie-Astra said. 'And I'm grateful for that.

My brothers froze her.' He looked over to Elan. 'Just like you did when we first arrived. But her eyes were shut and she couldn't see me. I'm afraid she's going to think I've abandoned her. She heard me say some awful things to my brothers. But I had to. Now I don't know how to save her.'

'You're a wizard; use your powers,' Jib challenged. 'You shouldn't have left her there!'

'I don't have any powers!' Onnie-Astra angrily shot back. 'They're gone! I was the most powerful wizard in the kingdom. Now I can't even light a candle!'

Elan sat at the table and considered. 'Do the twins know about this?'

'No,' Onnie-Astra quickly said. 'I shouted and bluffed. I threatened to kill them if they touched Elspeth. But if they knew the truth, they'd kill all of us. I just don't know what's happened to me. Was I a fox too long?'

Gwen shook her head. 'No, it wasn't that. I know what happened.'

'What?' Onnie-Astra asked. 'Tell me.'

Everyone in the room turned to her, waiting to hear the solution. Finally Gwen started. 'Yes, you were the most powerful wizard in the kingdom. But you were pure evil. Your feelings for Elspeth changed you. It defeated the evil in you. There's no room in your heart for it now.'

'That's impossible,' Onnie-Astra protested. 'Surely love isn't so strong.'

'Oh yes, it is,' Gwen said.

Onnie-Astra threw his arms in the air and cursed himself. 'So now when I need my powers most, they're gone. Without them, I'm nothing. I can't protect her.'

'We can,' Kira said as she looked over to Kahrin, Dane and Shanks. 'We've got our dragons. We can fight our way into the castle and free her. If we could bring down Lasser Commons, surely one castle with two old wizards can't be worse.'

'That was different,' Onnie-Astra said. 'We were up against old men and wounded soldiers at Lasser, not insanely powerful wizards who gain pleasure from killing.'

'There's also us,' Jib said. 'You're not the only one who loves Elspeth. We all do. And will fight together to free her.'

CHAPTER
~24~

Elspeth lay unmoving on the bed as she listened to the
cackling laughter of the twin wizards. They seemed
not to notice or care that she could hear every word
they said.

They were planning all the terrible things they
would do once Onnie-Astra freed them from their
prison. First would be her death, followed by the death
of their younger brother. Finally they would turn their
evil rage against everyone in the kingdom.

As she listened, Elspeth's mind was in great turmoil.
Throughout their long seasons together, Onnie had
never told her about himself, insisting she wouldn't
understand. But how difficult could it be to
understand he was evil?

He also said he would be back. But if the stories Elan
told her about the wizard Onnie-Astra were true, she
knew he would never return. He had been unleashed

on the unsuspecting kingdom. Was he killing Elan and Gwen right now?

Elspeth wanted to cry. But even that had been denied her. Frozen like a statue, all she could do was lie on the bed and listen to the horrible voices of the twins and await her painful death.

CHAPTER
~25~

Late into the day everyone remained in the cottage planning what they must do to free Elspeth from the twins.

Throughout the discussions, Kira, Gwen and Kahrin found themselves distracted and unable to think clearly with Onnie-Astra sitting at the table.

Finally when he saw the disruption he was causing, he asked Elan to cast a spell to make a mask for him. As Elan handed it over and Onnie-Astra drew it up to his face, Elan looked over at Kira. 'Onnie-Astra's face is one of the things that has always made him so dangerous. It has an enchantment all its own. That doesn't seem to have been lost with the rest of his powers.'

'It was a weapon I once used well,' Onnie-Astra admitted as he fitted the mask into place. 'Though, sadly, it never worked on my brothers. Now I dearly wish it did.'

'With or without it, we still need to get Elspeth away from there,' Dane said. 'And from what you tell us, it won't be easy.'

'No, Dane, it won't,' Onnie-Astra agreed. 'But there is one thing in our favour. My brothers' powers are trapped within the castle. All I have to do is get Elspeth out.'

Kira looked at Elan and Jib. 'What about you? Paradon said you had great powers. Can't you cast a spell that will bring her out of there without Onnie needing to return?'

It was Onnie-Astra who answered. 'No, that won't work. The spell I put around the estate not only keeps their magic from getting out, it also stops magic from getting in.' He then looked at Elan. 'However, if you can actually get inside the castle, your powers will work against them. But even if you do, the twins are more powerful than you and Jib combined.'

Everyone fell silent as they tried to figure out how to beat the undefeated evil twins. Finally it was Kahrin who made a simple statement.

'Your father put them together to make them strong?'

When Onnie-Astra nodded, she continued. 'What happens if you separate them again? Won't that make them weak?'

Elan opened his mouth to explain how it wouldn't work. But the words never came. He looked at Kahrin and frowned. 'It is so simple, it might just work.'

'You can't reverse my father's spell,' Onnie-Astra said. 'Only he could do it, and he's dead. And because I've lost my powers, I can't remove the spell around the estate.'

'Not reverse it,' Elan said excitedly to Onnie-Astra. 'Change it! Don't you see? If we can get into the castle, Jib and I can cast a new spell that will tear them apart. Once they are separated, their powers will be weakened. We can handle them while you get Elspeth out of there.'

'But how do we get in if magic protects the estate?' Kira asked.

'My spell keeps all other magic spells from getting on to the estate, not wizards on dragons,' Onnie-Astra explained. 'We can fly in and I will enter the castle with my father's Jewel of Power. All we'll need then is some kind of distraction to throw my brothers off. Then Elan and Jib can work their magic.'

'But if you go back and they find out it's a trick, they'll kill you,' Kahrin protested.

Onnie-Astra turned his masked face towards her. His voice softened. 'If my sacrifice means Elspeth will live, I would gladly do it.'

'Let's not talk of sacrifice just yet,' Elan said. 'Onnie-Astra is right. He must return to the castle. But you'll not have the real Jewel of Power with you. It would be far too dangerous if the twins got their hands on it—'

'He's got to carry something to show the twins,' Kira loudly protested. 'Otherwise they'll know something is up.'

Elan raised his hands. 'Calm down. He will have something with him. I'll make another Jewel of Power, one that looks identical to his father's, but without the power. It should convince them long enough for Jib and me to get in undetected.'

He then concentrated on Kira, Dane and Shanks. 'Then if you can create some kind of noisy distraction, we'll be able to surprise the twins and cast our own spell before they attack us.'

'Sound easy peasy,' Shanks said lightly as he slapped Dane playfully on the back. 'So easy in fact, I hardly think I need to go.'

Kira's eyes flashed with anger as she stood and faced the knight. 'You will go, Shanks-Spar! You will go and you'll help get my sister out of that place. Do you understand me?'

Shanks laughed once again and looked over to Gwen and Elan. 'Don't let her fool you. She likes me really.'

Just before sunset as the group prepared to leave for the twins' estate, Kira climbed on Jinx's wing and up into the saddlebox. Her eyes came to rest on Paradon's Eye sitting on the third seat. Jumping down from Jinx, she stepped up to Elan.

'When we left the future world, Paradon asked me to bring the Eye back with us. He said you'd know what to do with it.'

The shock was obvious on the wizard's face. 'You brought Paradon's Eye with you?' When Kira nodded, he asked her to show him.

'It's back there in the last seat,' Kira said as she stepped up to Jinx's head and calmed him down while Elan approached. 'You can climb up on his wing.' She then turned her attention to the dragon and scratched him behind the ears. 'It's all right, Jinx. Elan is our friend.'

As she stood at Jinx's head, Elan climbed lightly on the dragon's wing. 'My word, it is big!' he exclaimed. 'May I take it in the cottage?'

'If you can lift it,' Kira said.

Forgetting that unlike Paradon's spells, Elan's always worked, Kira was shocked to see him say a few words that lifted the large grey boulder out of the saddlebox.

As it floated in the air and moved away from Jinx, Kira saw all the dried and dead brambles falling away. That sight caused another lump to form in her throat and tears threatened to fall.

Leaving Jinx, Kira followed Elan back into the cottage behind the eye. As everyone gathered around, the Eye was lowered gently to the table.

'Elspeth always said it was much bigger than your stone globe,' Jib said to his father as he inspected the Eye. 'And look at how much brighter the colours are in it.'

'The Eye certainly is much older than my globe and contains more power. But it can't stay here. Not like this.'

'Why not?' Dane asked. 'If Paradon wanted you to have it, it must be important.'

'Oh, it is,' said Elan. 'But I have the younger version of the very same globe. The two can't exist in the same time together, it would be too dangerous.'

'What are you going to do?' Gwen asked.

Elan left the room for a moment. When he returned, he was carrying his stone globe. Removing the black cover, he put it on the table beside the Eye. 'These two are the same stone,' he said. 'Just from different times. I wouldn't be surprised if—'

Before he could finish speaking the two globes started to quiver. Soon they started to move, as if drawn together.

'Stand back!' Onnie-Astra shouted. 'They're going to fuse!'

Just as everyone dashed away from the table, the two powerful globes came together. The combined power of the merging stones knocked everyone to the floor as the cottage was filled with a blinding flash of many colours and a tremendous peal of thunder that echoed throughout the whole village.

When it was over and the colours finally receded, they slowly climbed back to their feet and cautiously moved closer to the table. Onnie-Astra looked over to Kira. 'Reminds me of the time Paradon redesigned the north tower for Jinx.'

Forgetting that Onnie-Astra was still 'Onnie' and had been there for Paradon's spell, Kira looked at him in surprise. 'At least we still have our hair and eyelashes.'

'True,' Onnie-Astra agreed. 'And we're not on fire.'

'But our table is,' Jib said, as he, Dane and Shanks quickly patted out the small fires around the single stone. When they were out, the wood beneath the stone was charred black and smouldering.

Jib gazed into the new stone and admired the vibrant colours swirling around within. The stone itself was much bigger than his father's globe, but smaller than the Eye had been. As though the two had mixed and found a middle size. 'That was amazing.'

Elan stared silently into the new Eye for a very long time. Eventually he looked back at Kira and the others. 'The Eye has shown me everything; such wonders and amazement.' Then he dropped his head. 'And such horror. The First Law of the kingdom is truly brutal and unjust.'

'It is,' Kira agreed. 'When we get home, we're going to challenge the king to stop it. Too many girls have been killed already.'

Elan nodded. 'And you will get home. The Eye has shown me how to do it. I've seen where you've come from, where you've been, and where you need to go. I have seen my great-great-grandson as well.' He smiled as he looked at Kira.

'Paradon cares for you all very much. He was wise sending this back with you. With his Eye, I can now see the spell I need to send you all home.'

'We just have to get Elspeth first,' Onnie-Astra added before Kira could.

'Indeed,' Elan agreed. Then he crossed to his

wife and embraced her. 'Time is on the wing. We must get moving.'

Gwen hugged and kissed him. Then she hugged Jib. 'Have you told Mariah where you are going?'

Jib dropped his eyes. 'Not yet. I didn't want to worry her.'

'She should be told,' Gwen said. 'If she is married to a wizard, she's got to learn to expect this. When you leave, I'll get her and bring her here. I'll explain everything. We'll both be waiting for your return.'

The goodbyes were brief and worry-filled, as everyone knew what they were up against. When Kira left the cottage and climbed up on Jinx, she felt nerves bunching up in her stomach. Onnie-Astra took the middle seat in the saddlebox and patted her on the shoulder. 'Don't worry, we'll get her back, Kira. We won't stop until we do.'

Kira turned in her seat and looked at Onnie-Astra. She wished he didn't have the mask on. She desperately wanted to see his face again. Shaking her head, she turned forward. 'Let's get moving.'

As Dane and Shanks climbed back on Rexor, Elan stepped up to them. 'Jib and I will meet you on the mountain to collect Harmony.'

Dane nodded. 'We're on our way.'

Taking the two dragons into the air, Kira led the way back up the mountain. The sky around them was turning dark red and purple as the sun set on the distant horizon. The colours it cast in the clouds and on the turning leaves of autumn only added to her sense of foreboding.

As they started to circle above the meadow, everyone watched Elan and Jib arrive on the mountain and climb on to Harmony's back. Once the red dragon joined Jinx and Rexor in the sky, Onnie-Astra set Kira on the course to his family estate.

The journey was long and little was said as everyone felt the fear gathering around them. The sun had long set and it was dark with only the bright moon and stars to light their way when Onnie-Astra finally tapped Kira on the shoulder.

'We're over the estate,' he said, pointing to a large area of dead forest. 'Take Jinx down away from the castle. We'll have to walk a bit, but at least my brothers won't be able to see us.'

Kira called to Dane and then Elan as she brought Jinx down lower. In the distance, she saw moonlight shining on the old castle. Most of the towers had collapsed in on themselves and the walls were crumbling.

'Over there,' Onnie-Astra said as he pointed to an

area where the dragons could safely land.

They approached an open area where the scattered dead trees looked like terrifying skeletons in the moonlight. There were pools of stagnant water scattered around and the stink of rot reached high into the air.

'What's that smell?' Kahrin asked, plugging her nose.

'Death,' Onnie-Astra answered darkly. 'Their powers can't get out of the castle, but their evil can. The twins are poisoning the area.'

Kira hated to ask Jinx to land on the foul ground. But this was where they had to be. Touching down lightly, the dragon started to whine.

'He senses the evil,' Onnie-Astra explained as he opened the hatch and climbed down on to the dragon's wing. 'Hopefully we won't have to be here long.'

'It's all right, Jinx,' Kira said lightly. She climbed down behind Onnie-Astra, approached Jinx's head and stroked his quivering neck.

Moments later, Dane and Shanks, Elan and Jib arrived.

'Nice place you got here,' Shanks said lightly to Onnie-Astra. 'Very homely indeed. Just the sort of place to raise evil wizards. No wonder you like it so much.'

Onnie-Astra remained still, but squinted

threateningly. 'My powers are gone, Shanks, not my temper. Tread lightly.'

Shanks stiffened his back and took a step closer to Onnie-Astra. 'Or what?' he said.

When Kira saw the challenge resting in his eyes, she quickly stepped between them. 'So what do we do now?' she asked, turning to Elan.

'We follow Onnie-Astra's lead and he takes us into the castle.'

From his pocket, Elan produced a beautiful sparkling jewel. 'Here, I've made this from what I remember of your father's jewel. I've put some power in it as well. If the twins touch it, they will feel it. But there's not enough to do any harm.'

Onnie-Astra received the large jewel. 'It looks exactly the same. But what if they want to test it?'

'We'll be with you, hiding. If they try to test it, I will cast the spell they want. They'll never know this isn't the real thing.'

'Thank you, Elan,' Onnie-Astra said. 'For everything.'

'Don't thank me yet; this isn't over.' Elan then turned back to Kira and her family. 'Once we are in there, I want you all to follow with the dragons. Land them on the roof and do whatever you can to get them roaring.

We need to distract the twins.' He paused. Then he said, 'This is going to be very dangerous. Unless we are able to separate them, we are facing a power much older and greater than our own.'

'They won't hesitate to kill you,' Onnie-Astra added. 'Don't think your youth will protect you.' He looked especially at Kira and Kahrin. 'They've killed children much younger than you.' He dropped his eyes in shame. 'As have I.'

Kira was stunned to hear this. Finally she said, 'We'll be careful.'

Onnie-Astra moved closer to her. Much to Kira's surprise, he put his arms around her and gave her a tight hug. 'I never hated you, Kira,' he whispered softly in her ear. 'Though you thought I did.'

'You just loved Elspeth more,' Kira replied.

'Yes,' he admitted. Then he moved away to say his goodbyes to Kahrin.

Before they left, Elan gave the group his final instructions. 'It should take us to the count of two hundred to reach the castle. Give us another count of one hundred after that. Then bring the dragons.'

With brief farewells spoken, Kira and her family watched as the three men started walking through the dead forest towards the castle.

'It still could be a trap to capture or kill Elan and Jib,' Shanks said darkly. 'I don't trust Onnie-Astra one bit. Especially after the way he has you girls falling all over him.'

Kahrin said nothing, but Kira looked at Shanks in shock. 'I wasn't falling all over him,' she challenged. 'He's Onnie. Our Onnie, that's all.'

'You always hated Onnie,' Shanks challenged. 'Now you go all weak at the knees whenever Onnie-Astra looks at you. It's disgusting.'

Kira was about to hit Shanks when Dane reached forward and caught her arm. 'He's right. Onnie-Astra's face makes you change. It makes all of us change. And, like Shanks, I don't trust him.' Dane then turned to his friend. 'But at this point, what choice do we really have?'

CHAPTER
~ 26 ~

Elspeth wanted to scream as a cold bony finger traced a line slowly down her cheek.

'Such a pretty girl,' Twin One said.

'Perhaps we should keep her for ourselves,' suggested Twin Two.

'Good idea,' said Twin One. 'It will torture Onnie-Astra to see her with us.'

'Much better than killing her straight away.'

Time seemed endless to Elspeth, as she lay unmoving on the bed. Onnie had been gone ages and she was convinced he wasn't coming back.

But the twins were still awaiting his return and making their terrible plans for the kingdom after their release. She prayed Onnie wouldn't come back. She would gladly face whatever the twins did to her, if it meant keeping them trapped in the castle.

Finally the cold fingers stopped touching her and

she heard the sound of the twins moving away from the bed.

'He's been gone too long. Onnie-Astra isn't coming back,' Twin One said.

'Yes he will,' Twin Two responded. 'For her he will. Stop saying he won't.'

'Don't tell me what to say,' the first twin responded. 'I'll speak as I wish.'

Elspeth listened in silence to the constant bickering of the twins. She heard them calling each other filthy names and threatening to cast vicious spells on each other. She was grateful for their short tempers. As long as they fought each other, they left her alone.

'You two haven't changed a bit,' a deep voice said, entering the chamber. 'After all this time, you still keep fighting.'

'Onnie-Astra!' Twin One said. 'You have returned.'

'You entered our castle quiet as a fox. We didn't hear you,' said Twin Two.

'I said I would be back,' Onnie-Astra responded softly. 'And I am.'

'He said you wouldn't,' Twin Two said about Twin One. 'He said you didn't care for the girl and would leave her with us.'

'I did not,' challenged Twin One.

'Yes you did,' argued Twin Two.

'Leave Elspeth with you filthy monsters?' Onnie-Astra cut in. 'I would rather see her dead first.'

That comment chilled Elspeth to the bone. Was Onnie planning to kill her in order to free himself from his promise?

'Did you bring Father's jewel?' Twin One asked anxiously.

'Yes, did you bring the Jewel of Power?' repeated Twin Two.

'I did,' Onnie-Astra said smoothly. 'Now, free Elspeth from the spell and I shall hand it over.'

'No,' the twins said as one. 'Give us the jewel first. Then you can have your precious girl.'

Elspeth wished she could see what was happening. She could hear the sound of Onnie's feet as they trod lightly on the chamber floor. She also heard the sound of cloth moving. Was he handing over the jewel? She tried to scream, tried to warn him it was a trap. But she could do nothing other than listen to the trap snapping shut behind him.

'See how it sparkles,' Twin One said.

'Such power,' agreed Twin Two. Then he added, 'Now, Onnie-Astra, remove the spell that keeps us imprisoned here.'

'Yes, free us!' demanded Twin One.

'Not yet,' Onnie-Astra said. 'You have the Jewel of Power. Give me Elspeth. Then and only then will I reverse the spell—'

'No!' shrieked Twin One. 'Remove the spell first.'

'Free us!' cried Twin Two.

'Not until I have Elspeth,' shouted Onnie-Astra. 'Give her to me!'

'You want your pretty girl?' asked Twin One.

'Then you shall have her!' cried Twin Two.

Elspeth suddenly felt herself being lifted off the bed and thrown violently across the room.

She could hear Onnie shouting and the sound of his running footsteps behind her. Right before she hit the floor, she felt his arms catching hold of her and stopping the fall.

'Elspeth,' he quickly whispered as he lowered her gently to the floor. 'Whatever happens, I love you.' Then just as quickly, his arms were gone and she was lying frozen on the cold stone floor.

'Your time has ended, brothers!' Onnie-Astra shouted. 'You will never leave here!'

'He didn't use magic!' cried Twin Two. 'He had to use his hands.'

'Why couldn't Onnie-Astra use magic to save

her?' demanded Twin One.

'Has he lost his powers?' asked Twin Two.

'Wait!' Twin One shouted. 'I smell something. What is it?'

Elspeth heard the awful sound of the twins loudly sniffing the air. They sounded like pigs in the barnyard searching for their food.

'Wizards!' Twin One cried. 'I can smell other wizards in here!'

'Who is it? Who is in here?' demanded Twin Two.

'Yes, show yourselves,' cried Twin One.

From across the room, Elspeth heard the sound of footsteps entering the chamber.

'It is I, Elan, son of Errin.' Elan called loudly. 'This is over. You have lost. Now give us the girl and we will leave you in peace.'

'Look brother,' cried Twin One. 'Errin's son is all grown up!'

'And is the younger man Elan's son?' Twin Two added. 'They look very much the same.'

'Could be,' Twin One answered. 'But why have they come here?'

'Onnie-Astra brought them,' cried Twin Two. 'He has betrayed us!'

'Yes, Onnie-Astra needs other wizards to fight his

battles,' agreed Twin One. 'He has no powers of his own!'

'But other wizards can not save him,' shouted Twin Two. 'We have more power than all of you!'

From her place on the floor, Elspeth heard the sound of Onnie rushing at the twins and shouting, 'Now, Elan, do it now!'

There were sounds of a scuffle as Onnie hit the twins. But then Elspeth heard Onnie, Elan and Jib suddenly start crying out in pain as the cackling sound of the twin's cruel laughter filled the air.

'You can't defeat us, Onnie-Astra!' the first twin shouted.

'You have no power!' cried Twin Two. 'We will kill you all!'

CHAPTER
~ 27 ~

Everyone waited, preparing to move on their dragons as they all counted down the final numbers.

'Two hundred and ninety-eight. Two hundred and ninety-nine. Three hundred!'

'Let's go!' Dane cried.

'Fly, Jinx,' Kira ordered as she pulled back on the reins. Quickly taking the dragons into the sky, Kira looked back and saw Harmony following them, even though she didn't have a rider.

'There it is,' she called over to her brother as they approached the crumbling castle.

'We can't land on the roof, it's ready to cave in,' Shanks shouted back. 'It won't hold the dragons. We'll fall right through.'

'If Elan needs a noisy distraction,' Kira shouted, 'we'll give him one. Dane, land Rexor over there, we'll land here. If we get them to fall through, that should be loud enough to distract them.'

'You're insane!' Shanks cried. 'We'll all be killed!'

'No we won't,' Kira argued. 'It's for Shadow!' Then she looked at Kahrin. 'Hold on tight. This is going to get rough.'

Kira ordered Jinx down out of the sky to land on the unstable castle roof. As his feet touched down, he started to roar and try to take off again.

'No, Jinx,' Kira ordered. 'Stay!'

Not far away, Kira watched as Dane had Rexor land on another part of the roof. Like Jinx, the dragon knew the roof was not strong enough to hold him and was trying to take off again. When Harmony landed between them, the combined weight of the three dragons was too much for the rotting timbers. They heard the sound of cracking and of roof tiles breaking away.

'It's starting!' Dane cried. 'Hang on!'

CHAPTER
~ 28 ~

Onnie-Astra, Elan and Jib were screaming and writhing in agony as the twins cast their spell against them. They were hardly aware of the roaring of the dragons and the sound of the castle's roof giving way.

But the twins heard it.

'Dragons?' Twin One asked, as he stopped casting the spell and curiously looked up to the ceiling of the bedchamber.

'Why do we have dragons in our loft?' questioned Twin Two as he also looked up.

'I don't know. Why did you put them there?' Twin One demanded of Twin Two. 'There's no room for dragons in the loft.'

'I didn't put them there!' Twin Two shouted. 'You know I hate dragons. You must have done it.'

'No I didn't!' argued Twin One.

'Don't lie to me!' Twin Two screeched. 'I know you're

up to something. You're always plotting against me!'

'I am not,' shouted Twin One. 'You are!'

Still lying frozen on the floor, Elspeth heard Elan, Jib and Onnie stop screaming as the twins argued and blamed each other for the sudden arrival of dragons. Then she heard Elan and Jib speaking together to cast a spell. The words were unfamiliar to her, but their effect was immediate. From across the room, she heard the twins start to cry out.

The louder their cries became, the louder Elan and Jib cast their spell. Finally Elspeth heard the sickening sound of tearing.

'Elan, noooooo—' the twins howled together.

As the twins started to come apart, their spell against Elspeth was broken. Suddenly she could move again. She opened her eyes and saw the madness in the room around her. Looking over to the twins, she saw a sight beyond imagining – the air around them was sparkling as they were being separated. Across from them, Elan and Jib were sitting up and holding their hands high as lightning sprang from their fingertips. Slowly standing, they advanced on the evil twin wizards.

'Run, Elspeth!' Elan cried as he saw her. 'You and Onnie-Astra get out of here!'

Climbing unsteadily to her feet, Elspeth looked

around and got her first look at Onnie as a man. But all she could see of him was his shining blond hair as his back was to her. As she watched, he drew something up to his head. When he turned towards her, she saw a black mask hiding his face.

'Elspeth,' he cried. Running to her, he caught her by the hand. 'We must leave here.'

'What about Elan and Jib?' Elspeth demanded, not wanting to leave the wizards to fight the twins alone. 'We must help them.'

From outside the chamber came the ferocious roars of dragons.

Elspeth looked back at Onnie. 'That sounded like Harmony.'

'Elspeth, get out of here!' Elan shouted again.

'Come, we've got to go,' Onnie-Astra said. 'Elan and Jib will concentrate better if we aren't here to distract them.'

Elspeth let Onnie lead her out of the chamber. When they entered the wide and crumbling corridor, her eyes flew wide at the sight of Kira, Kahrin, Dane and Shanks running towards her, followed closely by Jinx, Rexor and Harmony.

Dane and Shanks had their swords drawn and looked ready for battle.

'Kira?' Elspeth cried, unable to believe what she was seeing. Kira was covered in a thick layer of dust, cobwebs and roofing tiles. Everyone in the corridor was leaving a steady trail of debris behind them as they ran.

Kira stopped. Stunned, she tilted her head to the side and tried to focus her eyes on the beautiful young woman wearing the sparkling golden gown before her. 'Shadow? Could that really be you?'

Elspeth grinned and nodded.

Suddenly both girls ran to each other. Elspeth threw her arms around Kira and hugged her fiercely, never wanting to let go. 'Kira,' she cried. 'I thought I'd never see you again!'

When Kira pulled away, she looked up at her little sister who now stood a full head taller than she did. 'Shadow, you're all grown up!'

'And you're just as I remember you!' Elspeth laughed. 'If not a bit dustier.' She playfully patted Kira's shoulders, which caused dust and cobwebs from the collapsed roof to puff into the air.

After Kira, Elspeth reached for her brother and hugged him tightly. 'Dane, I'm so glad you're finally here. It's been endless waiting for you to come.'

'We've been trying to get back to you. I'm sorry it took us so long,' Dane said as he hugged her again.

Shanks then stepped forward and greeted Elspeth. 'We did try to get here sooner, but we've had a bit of trouble of our own.'

'Shanks got shot,' Kahrin said as she embraced Elspeth. 'He and Rexor almost died.'

'You did?' Elspeth asked.

When Shanks nodded, Elspeth hugged Kahrin again. 'When we get back to the mountain, you must tell me all about it!'

'We will,' Kahrin promised.

After she greeted her family, Elspeth ran over to Jinx. 'Oh, baby, how I've missed you!'

Jinx started to whine and press his head as close to Elspeth as he could. Then Harmony and Rexor moved forward, also seeking attention.

'Elspeth,' Onnie-Astra said as he approached and reached for her arm. 'All of you, we must leave here, it's not safe.'

'Where are Elan and Jib?' Kira asked.

Elspeth pointed back to the chamber. 'They're in there. Elan and Jib are doing something to the twins.'

'C'mon,' Shanks called to Dane excitedly. 'It's a fight. Let's help them!'

As the two dragon knights started to run towards the chamber, Elan and Jib burst into the corridor.

249

'Everyone, come, we don't have a lot of time,' Elan cried. 'The twins are apart. But when we tried to send them to opposite ends of the kingdom, the spell wouldn't work.'

'My old spell is still holding,' Onnie-Astra cursed. 'They can't leave the castle.'

Elan nodded. 'They're weak. But even now, they are casting spells to put themselves back together. We must be gone before that happens!'

From the bedchamber, everyone heard the sound of the twins cursing and shouting terrible threats and promises of the horrors yet to come.

'Quickly, get on your dragons!' Elan ordered.

Racing as fast as they could, Kira and Kahrin returned to Jinx and Dane and Shanks climbed on Rexor. Onnie-Astra and Elspeth crossed to Harmony and climbed on her back.

Elan then turned and looked down the long dark corridor. He held up his hands and cast a spell. The wall at the end immediately exploded, as huge chunks of the castle wall fell away leaving a gaping hole leading straight outside.

'Go! Take the dragons out of here,' he cried. 'Jib and I will follow you. Get back to the mountain!'

Following his orders, Kira directed Jinx forward. She

didn't need to coax him to get him to leap through the hole and fly outside. With Rexor and Harmony close behind, the dragons quickly made it to the safety of the open night sky.

Stealing a glance back to the castle, Kira saw bright lights shining from within and heard more explosions. She prayed that Elan and Jib were able to get away and would be meeting them at the top of the Rogue's Mountain.

It was nearly dawn by the time the dragons finally made it back to the meadow at the top of the mountain. When they arrived, Kira was grateful to see Elan standing with Gwen, while Jib stood waiting for them with his arm around a girl she didn't know.

'Gwen!' Elspeth shouted as Onnie-Astra helped her climb down from Harmony.

'Elspeth,' Gwen cried as she ran up to her and embraced her tightly. 'I've been so frightened for you.'

'I'm fine,' she said, embracing her again.

Onnie-Astra came up beside Elspeth. 'We're all fine. Thanks to you and Jib,' he said to Elan.

'No,' Elan corrected, 'Not us.' He then pointed to Kira and the family. 'Them. If they hadn't made the racket they did, I don't think any of us would be here now.'

Onnie-Astra turned to Kira and nodded. 'He's right. Thank you, Kira. That was both brave and insane. You could have been badly hurt.'

'What do you mean, could have?' Shanks complained as he held up his arm. 'I think I broke a bone!'

'Stop your moaning,' Kira said as she punched his sore arm. 'We all wanted to get Shadow out of there. We'd have done anything.'

Kira walked up to Elspeth and embraced her again. 'I don't think I'll ever get used to you being older and taller than me.'

Elspeth laughed and for the first time in her life, ruffled Kira's hair. 'I'll always be your little sister, Kira. Your Shadow.'

Everyone laughed as Kira and Elspeth clung to each other. Finally Elan came forward.

'It's been a long and exhausting night. But we're all safely together. I think this calls for a celebration.'

'Yes,' Mariah said, stepping forward. When she approached Elspeth, she offered her hand. 'I'm so sorry my father ruined the party for you. Maybe now we can finish what we started.'

Elspeth looked from Mariah, to Onnie and then over to Jib. She smiled, 'I'd like that.'

While the sun was rising on the mountain, Elan and

Jib cast spell after spell creating a great banquet in the meadow. The dragons were fed, watered and cleaned up after their ordeal with the castle roof, while tables were filled to bursting with food. Tunes were playing from unseen instruments as everyone celebrated Elspeth's rescue.

As Kira stood with Elan and Gwen, she watched Dane, Shanks and Kahrin filling their plates with food. On the grass, Jib danced with his new bride while Elspeth danced with Onnie-Astra. As she watched, she saw Onnie swinging her sister high up in the air and heard Elspeth's joyous laughter mixing with the laughter coming from behind the mask.

'I don't think I've ever seen Shadow look happier,' Kira said.

'She's in love,' Gwen explained. 'She's been in love with Onnie for ages, but never really knew it.'

'And he's loved her,' Elan said. Then he dropped his voice. 'Though he's about to break her heart.'

'What?' Kira asked. 'How?'

'Onnie-Astra knows with his face, he'll be a constant distraction to Elspeth. Which is why he hasn't removed his mask to show her.' Elan paused and looked at Kira. 'He's a distraction to you too. It's not his fault, but that face of his is dangerous.'

'He's not going to stay here, is he?' Kira asked.

Elan shook his head. 'No, he can't stay. He belongs back with you. But he also knows the trouble his face is going to cause. Especially with what is coming.'

'He can always wear the mask,' Kira suggested. 'I'm fine if I don't see his face. Or you could change it for him.'

Elan shook his head. 'Changing it won't end its charm. It's from deep within Onnie-Astra himself.' He then inhaled deeply. 'Kira, I've looked into the Eye. I saw what you are all facing when you return. Lord Dorcon and the king won't stop coming after you. The prophecy must be fulfilled.'

Kira gasped. 'You know about the prophecy?'

Elan nodded. 'Of the young girl with long braids of red hair, who dresses as a boy and rides a twin-tailed dragon? Of how she will defeat a corrupt king and bring an end to a wretched monarchy? Oh, yes. I have seen it all. I also know in order for you to fulfil the prophecy, you must not be distracted by Onnie-Astra's face.' Elan paused as he looked over to Onnie dancing with Elspeth. 'Onnie-Astra knows it too. And of the dangers he'll put you all in if he remains as he is.'

'So what do we do?' Kira asked, watching Elspeth's

radiant face as she held on to Onnie. 'It will kill her if he leaves.'

'Onnie-Astra could never leave. He belongs with her,' Elan said. 'But there's only one way he can stay, and he knows it. He's asked me to turn him back into a fox.'

'Elan, you can't!' Kira cried.

'I must,' Elan said. 'He's right. It is the only way.'

'But if you do that, he'll be stuck as a fox for the rest of his life.'

Elan shook his head. 'Not necessarily. If you all succeed and the prophecy is fulfilled, you can take Onnie to one of my descendents and have them break the spell.'

'But Paradon's powers don't work properly. He could kill him.'

'Not Paradon,' Elan said. 'His granddaughter. She has all the power you need to break the spell I will put on him.

Kira frowned. 'Paradon has a granddaughter? He never told me.'

Elan shrugged. 'I don't know how much I should be telling you, but I think it is important for you to know. The Eye has shown me that when he was much younger, Paradon was married. He actually has three children. Sadly, they were always ashamed of him and the failure of his spells. They hurt him, Kira. And when they had children of their own, they kept them away from him.'

Kira was shocked to hear this. She couldn't imagine anyone ever being ashamed of Paradon. He meant the world to her and her family.

'When it is over and the prophecy is done,' Elan continued, 'find his granddaughter. Take Onnie to her. Being of my bloodline, she'll be able to free him from my spell.'

It was all so hard to take in. Onnie was going to be turned back into a fox. Paradon had a granddaughter, and Elan knew about the prophecy. Suddenly she remembered what Paradon had told her of Elan's dark fate. She looked at Gwen. 'Will you please excuse us for a moment? I need to speak to Elan privately.'

Gwen nodded and pointed at Kahrin. 'I'll be over there with that young lady, if you need me.'

When she was gone, Kira looked back to Elan anxiously. 'So you know all about the prophecy?'

When Elan nodded, she continued, 'How much of it did you see?'

A deep sadness entered the wizard's eyes as he looked down on her. 'All of it. And before you speak, let me say, I already know about my place in it. It will be me who tells King Lacarian of the girl on the twin-tailed dragon who will end the monarchy. I didn't see when I'd do it. But I did see it.'

Elan paused and sighed heavily. 'Kira, it's because of me First Law started. I am responsible for the suffering and death of countless girls throughout the ages. Can you imagine how that makes me feel?'

'You're not responsible, Elan,' Kira quickly said. 'The kings are. Right up to the king of my own time, King Arden. It's them who did it, not you.' She paused before adding, 'King Lacarian is going to kill you.'

'I know,' Elan said. 'I saw that too. Perhaps it is why they say wizards should never be allowed to see their own deaths.'

'But now that you know, you can stop it,' Kira said hopefully. 'Elan, don't you see? You don't have to die. You have the power to stop First Law before it ever starts. Just don't tell King Lacarian about me and Jinx.'

Once again Elan sighed heavily as he reached for Kira's hand. 'If I don't tell King Lacarian, then everything you have ever known will be destroyed. You, Kira, will cease to exist.'

Kira frowned, not understanding. 'But I do exist. I'm standing right here in front of you.'

Elan chuckled, but it was filled with deep regret. 'Kira, you were born because First Law said your mother had to marry your father before she reached the age of thirteen. Did she choose your father for herself? Or did her parents choose him?'

Kira thought back to the stories her mother told. Her grandparents had arranged the marriage, not her mother. She shook her head. 'My mother's marriage was arranged.'

'Exactly. So if I stop First Law before it starts, then it's likely your mother would not have married your father. Then, my dear girl, you, Elspeth, Kahrin and Dane could not have been born.'

That comment stopped Kira. It was still so confusing, but she understood enough to know that Elan now held her life and the life of her entire family in his hands.

'You understand now,' Elan said. 'So you see, in order to protect you and the world you came from, a world which you are about to change, I must tell King Lacarian the prophecy. The rest is up to you to stop First Law and end the chain of abuse from the corrupt monarchy.'

'But he's going to kill you,' Kira insisted. 'Can't you at least change that?'

Elan shook his head. 'That you know I died by his hand means it is my destiny. I can't fight it.'

'Does Gwen know?' Kira asked in a whisper.

Elan shook his head. 'No, and I won't tell her until the time comes. It may not be for some time yet. I may even live to see Paradon's grandfather being born.'

Kira was left speechless as the impact of Elan's words settled in. It had been easy to hear the story when Paradon first told it to her so long ago. But now, standing before Elan the wizard and knowing he was going to be murdered by King Lacarian, it was different. And it hurt.

'Now, come,' said Elan brightly. 'Let's dance and sing and enjoy the moment. There will be time enough for tears later.'

The celebration lasted all day and well into the night. But finally exhaustion caught up with everyone. It had been agreed not to delay the departure any longer. The next day, Elan would cast the spell that would send them all home.

With everyone sleeping in the meadow, Kira and Kahrin lay up against Jinx. Kahrin was asleep, but Kira couldn't. Not far away, she saw Elspeth walking arm in arm with Onnie in the moonlight. As she watched, she saw Elspeth stop and start to shake her head violently.

259

Unable to bear the pain Elspeth was suffering, Kira turned away. She knew Onnie was telling her how Elan was going to turn him back into the fox. Elspeth's sobs were the last things she heard before she drifted off into a deep troubled sleep.

As dawn arrived on the mountain, Kira awoke. Sitting up and stretching, she saw Elspeth and Onnie sitting together, holding hands and leaning against Harmony. They looked as though they hadn't slept at all.

Feeling her awake, Jinx turned his head back and gently nudged her. 'Morning, baby,' Kira said softly as she caught hold of his wing and hauled herself up. 'We're going home today.'

'Finally,' Shanks said as he and Dane drew up to her. 'This whole thing has been too strange for my liking. Give me a good sword and battle anytime over all this time travel and wizard stuff. I don't think I'll ever get used it.'

'I kind of like it,' Dane said. 'You can't say it was boring.'

'No, boring isn't the word I would use to describe it,' Shanks agreed. He then looked at Kira's face. 'Hey, you look like a dragon just ate your cat. What's wrong?'

Kira pointed over to Elspeth and Onnie as Elan

stepped up to them. 'Elan is about to turn Onnie back into a fox.'

'What?' Dane said. 'Why?'

'I know why,' Shanks said. 'It's because of the way you girls look at him, isn't it?'

When Kira nodded hesitantly, Shanks shrugged. 'I don't get it. Dane, could you please tell me what Onnie-Astra has that I haven't?'

Kira answered quickly for her brother. 'I'll tell you. It's good manners, beautiful eyes and a handsome face. Oh, and a lovely voice. Basically he's everything you're not.'

'And yet,' Shanks teased, winking at her, 'you like me just the same.'

Kira's eyes flew wide, but her cheeks turned red. 'In your dreams, Shanks-Spar!' Stepping away from her brother and Shanks, she walked hesitantly towards Elspeth.

'Kira, wait,' Gwen called as she approached. 'Leave them be. Give them these last few moments alone together. Elan is about to cast the spell.'

Standing with Gwen, Kira watched as Elspeth rested her head on Onnie's chest. From where she stood, Kira could see the tears streaming down Elspeth's cheeks. Soon Onnie drew his hand gently over her eyes to get her to close them. When they were, he removed his mask.

Kira's heart skipped a beat when she saw his beautiful face again. Only then did she realize Onnie had been right. He was a distraction. Watching him with her sister, Kira's own eyes filled with tears as Onnie-Astra kissed Elspeth and pulled her into a tight embrace. He then looked back to Elan and nodded.

Raising his hands in the air, Elan cast the spell. A moment later, the air sparkled and Onnie-Astra was gone. On the ground at Elspeth's feet was the familiar red fox with the black mask lying beside him. Falling to the ground, Elspeth scooped him up in her arms and pulled him to her chest.

Elan reached out and petted the fox once before turning to cross over to Gwen.

'That was the hardest thing I've ever done in my life,' the wizard said sadly as he put his arm around his wife. Then he looked at Kira. 'Fulfil that prophecy as quickly as you can. It's too cruel to keep those two apart.'

Kira nodded, 'I will.'

She crossed over to Elspeth. 'Shadow?' she said gently as she lowered herself to the ground beside her sister. Elspeth looked miserably at Kira, but couldn't speak.

'We'll go home and end this,' Kira said softly. 'Then we'll find Paradon's granddaughter and turn Onnie back.' Without any hesitation, Kira reached forward and stroked the fox's soft red head. 'It won't be long, Onnie. I promise.'

In response, the fox howled mournfully before giving Kira's hand one single lick.

By midday, the dragons and their riders were finally ready to leave the time of Elan.

The wizard had summoned up the Eye from his cottage and it sat in the middle of the meadow, almost in the same place it had been with old Paradon in the future.

Kira looked over to Elspeth. She was standing beside Harmony, dressed the way she always remembered her. Gone was the beautiful golden gown. Instead she wore her leather trousers and rough-skinned top. Her knight's dagger was at her waist and she carried her bow and quiver of arrows. Her long flowing hair had been restored to the two braids. Elspeth was back to being Elspeth again – except for the haunted expression in her eyes.

Kira wondered how long it would take for that to finally pass. Onnie was in the pouch on her back with his paws resting lightly on her shoulders. Like Elspeth, there was an air of profound sadness around the fox.

The goodbyes were tearful and pain-filled as Elspeth embraced and kissed Elan, Gwen and Jib a final time before crossing to Harmony and climbing slowly on to her back. When it was Kira's turn, she felt her own sadness surface as she looked at Elan and knew the sacrifice the wizard was going to make on their behalf.

After thanking Elan, she climbed on Jinx's wing and looked back at Kahrin seated behind her. 'You ready to go home?'

Kahrin nodded. 'I just wish Elspeth wasn't so sad.'

'Me too.' She looked over to her sister and saw the pain resting on her face. 'She'll be all right soon. Onnie is still with her.'

Kira faced forward again and looked at Elan as he stood before the Eye. 'Godspeed,' he called as he raised his hands in the air and started to cast the spell. As the Eye started to glow and the colours flowed out of it, Kira heard Elan, Gwen, Jib and Mariah calling their final farewells.

Moments later, the tendrils from the Eye reached forward and wrapped around the three dragons and their riders. Then they were gone.

Every other time they travelled in the Eye, the dragons had been flying. This time, they were standing and unmoving as the colourful sea of time passed around them. Soon they all heard the familiar peals of thunder as the colours faded and the world around them came into focus.

With the last of the colours gone, Kira looked around and was grateful to finally see the courtyard of Paradon's floating castle.

'Thank you, Elan!' Kira cried as she excitedly opened the hatch to the saddlebox and climbed down from Jinx. Helping Kahrin down, they heard a much-loved voice calling from the open doors of the castle.

'Welcome home!' Paradon cried excitedly. 'Welcome home!'

Turning, Kira saw the Paradon she remembered. Not the pain-filled, wizened and impossibly old man from the future, but her Paradon. He was still old, but strong and smiling and running towards her.

'Paradon!' Kira squealed.

Jumping down from Jinx's wing, Kira ran at the wizard and threw her arms around him and hugged him fiercely. 'Oh, Paradon, how I've missed you!'

'I've missed you too,' Paradon said as he kissed her cheek. 'This old castle hasn't been the same since you left. It's been the longest three seasons of my life!'

'Three seasons?' Dane asked as he stepped up to the wizard and greeted him. 'We've really been gone three seasons?'

'Indeed you have,' Paradon chuckled. 'I can't tell you how frightened I've been for you all. I saw the spell going wrong and couldn't stop it—' Halfway through his sentence, Paradon looked over and saw Elspeth walking slowly up to him, clutching Onnie in her arms.

'Elspeth?' Paradon frowned. 'My word, child, what happened to you?'

Unable to speak, Elspeth ran the distance between them and hugged the wizard. Her tears started to fall as Onnie howled, held between the two.

'Talk to me,' Paradon said as he brushed away her tears. 'What happened?'

Kira explained for her sister. 'While we were only in the future a short time, she and Onnie were stuck in the past for over eight winters.'

'Eight winters?' Paradon repeated. When everyone nodded, he smiled sadly at Elspeth. 'Oh, my dearest girl, I am so sorry.' He then motioned back to the castle. 'Come inside and bring your dragons with you. You mustn't be seen out here. Then you must tell me everything.'

The group entered the castle and led the dragons into the great hall. They sat down and tried to explain as best they could, all the events that had occurred since they first entered the Eye.

Kira started speaking first as she told Paradon about the events in the future world and how a very much older version of himself had sent them back to Elspeth. She then told him what she knew of Elan and how he, Jib and Onnie-Astra had helped them recover Elspeth from the evil twins.

When Kira finished, Paradon crossed to Elspeth. Offering his hand, he drew her up to stand with him. 'I am so grateful you found Elan,' he said softly. He then looked at Onnie, still clutched in her arms. He reached out and stroked the fox's head.

'Onnie-Astra,' he repeated. 'I remember stories of

that name when I was just a boy. But I never imagined it could be you. I'm so sorry, my old friend.'

He stroked Elspeth's cheek again. 'I'm truly sorry for both of you. I would never have wished that pain on you. You have my word, we will do as Elan suggested and find Sara. She will restore you.'

'Sara?' Kira asked.

Paradon nodded. 'My granddaughter. Sadly, I've never met her and don't know where she lives. But now that you are back, the Eye will show me. She can break Elan's spell and restore Onnie to his true form.'

Before Paradon walked back to Kira, he took Elspeth's hand and smiled gently at her. 'Perhaps when you are feeling better, you might tell me everything you can about your life with Elan, Gwen and Jib. There are stories that have been passed down through my family, but you actually knew them.'

'We will,' Elspeth promised softly.

'So what happened here after we left?' Shanks asked.

Paradon gave Elspeth's hand a final squeeze as he turned to face the others. 'Well, as we suspected, Lord Dorcon was none too pleased with your departure. He and his men finally broke down the portcullis and entered the grounds. After that, it didn't take them long to get into the castle itself. But they couldn't get in my tower. After a time, they left, leaving several knights posted here. I was able to cast a few spells that finally drove those men away as well.'

'So it's over?' Kahrin asked. 'Are we safe?'

Paradon sighed heavily before shaking his head. 'No, I'm afraid not. I've seen through the Eye that the king has men posted in the forest around the castle. They know better than to approach after what happened last time, but they are out there watching us. Every day I see dragon knights flying overhead, checking the courtyard. No doubt your noisy and bright arrival today has announced your return.'

'Then we did it for nothing!' Kira said angrily as she rose and started to pace the wide floor of the great hall. 'Shanks and the dragons were shot and nearly killed. Elspeth and Onnie went through hell, and all for nothing. We're right back where we started! Soon, Lord Dorcon will be back at our door, sending his men in to get us!'

'Calm down,' Paradon said. 'It's true that the danger hasn't passed. But we have more time than we did before. And Lord Dorcon's men will not launch another assault against this castle. I never realized I could defend her as well as I could. My magic is far from perfect, and the spells didn't come out the way I planned. But it worked enough to drive Lord Dorcon's men away.'

'So that leaves us trapped in here?' Dane asked. 'We're safe in the castle, but only in the castle. We'll be killed the moment we step outside the grounds.'

Paradon looked at Dane and nodded slowly. 'For the time being, that's exactly what the situation is.'

'This is no life for us,' Shanks said. 'We're dragon knights, not cowards. We don't hide from fights.'

'Shadow, Kahrin and I aren't dragon knights, but we won't hide either,' Kira said. 'And what about the prophecy? How are we going to fulfil it if we're stuck in here?'

Paradon held up his hands to calm everyone down. 'Please don't see it as cowardice to remain here for a bit. We must use this time to plan our next move. And to see what the king has got in mind for us.'

Elspeth frowned as she looked at Kira. 'What prophecy? What are you talking about?'

Kira suddenly realized Elspeth was now the only member of the family not to know Elan's prophecy. She caught Elspeth by the hand.

'Shadow, sit down for a moment. I need to tell you something.'

Elspeth sat beside Kahrin as Kira and Paradon

told her the details of the ancient prophecy foretold by Elan.

Elspeth looked at Kira in disbelief. 'You knew this all along and didn't tell me? Why?'

Kira sighed. 'You were so young and we'd only just come to the castle when Paradon first told me. We thought it best to keep it from you because we didn't want to worry you.'

'Worry me?' Elspeth challenged as she stood and turned on Kira. 'Worry me? You should have told me, Kira, especially as Elan is part of it. He's going to be killed by King Lacarian! I've got to warn him!'

'I did warn him,' Kira said. 'Shadow, he'd already seen it in the Eye. He knew everything about the prophecy and his part in it. He knew King Lacarian was going to betray him and First Law was going to start. He knew all of it and though he wanted to stop it, he knew he couldn't.'

'But we can save him!' Elspeth cried. Then she looked pleadingly at Paradon. 'You've got to send me back there. Elan is a good man. He and Gwen took me in and treated me like family. I can't let the king hurt him.'

Paradon shook his head sadly. 'I'm so sorry, Elspeth, but it has already happened, a very, very long time ago.

Elan is gone. So are Gwen and Jib and Jib's children and their children. They were my ancestors. Elspeth, you shouldn't have even been there in the first place. It was my mistake. I'm so sorry, but there is nothing more to be done.'

'But there's got to be something we can do!' Elspeth cried.

'There is,' Kira said. 'Shadow, right before we left, Elan begged me to fulfil the prophecy. He was counting on us to end First Law against girls and free the people of this time. He said if we do that, he would rest easy.'

In her arms, Onnie started to yip. Elspeth looked down on him, and then nodded her head before looking at Kira. 'Onnie says it's up to us. Once we end First Law, we can find Sara and turn him back.'

Kira nodded and then looked to the others in the room. 'Then we'll end this. Once and for all!'

CHAPTER
~30~

Kira was grateful to be back with Paradon in the castle. But everything had changed. Elspeth was different. She spent more and more time alone with only Onnie and Harmony for company, and asked Paradon for her own private chamber. Before long, Rexor was also spending each night in Elspeth's new chamber.

Kira also noticed more and more animals finding their way into the castle to spend time with her sister. She was growing accustomed to seeing hawks, owls, ravens, rodents and any creature that could make it into the castle, quietly following her sister through the corridors or perching on chairs around her.

Jinx continued to stay with Kira and Kahrin in their chamber while Dane and Shanks had taken over one of the zigzag towers to call their own. But with the king's knights flying overhead several times a day, and men hiding in the forests, it was impossible to take the dragons out for exercise.

Late one evening after everyone had gone to bed, Kira found she couldn't sleep. Rising quietly, she crossed to Jinx and ordered him to stay and protect Kahrin while she went for a walk.

She wandered through the empty corridors of the castle and found herself at the entrance to the north tower. Climbing to the top, she was startled to see Elspeth, Onnie and Harmony there, staring out into the night. As she stepped out on to the tower roof, Harmony started to growl softly.

'Harmony, stop it,' Elspeth said.

'Shadow?' Kira called. 'May I join you?'

Elspeth looked at her and nodded. 'You know you don't have to ask.'

'I know. It's just that a lot has changed. You're spending all your time alone with Onnie and I didn't want to disturb you.'

Elspeth sighed. 'I'm sorry. I just don't know what's wrong with me. I feel like I don't belong anywhere any more.'

When Kira stepped closer to Elspeth, she noticed all the owls perching on the short wall beside her. 'I think you were alone on the mountain too long. It'll take time to get used to living with us again.'

'I hope you're right,' Elspeth said.

As Kira drew near to an owl, she looked over to Elspeth. 'Do you think I could pet one?'

When Elspeth agreed, Kira reached out and started to gently stroke the soft chest feathers of a wild owl. 'They really do like you, don't they?'

Elspeth nodded. 'A long time ago, I started to develop my skills with animals. Only now it seems they follow me everywhere I go, whether I want them to or not.'

'That's not such a bad thing,' Kira said. 'I like having the castle full of animals. Besides, it really bothers Shanks when he sits in bird's mess. So that's a plus.'

Elspeth chuckled softly as she held on to Onnie, lightly scratching his chin. 'You really do like him, don't you?'

Kira blushed. 'Me like Shanks?' When Elspeth nodded, Kira shook her head. 'Never.'

In her arms, Onnie yipped and wagged his bushy tail. Elspeth leaned down and kissed the top of his head. 'Onnie says he doesn't believe you.'

'What does he know? He's just a red rat!' Kira teased, as she stuck out her tongue at the fox.

For the first time since they'd returned, Onnie squinted back at her. It made Kira smile to think things were finally getting back to normal. She reached out and stroked the fox's soft fur. Then she looked back to Elspeth. 'I really don't like Shanks at all.'

'No, of course not,' Elspeth teased. 'And he doesn't like you either.'

'What do you mean?' Kira asked.

'You know exactly what I mean. I don't think he's taken his eyes off you since you first met.'

The blush in Kira's cheeks darkened. 'Well, it doesn't matter. We've got to concentrate on more serious things.'

'Yes we do,' Elspeth agreed as she looked out over the dark forest. 'The owls tell me there are a lot of men out there. They're watching us and waiting for us to leave so they can attack.'

The smile left Kira's face and she felt a shiver moving down her spine. 'Have they moved any closer?'

'No,' Elspeth answered. 'But I did have an idea I wanted to try. Now that you're here, how about we have some fun?'

Kira looked up at her sister. 'What were you planning?'

Suddenly a wicked grin spread across Elspeth's face. 'This . . .'

As Kira watched, Elspeth held her hand out over the

side of the tower. 'Find the men,' she called softly. 'Drive them away from this place.' In her arms, Onnie started to howl and yip excitedly.

At first nothing happened. Then after a while Elspeth started to grin. 'Wait . . . Wait for it . . .'

Kira stood beside her sister looking out into the night. Suddenly the silence was shattered by the sound of howling wolves and the frightened cries of men.

'What's happening down there?' Kira asked.

'Go away!' Elspeth shouted. 'Leave us alone!' Then she looked at Kira and burst out laughing. 'The wolves are chasing the men away. I've asked them to clear the forest and keep them out. Now we can take the dragons out for some exercise.'

Kira looked over the forest in wonder. She couldn't see the men fleeing, but she could hear the sound of their cries as the wolves chased them. She looked back at Elspeth in awe. 'I sure wish I could do that.'

'It really doesn't frighten you?' Elspeth asked, growing serious.

Kira looked at her sister in shock. 'Frighten me?' She shook her head. 'Shadow, have you forgotten our time together on the Rogue's Mountain? You know you could never do anything to frighten me. You're my sister and I love you. I've always envied what you can do with animals.'

For the first time in ages, Elspeth looked at Kira and gave her a smile that reached all the way to her eyes. 'The whole time I was with Elan, the villagers called me Animal Girl and were scared of me. It makes me realize just how much I missed you, and how glad I am that we're back together.'

Pouring Onnie to the ground, Elspeth pulled Kira into a tight hug. 'How about we learn to fight better so we can finally fulfil Elan's prophecy and free Onnie!'

As Kira returned the hug, she laughed. 'You don't need to learn to fight. With animals doing whatever you ask them to, you've got an army all of your own!'

With the king's men kept from the castle, the dragons were finally allowed out at night for some much needed exercise. During the day, the king's dragon knights continued to fly over the courtyard, but they kept their distance.

As they had done before, Dane and Shanks instructed the girls in sword fighting as well as hand-to-hand combat. Gathered together in the great hall, Elspeth was wrestling with Dane while Shanks took on Kira as they tried to pin each other down.

With Onnie and Kahrin offering encouragement

from the side, Elspeth was able to get the better of Dane time and time again.

Holding him to the ground, Dane surrendered.

'You're a girl,' he complained, as Elspeth climbed off and helped him up. 'You're not supposed to be stronger than me.'

'Yeah,' Shanks agreed as he suddenly made a move that caught Kira off guard. Knocking her legs out from under her, she fell to the floor. Moments later he was sitting on top of her and holding her shoulders down. 'See, this is how it's supposed to be. Men are stronger than girls.'

This made Kira angry. Arching her back, she pushed up with all her strength and was able to dislodge Shanks. Flipping him over, she quickly climbed on top to pin him down.

'What were you saying about girls?' she demanded.

Beneath her, Shanks started to laugh. 'I said men are better at everything. I only let you win so you wouldn't run off in a huff.'

'You did not!' Kira cried. 'I beat you fairly. You didn't let me win!'

'Of course I did,' Shanks teased as his laughter increased. He reached up and caught hold of her two long braids. Giving them a playful tug, he continued,

'You don't think you could actually beat a knight of the realm, do you?'

Kira was about to retort when Jinx growled softly. Paradon had arrived in the great hall. Everyone saw the grim expression on his face.

'We've just received this from one of the dragon knights,' the wizard explained as he held up a parchment. 'It was attached to a lance he threw down into the courtyard.'

'What's it say?' Shanks asked as Kira climbed off and allowed him to get up.

Paradon shook his head. 'I don't know. I can't read.'

'I can,' Elspeth said. 'Gwen taught me.' Crossing to the wizard, she caught hold of the parchment and unrolled it. Reading the message, her eyes went wide with fear. 'They can't!'

'What is it?' Kira demanded.

'The king is going to kill Mother.'

'What!' Dane shouted as he reached for the scroll. He unrolled it and started to read the message aloud.

By proclamation of the King

The prisoners, Alisandra, wife of the traitor Darious, and Treyu, the former instructor to the palace dragon stables who aided in the escape of Dane, son of the traitor

Darious, are to be executed for crimes of treason against King Arden and the kingdom. The time of the execution will be at dawn on the next new moon.

Throwing it away, Dane looked at Paradon. 'They can't do that. Mother hasn't done anything wrong.'

'She doesn't have to for the king to execute her,' Paradon explained. 'This isn't about your mother or the instructor.'

'No, it's about us,' Kira angrily cut in. 'Lord Dorcon and the king know they can't get us while we're here at the castle. So they're setting at trap they know we can't resist.'

Paradon nodded. 'I've been watching him in the Eye. King Arden is desperate. His attempts to kill the Rogue have failed. The people at the palace are starving and starting to riot. The war is lost and you have returned to the kingdom. He believes the prophecy is coming and he'll do anything to stop it. If he just wanted to kill your mother and the instructor, he would have done so already. This message is his way of challenging you to the final fight.'

'If it's a fight he wants,' Kira said furiously, 'we'll give it to him. This ends now!'

CHAPTER
~ 31 ~

'We can't fight them outright,' Paradon explained as they all gathered together in the great hall to work out their next move. 'Their numbers are far too great. We'll have to fight them using our brains and stealth.'

'And dragons,' Kira added as she stroked Jinx's thick neck. 'Jinx helped us at Lasser, in the future against the choppers and then at the twins' castle. We should let them all help us again.'

'Yes,' Paradon agreed. 'But only to get us to the palace. Once we make it there, they can't help us any further. We'll have to go in alone.'

'Why?' Shanks asked. 'The dragons are our best weapons.'

Paradon started to pace the area. 'Because a frontal attack on the palace will fail. When we arrive, we must enter using a different route.'

'What route?' Dane asked. 'With the portcullis

fortified, and the way into the dragon stables secured, there is only one way in for us: using the dragons to land in the courtyard.'

Paradon shook his head. 'No, that's just too dangerous and what they'll be expecting. There is another way in. Don't forget, I used to serve King Arden and his father before him. After what happened to Elan . . .'

Paradon paused when he saw both Kira and Elspeth react to the mention of Elan's name. The memory of the powerful wizard was still too fresh and the knowledge that he had been betrayed and murdered by King Lacarian was still too painful. 'I'm sorry, girls,' he continued, 'but after he was killed by King Lacarian, the next wizard to serve the king made a few changes to the palace that the king never knew about. He created secret escape tunnels that go in and out. It's these tunnels we will use.'

'But won't his current wizard also know about the tunnels and warn him?' Dane asked.

Paradon shook his head. 'I was the last wizard to serve King Arden. He never liked wizards and hates magic. So once I was gone, he banned all other wizards from visiting the palace. This has actually helped us greatly. If he had a palace wizard, King Arden would have used him to stop us ages ago.'

'With or without a wizard at the palace,' Dane continued, 'when we do get in there, the first thing I'm going to do is find Lord Dorcon. Then I'm going to make him pay for what he did to Father.'

'And to you,' Kahrin added, looking at Dane's scarred face.

'And for what he did to Blue on the Rogue's Mountain,' Kira added. 'I want to be there too. He's going to see all of us when he is punished.'

Dane nodded and looked back at Paradon. 'When do you think we should go?'

Paradon rubbed the stubble on his chin. 'Well, the moon is almost full, so we have a bit of time.'

In Elspeth's arms, Onnie started to yip frantically. 'Onnie says we should leave as soon as possible,' she said. 'He said we shouldn't give the king time to prepare.'

Paradon crossed over to Elspeth and Onnie and stroked the fox's head. 'I agree that we shouldn't delay. But we mustn't think for one moment that the king and Lord Dorcon aren't already prepared for us. They would have set their trap long before they sent the message to us.'

Shanks stepped forward and faced Dane and Kira. 'He'll probably have moved your mother and the instructor down to the dungeons since that is the most secure place in the palace.'

'And increased the guards,' Dane added.

'This rescue won't be easy,' Paradon said. 'In fact, I believe it's going to be the hardest of all. Lasser was dangerous, but the guards were ill prepared for a dragon attack. Going after Elspeth at the twins' castle was equally dangerous, but you had two powerful wizards with you. This time, you will have only yourselves, your wits and me.'

'You're coming with us?' Kahrin asked.

Paradon nodded. 'I've come to realize that staying with the Eye to use my powers isn't always the best option. It worked at Lasser because there were only the two of you,' he said to Kira and Elspeth. 'But this time, there are more of you going. We all stand a better chance if I am with you.'

Hearing this made Kira feel instantly better. 'If you are with us, we can't possibly fail.'

For the next few days, Paradon drew up diagrams of the palace and instructed everyone on the locations of the various escape tunnels running beneath it. He made sure everyone knew their location in case they ever got separated.

As the time of departure drew near, they discussed their final plans.

'All right,' Shanks was saying. 'We know the palace dragons won't fly at night, so that will be our time to move.'

'How long will it take us to get there?' Kira asked.

'It took us four days to get here the first time we came,' Dane answered. 'So it should take us the same amount to get back.'

'Perhaps longer,' Paradon added. 'I don't think it's wise to take the same direct route you and Shanks used. We all know this is a trap. But none of us can be sure where it's going to be sprung. Though I would think it will be at the palace itself and not on the way there. I suggest we fly around the palace and come at them from the south.'

'But that will add another day,' Dane argued. 'They might execute Mother and the instructor in that time.'

'Not if we leave tomorrow night,' Elspeth suggested. 'Then it would give us plenty of time to fly the dragons well around the palace and come at them from behind.'

Paradon nodded thoughtfully. 'Does anyone have any objections to that?' When no one spoke, he continued, 'Fine then, we'll leave tomorrow night.'

As they had done before, everyone gathered together in the great hall to finish getting ready to go. Little was said as they carefully packed the dragons' saddleboxes with extra arrows and weapons.

Kira quietly watched her family preparing for this final, critical battle. She never spoke of her feelings but, as she stood with Jinx, she couldn't shake the sickening feeling that something was about to go terribly wrong.

Going to Lasser had been bad. But as she and Elspeth had never gone into battle before and didn't know what they'd encounter, it wasn't so terrible. Working with Elan, Jib and Onnie-Astra to free Elspeth had also been very frightening. But deep in her heart, she knew they would succeed.

But this time was different. This time they were going after a king.

As she stroked Jinx's thick neck, Kira felt more fear, more dread than she'd ever felt before. It was like a heavy rock sitting in the pit of her stomach. Was it because this was her chance to finally fulfil the prophecy? Did she feel this way because Elan was somehow counting on her to succeed? She didn't know. All Kira did know was that she was terrified.

'Are you all right?' Kahrin asked as she came up behind her carrying a quiver filled with arrows.

Shaken from her thoughts, Kira looked back at her younger sister and nodded. 'Just a little nervous, that's all.'

'Me too,' Kahrin admitted. 'If it goes wrong, do you think they'll put us in prison like they did to me at Lasser?'

Kira shrugged. 'I don't know. The king and Lord Dorcon are really angry. I don't know what they'll do.'

'I think they'll kill us,' Kahrin suggested flatly. 'But that's definitely better than prison.'

Kira looked at Kahrin and knew her sister understood what she was saying. Her experiences at Lasser Commons had left deep wounds that even now, were still coming to the surface.

'Whatever happens, Kahrin, has to happen,' Kira said softly. 'We can't let the king hurt Mother or continue with First Law. Too many girls have died already . . .' Kira paused and reached out to her sister. 'You know, you don't have to come with us. After what you've been through, I know everyone would understand. You can stay here at the castle and be safe.'

Kahrin inhaled deeply and squared her shoulders. Suddenly she reminded Kira of Elspeth when she was much younger. 'No,' she said. 'I'm not going to stay here. I'm going to fight with you. Even if I die, it's better than being left alone again.'

Kira pulled Kahrin into a tight hug. 'You're not

going to die, Kahrin,' she said softly. 'I promise you, I won't let the king or Lord Dorcon hurt you.'

Dane came up and tapped Kira on the shoulder. 'You ready to go? The sun is almost down.'

Kira looked at Kahrin. 'Are you ready?' When Kahrin nodded, Kira looked at her brother. 'We're ready.'

Once the sun had set, the dragons filed quietly out of the castle and into the courtyard. Kira, Paradon and Kahrin were on Jinx, while Dane and Shanks were on Rexor. Dane was at the head of the dragon in the saddlebox, while Shanks held his bow at the ready in the rear. Finally Harmony emerged with Elspeth and Onnie.

Gathered together in the centre of the courtyard, everyone looked at Elspeth. Kira saw her sister close her eyes and raise her head up. A little while later, several owls swooped down from the sky. One landed on Elspeth's outstretched arm.

Finally nodding her head, Elspeth released the owl and turned to everyone. 'The forest is clear. There are no men in it. They say the sky is clear of dragons as well.'

'That's a very handy talent you've got there,' Shanks said. 'When this is over, will you show me how to do it?'

Kira looked over to Shanks. 'If she can't show me

how to do it and I'm her sister, what makes you think you can learn?'

'I'm a man, I can learn anything.'

Suddenly angry again, Kira challenged, 'Shanks-Spar, when we get back, I'm going to show you what girls can really do! That'll wipe that smile off your face.'

'Promises, promises,' Shanks teased.

Paradon cleared his throat, cutting off further arguments. 'Are we ready to go?' With everyone agreeing, he tapped Kira on the shoulder. 'We've a long journey ahead of us. Let's get moving.'

Kira looked back at the wizard and saw the worried expression on his face. She nodded, then faced forward and pulled back on the reins. 'Let's go flying, Jinx.'

The first long night of the journey was uneventful. As the pink rays of dawn lit the horizon, Paradon pointed out a clearing in the forest for the group to land. When they were down, they walked the dragons into the protective cover of the trees to be fed and rested.

They gathered together around a small campfire. Little was said as they gazed into the flames and worried about the fight to come. After a brief meal, everyone settled down for some much needed rest.

The second and third night on the journey were

much the same. By dawn they were able to find the safety of forest cover for the dragons. But on the fourth night the forest gave way to open, abandoned farmland. Without the cover of trees, they landed the dragons at an empty barn.

It was a tight fit getting all three large dragons inside, but as the sun crept higher in the sky, everyone settled down to rest. Elspeth was curled up with Onnie under Harmony's wing while Kira and Kahrin slept beside Jinx. Dane, Shanks and Paradon lay in their bedrolls close to the fire, opposite Rexor. It wasn't long before everyone fell into a deep and exhausted sleep.

The sudden and loud barking of dogs woke Kira with a start. Sitting up, she looked over and saw Elspeth already on her feet. A large raven swooped down from an upper window of the barn and landed on Elspeth's arm and cawed loudly.

'Get up, everyone!' Elspeth cried. 'Knights are coming!'

Behind the barking of dogs, Kira heard the cawing of more crows and screeching of predatory birds. It sounded like every animal outside the barn was trying to get in and warn them of the impending danger.

In response to the noises, all three dragons started to growl and then roar.

'Get to your dragons!' Paradon ordered as he ran to open the barn doors. 'We may still have time.'

As soon as the two doors opened, Paradon cried out in pain. Kira turned and saw an arrow protruding from his chest as he fell to the floor.

'Paradon!' she howled.

Kira raced over to the wizard and saw blood coming to the surface of his wound. He was unconscious.

'Dane, help me!' she cried.

With Dane's help, they started to drag the wounded wizard back inside. Before they could close the doors again, Kira and Dane watched as a legion of knights arrived and encircled the barn. Above them, the sky was filled with dragon knights. Their riders were pointing drawn bows at them.

Then Kira's eyes came to rest on the most frightening sight of all. Lord Dorcon. Fully armoured with his visor down, she could only see his blazing eyes.

'Surrender!' he shouted. Seated on his high warhorse, he was holding his sword in the air. 'Come out or we'll burn you out!'

Kira looked desperately back to Dane. 'What do we do?'

'We fight!' Shanks cried. Seated on Rexor, he fixed

an arrow in his bow. 'Dane, come on, this is what we've trained for.'

'There are too many!' Kira cried. 'Shanks, we'll all be killed.'

'Better to die than be captured,' Shanks said.

'No!' Elspeth shouted. 'All of you stay here and take care of Paradon. They have dragons and horses. I can make the animals defy their riders. We won't have to fight.'

Kneeling beside the fallen wizard, Kira watched Elspeth climb on to Harmony's back. Onnie was in his pouch with his paws resting on her shoulders. Closing her eyes, Elspeth raised her hands in the air. 'Dragons and horses go!' she commanded. 'Leave here now.'

Daring to steal a glance outside, Kira saw the horses starting to rear up and fight their riders. Looking into the sky, she saw the dragons defy their knights and start flying away from the area.

'It's working!' Kira cried. 'Shadow, it's working. Whatever you're doing, keep doing it!'

Without speaking, Elspeth directed Harmony forward. Her hands were still held high as she continued to order the horses and dragons away from the area.

Outside the barn, Kira watched in pleasure as Lord

Dorcon's stallion reared up and fought the evil knight. Lord Dorcon was then cast out of the saddle and he landed with a loud thump on the ground.

'Now's our chance,' Shanks called. 'Dane and I will help drive them away. Kira and Kahrin, you stay with Paradon.'

'I'm fighting too,' Kahrin said. Reaching for her bow, she crossed to the entrance and hid behind one of the open doors. She fixed an arrow in her bow and fired at the closest knight.

Checking on Paradon again, Kira saw that although it was weak and shallow, he was still breathing. She was hesitant to leave him, but finally drew away to collect her own bow and join Kahrin at the door.

Drawing their swords, Dane and Shanks charged outside to face the men who'd fallen from their horses. Soon both were fighting the knights as their swords flashed in the sunlight.

With her hands still held high, Elspeth commanded the birds of the area to launch an attack. Ravens and hawks dived at the knights, driving them away.

'It's her!' Lord Dorcon howled at his men as he climbed to his feet and pointed at Elspeth. 'She's doing it. Get her!'

Hearing Lord Dorcon's words, Kira looked at

Kahrin. 'Keep firing at the men, but stay here with Paradon.'

Before Kahrin could protest, Kira ran over to Rexor. Taking hold of his reins, she ran him to the front of the barn. 'Go get them, Rexor! Help Shadow!'

Kira knew he couldn't understand her words, but when the dragon saw the fight outside the barn, he raced outside to attack the charging knights as he had done in the future world.

From Rexor, Kira ran back to Jinx. She climbed into the saddlebox and reached for the reins. 'Go, Jinx,' she ordered. 'Go outside and help Shadow.'

The blue twin-tailed dragon moved instantly. Charging forward, Kira directed him towards the first knight she saw. Kira didn't need to tell Jinx what to do. He did it instinctively as he dispatched the knight.

Turning him around, Kira sought out Lord Dorcon. This was it, the end of the fight. He had been after them long enough. Now he would face her dragon's rage.

But as she saw Lord Dorcon standing amongst his many other knights, her blood ran cold. Lord Dorcon was holding a bow with the arrow pointed directly at Elspeth's back. Before Kira had a chance to warn her sister, Lord Dorcon released his arrow.

CHAPTER
~32~

Everything was happening too quickly. Unable to warn her sister in time, Kira watched the arrow strike Onnie first, before passing threw him to hit Elspeth. A second arrow quickly followed the first, once again hitting both Onnie and Elspeth.

By the time the third arrow struck, Elspeth was falling from Harmony's back.

'Shadow!' Kira screamed. 'No!'

Elspeth hit the ground at Harmony's feet and the red dragon started to whine. Harmony turned back and gently nudged her. But Elspeth remained still. Finally the dragon let out a ferocious roar as she turned and viciously attacked the nearest knights. Jinx was the next to roar in reaction to Elspeth, quickly followed by Rexor. All the dragons seemed to know something was terribly wrong.

With Elspeth down, the spell controlling the animals

was immediately broken. The dragon knights in the sky regained control over their mounts and turned them back to the fight. On the ground, the bolting horses were also brought under control as more knights quickly returned.

Jumping down from Jinx, Kira ran over to Elspeth. She heard Dane and Shanks continuing to fight around her, while Jinx, Rexor and Harmony went after the attacking legion with more fury than Kira had ever seen before.

Kneeling at her sister's side, Kira's eyes filled with tears as she saw the three arrows poking out of Onnie and Elspeth's back.

'Shadow?' she called weakly. She could see no signs of life from her sister. With trembling hands, Kira reached out and felt for a pulse at Elspeth's neck. 'No,' she whimpered when she could find none. 'No, please . . .'

Kira next reached for Onnie. As his head flopped in her hand, she realized that, like her sister, he too was dead.

She threw back her head and howled in heart-wrenching grief. They had fought together so hard for so long. Now it was over. Lord Dorcon had won. He had killed her father and now Elspeth and Onnie.

'Where's your prophecy now, Elan!' she cried furiously as she stood and turned to the battle. Drawing her dagger, she prepared to enter the fight. But looking at the terrible scene around her, she saw they had already lost. Dane and Shanks were badly outnumbered and it was only a matter of time before they were captured. Kahrin had already been caught and was being dragged from the barn by several knights.

Dragon knights were landing on the ground and using their long deadly lances against the three dragons. Harmony was the first to fall as two lances deeply pierced her side. Howling in agony, she fell to the ground. Using the last of her fading strength, the dying dragon hauled herself over to Elspeth. As she reached Elspeth's side, Kira heard Harmony let out one final grunt before becoming still.

Not far away, Rexor had been wounded and was now under the control of the dragon knights. She sought out Jinx amongst the madness and saw him take on several dragon knights and their mounts. Like the Rogue, Jinx was bigger and stronger than the other dragons. But he was only one against many. Those knights who weren't trying to stab him with their lances were shooting arrows into him as they attempted to kill him.

'Leave him alone!' Kira cried. Raising her dagger, she ran at the closest knight trying to kill her beloved dragon. 'Go, Jinx!' she ordered. 'Fly away from here. Go now!'

Suddenly a knight came at her from behind. He knocked Kira to the ground and she felt his heavy weight crushing down on her. Struggling to escape, her worst fears were quickly realized when she discovered it was Lord Dorcon.

'It's over, Kira,' he boasted. 'You're finished. I've got you now.'

'No!' she howled. Kira's dagger was trapped beneath her. As she struggled in Lord Dorcon's arms, she tried to get it free to kill him. But the more she struggled, the tighter he held her.

'Your father is dead, as is your friend over there with the fox—'

'She was my sister!' Kira cried in fury. 'You killed Elspeth!'

That comment seemed to confuse him. 'Elspeth?' he repeated. 'Impossible! She was the youngest of the family.'

'It was Elspeth,' Kira argued, still trying to get at her dagger. 'You killed her and now I'm going to kill you!'

'Don't be a fool. You can't win against me. You never could.'

Kira cried out as Lord Dorcon wrenched her arms painfully back behind her. Unable to reach her weapon, she was hauled roughly to her feet.

'Let me go!' she shouted as she fought against the strong and brutal arms that held her tight.

'Let you go?' Lord Dorcon laughed. The sound was harsh and shallow behind the visor. 'Why would I do that? Look around you, Kira. It's over, you've lost.' Then he tightened his grip on her arms as he leaned down to whisper in her ear. 'All of this is your fault. Your sister is dead. Her fox and dragon are dead, all because of you. Not me. If, back on your farm, you hadn't run away, none of this would have happened.'

Kira couldn't help but look at the destruction around her. He was right. It was her fault. Elspeth and Onnie were dead. So was Harmony. Paradon was badly wounded, as was Rexor. Dane, Shanks and Kahrin were gathered together and being put in chains. None of this would have happened if she hadn't run so long ago.

As her eyes trailed up into the sky, Kira could see Jinx circling above them. He was roaring and trying to get back to her, but every time he tried, more arrows flew at him and pieced his blue scales.

'Believe me,' Lord Dorcon continued, 'it won't be long before that blue monster is dead also.'

'You're the one who's going to die,' Kira said, though there wasn't a lot of confidence in the statement.

'Really?' Lord Dorcon said in amusement. 'And how do you see that happening when I have won?'

'Because you're evil. And evil always loses.'

'Not this time,' Lord Dorcon said smugly. He then turned to the dragon knights. 'Take the prisoners back to the palace and put them in the dungeon. I will keep Kira with me. We'll follow you on horseback.'

Kira watched as Dane, Kahrin and Shanks were hauled up and on to palace dragons. Still unconscious, Paradon was also put on a dragon's back behind a knight.

Moments later, the knights directed their mounts into the sky. Jinx roared at the departing dragons, but continued to stay in the sky above Kira. Only the knights firing their arrows at him kept him from landing.

'My Lord?' one of the knights asked as he stood before Elspeth. 'What about her? Should we bury her?'

Lord Dorcon gave Kira's arm another painful squeeze. 'Would you like my men to bury your sister with her fox?'

Unable to speak, Kira looked at Elspeth's body as tears streamed down her cheeks.

Lord Dorcon then looked at one of his men and roughly shoved Kira over to him. 'Hold her for me.'

When the knight caught hold of her arms, Kira watched Lord Dorcon striding over to Elspeth's body. 'So this is Elspeth?' he asked, looking back to her. 'Youngest daughter of Captain Darious?'

Kira said nothing.

The knight holding her shook her violently. 'Answer him!' he ordered. 'Is that the captain's youngest daughter?'

'Yes!' Kira spat, trying to pull away from the knight. Then she shouted at Lord Dorcon, 'Don't you dare touch her!'

Lord Dorcon looked at Kira and laughed cruelly. 'I wouldn't wipe my dirty boots on her! But I will take my arrows back!' He bent down and violently yanked the three arrows out of Elspeth and Onnie.

When he walked back to Kira, he stood before her. Holding up the bloody arrow tips, he wiped the fresh blood on her leather top. 'Something to remember your sister by.' He then called back at his men. 'Leave their bodies for the animals to eat.' Studying Kira closely, he waited for a reaction. When nothing happened, he finally said, 'Put the chains on her. It's time to head back to the palace.'

While his men put the shackles on Kira, Lord Dorcon climbed on to his tall warhorse. Kira was hoisted up to sit in the saddle in front of him. When she was in place, he put his arms possessively around her as he reached for the horse's reins.

'I think it will be nice for us to ride together, don't you?' he teased cruelly 'It will give us time to get to know each other better.'

Saying nothing, Kira's eyes lingered on the bodies of Elspeth, Onnie and Harmony as Lord Dorcon and his legion of men started to ride away from the barn.

CHAPTER
~33~

Dane sat behind the dragon knight, looking over to Shanks and Kahrin being transported on the other dragons as they were flown back to the palace.

Tears stung his eyes as he fought to get the image of Elspeth out of his mind. His sister was dead. The only thing that gave him any relief from the overwhelming grief was the knowledge that, wherever she was now, Onnie-Astra was with her.

The shock of the barn disaster had been so profound, Dane had failed to see who was taking him back to the palace. But not long after they entered the sky, the knight turned in his seat.

'I'm so sorry, Dane,' the knight said as his eyes came to rest on Lord Dorcon's brand on his face. 'For everything.'

Dane sucked in his breath when he saw it was Tobias, the smallest and, perhaps, bravest of the dragon knights who had trained with Dane and Shanks at the dragon stables. 'Toby? Is that really you?'

Tobias nodded. 'We were ordered back from the front to get you. Dane, what's going on? They're calling you and Shanks traitors.'

'We're not traitors,' Dane said bitterly. 'King Arden is the real traitor. He's betrayed all his people. He's driven them to starvation and death because of this foolish war against King Casey.'

'The war is over,' Tobias explained. 'We've lost. Now all we're doing is fighting to keep them from invading us.'

'I hope King Casey does invade us,' Dane said. 'He can't be any worse than King Arden.'

'Maybe not,' Tobias agreed. Then he said, 'Dane, I don't understand. What happened to you?'

Seated behind his old friend, Dane told Tobias all the events that had occurred since he was first taken from the battlefront to face Lord Dorcon.

When he finished, Tobias whistled. 'That's not what we were told.'

'But it's the truth,' Dane finished softly. Soon his voice started to break. 'Lord Dorcon has killed my sister Elspeth and taken Kira. I don't know what he's going to do to her. I know he's going to execute the rest of us, but he really hates her. I'm afraid he's going to do something much worse.'

'Maybe not,' Tobias said. 'Dane, a lot has changed since you and Shanks disappeared. Some of the people at the palace see your sisters as heroes for saving their daughters who were being held at Lasser. Others are talking about a revolt. Too many people have died. Even more are starving.'

'Then what's everyone waiting for?' Dane demanded angrily. 'Surely you can see the king is evil. Why hasn't anyone risen against him?'

'It's not that simple,' Tobias said. 'People are afraid. They're not organized. We all know something is wrong, but we also know the king has spies everywhere. If they heard any of us talking of revolt, we'd be killed.'

'So instead the king is allowed to starve his people to death and kill whomever he chooses!' Dane argued. 'Toby, we were all brave dragon knights. We knew right from wrong. What happened to you and the others?'

Tobias looked back at Dane apologetically. 'I told you, it's not so easy for us. The king is holding our families as hostages. If we made a move against him, he'd kill them all.'

'He's already responsible for the death of my father and sister!' Dane challenged. 'But I'll still fight him till my last breath.'

Tobias became silent. Beneath them, Dane could see they were approaching the palace. Seeing it again caused a shiver to run down his spine. Finally Tobias looked back at him.

'I can't make any promises, but I'll speak with a few other knights I can trust. Maybe now is the time to make our move.'

'Please,' Dane said. 'We've got to do it before it's too late.'

CHAPTER
~34~

Kira's heart and spirit were broken as she rode with Lord Dorcon back to the palace. She knew he'd chosen to go by horse so he could torment her longer than he could if they travelled by dragon.

As she raised her eyes, she could still see Jinx flying overhead trying to get back to her. Countless arrows stuck out from his sides, wings and tails, and yet he refused to abandon her.

'He is devoted, I'll give him that,' Lord Dorcon said, as he too looked up to gaze at the blue dragon. 'But then again, all the twin-tailed dragons were. That is, until we killed them.'

Kira tried not to speak. Each time she did, the evil knight used it as an opportunity to hurt her, either with words or physically. Instead she dropped her eyes.

'You know, Kira,' he continued conversationally, 'I had considered having my knights finish him off like they did the red dragon. But then I thought it would be more sporting to kill him at the palace. That way the king could enjoy his destruction as well.'

'The king is too frightened to dare look at him,' Kira finally spat, looking back into the cold grey eyes of Lord Dorcon. 'Jinx will fulfil the prophecy with or without me! Just you watch. He'll kill King Arden and end his wicked monarchy once and for all.'

As he had done before, Lord Dorcon squeezed his arms tightly around her until it drove the wind painfully from her lungs. 'What prophecy?' he demanded. 'What are you talking about?'

'So King Arden doesn't trust you enough to tell you,' Kira challenged as she faced the armoured knight. 'He never told you the prophecy.'

She grunted as Lord Dorcon squeezed her tighter. 'Tread lightly, Kira,' he warned. 'I can kill you any time I please.'

Kira bit back another comment. It would have been too easy to end it. But her family still needed her. She had to get away somehow. Instead she calmed herself and looked back up to her beloved dragon.

'Tell me,' Lord Dorcon demanded. 'What prophecy?'

Once more Kira turned in the saddle to look up into the only part of his face she could see through the visor;

his cold grey eyes. Finally she started to speak. 'Long ago, a great wizard called Elan foretold that a twin-tailed dragon would end King Arden's reign. He will destroy the monarchy and bring peace to the land.'

'Impossible!' Lord Dorcon spat.

'It will happen,' Kira challenged. 'Ask the king if you don't believe me. His ancestor King Lacarian betrayed Elan after he told him what he'd seen. But it was too late. The prophecy will happen. Arden is going to die, and Jinx is the one to do it.'

'That old wizard Paradon has been filling your head with lies,' Lord Dorcon said. 'King Arden is not the one who is going to die. You are.' He began to squeeze her even tighter, driving the air from her lungs. Kira's blood started to pound in her ears. She struggled against him and tried to fight his strong arms, but before long the lack of air took hold and her world went black.

It was the sounds of Jinx roaring that roused Kira. She was still seated on Lord Dorcon's horse and the evil knight still had his arms tightly around her.

'Have a nice nap?' he teased.

As Kira took in a shaky breath, she felt her arms start to throb from where he had crushed her. Looking up, she could see Jinx soaring overhead, still trying to get back to her. There were even more arrows sticking out of him.

'By rights, that blue monster should be dead,' said Lord Dorcon. 'I don't think I've ever seen a dragon lose so much blood and still keep flying. It's quite extraordinary really.'

Kira bit back a comment. She knew it was what Lord Dorcon wanted. But as he spoke, she found it harder and harder to keep silent.

'Of course,' Lord Dorcon continued, 'when we reach the palace, it might be interesting to discover just how much blood a dragon like him can lose before he succumbs. It would make for a good experiment.'

Finally Kira couldn't hold back. 'Jinx may die, and so will I, but not before he kills you and the king! The prophecy is coming and you know it.'

From behind her, Lord Dorcon's breathing changed. His arms started to squeeze again as he warned, 'One more word about that ridiculous prophecy and I'll have my men kill your dragon right now. Do you understand me?'

Kira stole a glance up at her beloved Jinx. She knew Lord Dorcon meant every word he said. She fell silent and concentrated instead on the road ahead.

It was long passed dark when Kira finally saw the light of the palace torches shining in the distance. Sometime before sunset, her heart sank even further when she saw Jinx starting to falter in the sky. Finally he roared a single time before flying away unsteadily.

Seeing him go, Lord Dorcon seemed relieved. He taunted Kira, saying that the great blue monster had found somewhere to die. She had so desperately wanted to believe he was wrong, but the blood spatters on her and everyone riding with her proved that Jinx had lost too much blood.

Sitting with Lord Dorcon, her tears fell silently down her cheeks as she grieved for yet another painful loss.

Kira was hardly aware of arriving at the magnificent palace when the heavy portcullis was raised and Lord Dorcon and his men entered the courtyard. Looking around, she saw the faces of the villagers who had come out to see her. Holding up torches, their faces were almost as sad as hers. Seeing this made her defeat that much greater.

When the horses stopped, Lord Dorcon climbed down and drew Kira down beside him. Still in chains, she didn't have the strength or will to fight him any more. She had lost everything. She knew it, and so did he.

'Would you care to see your new quarters?' Lord Dorcon teased.

Unresponsive, Kira kept her head down.

He started to chuckle. 'Be careful, Kira. One might think you're grieving more for that blue monster than for your own dead sister.'

Again Kira remained silent as Lord Dorcon continued to taunt and bully her. Instead she let him drag her through the parting crowd of villagers and escort her into the palace.

'The rest of your traitor family are down in the dungeon, so obviously I can't take you there. Instead, the king and I have decided on a much nicer place for you to stay.'

Silent and uncaring, Kira was dragged through the richly decorated palace corridors. True to his word, instead of going down into the dungeon, Lord Dorcon's wide gate hauled her towards stairs leading to the top of one of the palace towers.

As the long staircase spiralled up, he continued to tease her about his plans for her punishment. But his words never reached her. Kira was lost to overwhelming grief.

When they finally reached the top of the tower, Kira was taken into a small room. She could see shackles hanging from high up in the wall. As Lord Dorcon drew her closer, he caught hold of her wrist and raised it up to the first shackle.

'I'm sure this won't be the most comfortable place you've slept, but then again, you don't deserve better.'

When her other wrist was chained to the wall, Lord Dorcon stood before her. He inhaled contentedly. 'Finally, Kira, you are here with me. Now, be sure to have a good night's sleep, for tomorrow the king will decide your fate – though I wouldn't count on any mercy if I were you.'

He finished speaking and began to chuckle again. 'After all the trouble you've caused us, you'll be lucky if all he does is have you executed. Of course, I've made a few suggestions of my own.' He leaned closer to her ear and whispered softly, 'We'll see if he will grant my special request. Until then, have a lovely night.'

Lord Dorcon's evil laughter was the last thing Kira heard as the tall knight left the room. Slamming the door behind him, she heard a key turning in the lock. Left alone in the dark cell, Kira looked across to the only window in the room. She could see the light of the torches from the courtyard and hear the sound of hammering and workmen's voices rising up from below.

'Shadow,' Kira moaned as the visions of the morning's disaster at the barn surfaced once again to torment her. 'Shadow, I'm so sorry for everything . . .'

CHAPTER
~35~

Chained to the tower wall, Kira was unable to sit or sleep all night. But even if she had been allowed to sit or lie down, she knew she couldn't have slept anyway. Too much had happened.

'We were wrong, Paradon,' she said softly as she stared out the barred window and watched the first rays of dawn lighting the distant sky. 'It wasn't me in the prophecy. I've failed.'

The sound of hammering had continued all night. As the sun rose higher in the sky, it became even more rushed and active. But mixed amongst the sounds of the workmen, she could hear the soft sound of weeping and the moaning of people in the courtyard.

Left only to her thoughts, Kira worried for the survivors of her family. Were they all right? Had her mother been executed already? Was Paradon alive? She recalled the sight of the arrow protruding from the wizard's chest. As he'd been dragged over to the dragon, Kira hadn't been able to see if he was still breathing or not.

'How could it all go so wrong?' she asked herself quietly. Her tears had long since ended and there were none left to cry. All she could do now was stand and await her fate.

Kira didn't have long to wait before she heard the sound of a key entering the lock on her door. Soon several of the king's guards entered, followed by Lord Dorcon. This was the first time Kira had seen him outside of his armour, and the first time she'd ever seen his face. He was younger than her father, with a sharp nose and thin lips. But as always, it was his cold grey eyes that were the most striking feature of the evil knight.

As he entered her cell, he was dressed in his court finest. His black hair had been neatly trimmed and combed and his eyes blazed with excitement as he drew near.

'Good morning, Kira,' he said lightly. 'I trust you slept well.'

As she watched him move closer, Kira promised herself she would remain silent. She wouldn't give him the satisfaction of drawing comments from her. But when he approached the wall and turned back to the door and knelt, she felt her heart start to pound.

Across the small cell, one of the guards lowered his head. Then the other guards also dropped to their knees. 'His Royal Highness, King Arden,' he announced.

Kira's eyes shot to the door. When King Arden entered, she was shocked to see the man that she had loathed and feared all her life.

The only word Kira could think of to describe him best was 'insignificant'. He was short, younger than she imagined, not fat, but soft and weak-looking with mousy-brown hair and pale watery eyes. On his head was the crown everyone said he never removed. It was too large for him and hung down too low. It pushed his ears out sideways and made him look more like a court clown than the kingdom's ruler.

When he entered her cell and drew near, she could see definite hesitation in his manner as he regarded her. King Arden was frightened of her! That thought alone almost made it all worth it.

'Bow your head when you stand before your king,' Lord Dorcon ordered.

Kira looked from the king to Lord Dorcon then back to the king. 'You are not my king,' she said softly. 'Nor do you deserve my respect.'

'Insolence!' Lord Dorcon barked as he rose to strike her.

'Enough,' King Arden said, raising a soft weak hand. 'Lord Dorcon, control your temper. You'll have plenty of time to punish her later.'

Kira noticed the soft light voice of the king. There was no power behind his command. As she watched him, she wondered how he had managed to rule the kingdom with such fear for so long.

King Arden then concentrated on her. 'I am your king, young lady, and you will respect me.'

'My father served and respected you,' Kira spat, 'and look how his service was repaid. You branded him a traitor and Lord Dorcon murdered him. Why should I respect you?'

The king ignored her comment and looked up to Lord Dorcon. 'She does have her father's fire,' he said casually, 'and a temper to match that red hair of hers.'

Lord Dorcon's eyes bored into Kira. 'She is insolent and rude. A savage. She must be punished for her crimes.'

'Oh she will be,' King Arden said casually. Then he dropped his voice. 'In ways that will make her wish she'd never been born.'

'Do what you will,' Kira retorted angrily. 'It won't

change the prophecy. You are going to die, King Arden. Even if I don't live to see it, it will happen. King Lacarian knew it and, deep down inside, so do you.'

In a move faster than she imagined possible for one so tall and large, Lord Dorcon drew his dagger and pressed it to her throat in an instant. 'One more word, Kira, just one, and I'll cut out your tongue.'

Kira felt the cold sharp blade pressing to the soft skin of her throat. Looking into Lord Dorcon's blazing eyes she knew he wanted to do it.

'Ah, yes, the prophecy,' King Arden said casually as he stepped closer to her. 'Of course, Paradon has taught you well. You dress as a boy, fight like a boy, you are unmarried and have even trained a dragon to fight for you. Those are all breaches of First Law and, as you and I both know, part of the prophecy. But that doesn't make you *her*.'

Kira noticed how Lord Dorcon's eyes shot to the king. She realized this was confirmation of the prophecy she had told him on the way to the palace. She then wondered if he felt betrayed because the king hadn't told him about it before.

'Lord Dorcon tells me your blue dragon is dead. How can you fulfil the prophecy without a twin-tailed dragon? You are nothing, Kira, daughter of Captain

Darious, nothing but a traitor who has broken every part of the First Law. You are just a girl. And like all girls, you have no strength and no power. You are weak, and you are completely defeated.'

'And yet you are still frightened of me,' Kira spat before she could hold back.

Immediately she felt Lord Dorcon's hand tense as the blade was about to cut into the skin of her throat.

'Wait!' King Arden ordered. 'Hold your dagger, Lord Dorcon!'

Kira watched Lord Dorcon's face. She could see the rage blazing and the desire to hurt her boiling over. But then she felt the pressure on the blade lighten.

'Give me your dagger,' King Arden commanded as he held his hand out.

Lord Dorcon hesitated for a moment before handing it over to the king. When the king concentrated on her, she felt fear coursing through her entire body. This was it. The end. It wouldn't be Lord Dorcon who killed her. It would be the king himself.

'I have thought long and hard on what your punishment should be,' King Arden said as he moved another step closer. 'Of course, you deserve to die after all you have done against me. Death is the only suitable punishment.'

Straining against the chains that held her, Kira tried to shy away from the approaching blade. But as she moved, Lord Dorcon's hand landed painfully on her shoulder and held her still.

As the distance shortened and the blade moved closer to her neck, Kira suddenly relaxed. If she were going to die, she would make her father proud by dying bravely and not showing any fear. Standing erect, she closed her eyes and waited for the dagger to do its worst.

CHAPTER
~36~

Kira waited for the king to slit her throat. Instead she felt a firm tug on one of her long braids and felt the sharp blade slicing through her hair. Opening her eyes, she watched in shock as the king caught hold of the second braid and quickly cut it off as well.

When he finished, he threw the two long lengths of red hair to the floor of the cell.

'The prophecy says an unmarried girl astride a twin-tailed dragon, dressed as a boy but with two long braids will destroy me. You have no dragon. You have no weapons, no braids. Soon you will be out of those clothes and dressed as a woman should dress. You are not the girl from the prophecy, Kira. You never were.'

'Your Majesty,' Lord Dorcon sputtered. 'Her punishment! Kira must be executed.'

Still not believing what she was hearing, Kira watched Lord Dorcon's face turn red.

'She will be punished, Lord Dorcon, make no mistake about that. But it is up to me to choose the manner of that punishment. And I have.' He then turned to her again. 'Kira, you are almost fourteen and yet still unmarried. First Law says you must be married before your thirteenth birthday. You have broken the First Law in many ways and you must be punished for this. The first part of your punishment is that you are to be married immediately.'

'Married!' Lord Dorcon spat. 'Your Majesty, you can't. Kira has betrayed you in every way. Surely she must die!'

Suddenly the king turned on Lord Dorcon. 'You have betrayed me also.'

'Me?' Lord Dorcon cried. 'How?'

'In your failure to capture this girl sooner. She sacked Lasser Commons. She has created sympathy for her cause amongst my people here at the palace. Should I kill her now, she would become a martyr. There would be a revolt. Kira must not die yet. Instead she will be made to conform to First Law. The people will see this and realize that I can be a just and fair king whose only duty is to serve and protect my people.'

'Who is she to marry?' Lord Dorcon demanded.

Before answering, the king smiled cruelly. 'You, Lord

Dorcon. Kira will marry you.'

'Me?' the tall knight cried. 'No! Please, Your Majesty, wait. I can't.'

'Are you defying your king?' King Arden demanded darkly. Behind him, the guards moved closer and held up their weapons threateningly.

'No, Your Majesty,' Lord Dorcon sputtered. 'Please, I beg you to reconsider. I can't marry her. Not Kira—'

'You can and you will marry her!' the king shouted furiously. 'Had you captured her when I ordered you to, none of this would have happened. Now I have no choice but to let her live.

'You have left me the laughing stock of the kingdom, Lord Dorcon. Consider yourself fortunate not to be chained to that wall and facing your own execution. Now you will marry Kira and for one full winter, you will not harm her. After that, I don't care what you do with her. But for now, you will do as I command.'

The king then turned to his guards. 'Bring in the seamstresses and court ladies. Get this filthy savage out of those clothes and dress her as a woman. We have an execution and celebration to plan for.'

'Execution?' Kira repeated.

The king turned to Kira as though she were an afterthought. 'Yes, Kira, execution. Your mother and the palace instructor's executions will go ahead as planned. Only now there will be a few more heads to roll. Your brother, the wizard and the knight Shanks-Spar, will all join them on the scaffold. I haven't yet decided the fate of Kahrin. Your cooperation will determine whether she lives or dies.'

As the king turned to leave, Lord Dorcon threw himself down on his knees. 'Please, Your Majesty, I beg you, don't make me do this. I have served you well all my life. Don't make me marry Kira.'

King Arden looked down on the tall knight. 'You will do as I command, or you will join the rest of her family on the scaffold. The choice is yours, Lord Dorcon.'

When he finished speaking, the king and his guards left Kira and Lord Dorcon alone in the cell.

Hardly believing what she'd just heard, Kira watched as Lord Dorcon slowly climbed to his feet. His face was red with fury. As he turned to her, his eyes blazed with pure hatred.

'You have destroyed me, Kira,' he said softly. 'But this is far from over. I will do as my king commands and marry you. You will live safe and unharmed with me for one full winter. After that, you will experience the full depth of my rage.' Saying nothing more, he picked up Kira's two long braids and stormed out of the cell.

Left alone, Kira stood in shocked silence. Her throat hurt from where Lord Dorcon's blade had pressed against the tender skin. But that pain was nothing compared to the hurt she was suffering at the loss of Elspeth, Onnie and Jinx, not to mention the terror of the upcoming execution of her entire family. She thought she was out of tears, but as the full horror of the king's words settled in, her eyes filled once again and she lowered her head in complete despair.

CHAPTER
~37~

Dane paced the confines of the dark and smelly cell while Shanks sat in the back corner picking at straw.

In the cell across from him, he could hear Kahrin's light voice. She had been imprisoned with Paradon and was begging the wizard to wake up. But Paradon was not responding. He had remained unconscious since he was shot in the chest with the arrow. No doctors had been in to see him and the arrow remained imbedded in his body.

Their mother was in the cell next to Kahrin. They had managed to speak a bit, but every time he called out to her, a guard would come to silence them. When the guard entered his mother's cell and struck her, Dane cursed him and swore revenge. He then begged his mother to remain silent.

Dane also knew his instructor was in the cell next to his. But once again, any attempt at conversation was cut short by violence from the vicious guards.

'Dane, will you please sit down, you're driving me mad,' Shanks said irritably. 'You're not helping them or yourself by causing trouble.'

Dane looked at Shanks and knew his friend was right. But he couldn't rest. Lord Dorcon had Kira in some other part of the palace and he couldn't find out what was happening to her. If she were down in the dungeon, even though their future was grim, at least they would face it together. But not knowing her fate was torture.

Finally he moved to the rear and sat beside his friend. 'I just wish I knew what was happening to Kira,' Dane said.

Shanks dropped the piece of straw he was shredding and suddenly slammed his fist into the wall. 'If that monster touches her, I don't care what they do to me. I swear I'm going to kill him.'

'He's mine first,' Dane said angrily. 'But it's the not knowing what's happening to her that's killing me.'

'And they know it,' Shanks agreed. 'That's the whole point.'

From out in the corridor, they heard the sound of voices. Dane immediately recognized Tobias. They heard footsteps approaching. Instantly on their feet, both Dane and Shanks crossed to the cell door.

'Stand at the back,' the guard barked through the small window. 'You've got a visitor.'

Moving to the rear of the cell, they watched the door open and Tobias enter. When the door closed behind him, he turned back to the guard. 'That will be all for the moment. I'll call you when I'm ready to leave.'

'Yes, sir,' the guard said.

Dane had not noticed it before, but looking at his uniform and the insignias blazing on the breast, he realized Tobias had moved up in rank. He was still desperately young, and painfully small, but he wasn't without power and influence.

'Toby!' Shanks called as he raced forward and ruffled his friend's hair. 'Look at you. We'll be calling you Captain before you know it!'

Tobias didn't smile. Instead he directed them to the back of the cell. He started to whisper. 'I don't have a lot of time. I've been sent down here to pass along a message meant to torment you. But I'm also here to offer a bit of hope.'

'What is it?' Dane asked.

'The king has just announced that he's pardoned your sister. He says Kira has renounced her traitor ways and is now ready to conform to First Law. He says she's getting married.'

'Married?' Shanks repeated quickly. 'To who? You?'

Tobias looked at both Dane and Shanks and shook his head apologetically. 'I wish it were me, but it's not. She's going to marry Lord Dorcon.'

'What!' they both cried.

When Tobias nodded, Shanks stepped forward. 'She can't!' he spat furiously. 'She hates him—'

'And he hates her!' Dane finished.

'Maybe so,' Tobias agreed. 'But they are still going to be married two days from today.'

'We've got to stop it!' Shanks cried. 'I won't let him near her!'

Seeing Shank's violent reaction, Tobias reached out and caught hold of his arm. 'It gets worse,' he said softly.

'What could be worse than that?' Dane demanded.

'On the morning of the ceremony, they are going to execute both of you.' He then looked at Dane. 'And your mother, the wizard and the instructor who helped you escape from the dungeon.'

'What!' Shanks cried.

Once again, Tobias nodded. 'I'm so sorry.'

Dane remained silent. Locking his hands behind his back, he started to pace. Faster and faster until he looked like a caged wild animal. Finally a thought struck him and he came back to Tobias. 'Why are you here telling us this?' he angrily demanded. 'No one is allowed down here to see us. Why you?'

Tobias lowered his head in shame. 'I was ordered to tell you. It's all part of your punishment. The people of the kingdom think you are all freedom fighters, so the king can't have you physically tortured before your execution.'

'So he's going to hurt us by telling us about Lord Dorcon and our execution,' Dane challenged.

'Yes,' Tobias softly agreed.

'It won't happen,' Shanks said, furiously shaking his head. 'I won't let it. He's not going to touch her. Not my Kira.'

Dropping his voice, Tobias leaned closer to both Dane and Shanks. 'I've spoken to some of the other knights I know I can trust. They all remember you both and don't want to see this happen either. On the day of the execution, we are going to make our move against the king. This is the opportunity we've been waiting for. Everyone at the palace has been ordered to attend the execution and marriage ceremony. When they see us fighting, we're hoping they will rise up against the king.'

'And if they don't?' Dane asked.

Tobias shrugged. 'Then we all die together.'

CHAPTER
~ 38 ~

Kira had been unchained when the seamstresses arrived at her cell to take her measurements for her wedding dress. With multiple guards on her door and bars on the window, she wasn't chained again when they left, as the king knew there was no way she could get out of the cell.

Standing at the small window overlooking the courtyard, she watched as the builders put the finishing touches to the scaffold. Not far from where most of her family was to be executed, she also saw the decorations going up and preparations starting for her upcoming wedding.

'*Wedding*,' Kira moaned as tears trailed down her cheeks and she leaned her head heavily against the cold bars of the window. She was actually going to marry Lord Dorcon. From the moment the king had made the proclamation, she tried to figure a way out. But each time she thought she had an idea, it always came back to the same thing. If she did anything against the king, Lord Dorcon or even herself, Kahrin would suffer. As it was, Kira had been told that Kahrin would spend the rest of her life in the dungeon. But one word against her upcoming marriage would condemn her sister to slow torture and death.

So Kira kept her mouth shut and allowed the seamstresses and court ladies to fuss over her. She was bathed and perfumed. Her fingernails trimmed and cleaned, her short hair had been cut again to a complimentary style, and her boy's clothing had been taken away and replaced by a load of beautiful gowns. The court ladies had been very thorough in their efforts to make it appear that Kira had reformed and was now ready to take on the duties of a woman living under the leadership of King Arden.

She looked down on the beautiful blue gown she wore and felt sick. At any other time in her life, she would have been thrilled. Now the smooth silky fabric felt worse to her than the chains on the wall had.

Standing at the window, Kira heard a key being inserted in the lock. She then heard the deep, terrifying voice of Lord Dorcon as he ordered his men to remain in the corridor.

Turning to confront him, Kira saw his immediate reaction to her new appearance show on his face. He smiled and nodded approvingly.

'So there was a woman under all that filth after all,' he said pleasantly. 'I must admit I'm shocked. Kira, you really are quite beautiful.'

'Go away,' Kira said as she turned away from the sight of Lord Dorcon and returned to staring out the window.

'Is that any way to treat your future husband?'

Without facing him, she spat, 'You'll never be my husband.'

'The king says differently. And now seeing you in your lovely gown, I certainly agree with him.'

That comment made Kira shiver. There was something vile in his voice that frightened her more than all the threats he'd made to her in the past. 'Why have you come here, Lord Dorcon?'

'I've come to see my fiancée and offer a small token of my . . . affection.' Moving closer, he stood directly behind her and gazed out the window to see what she was looking at. 'The scaffold is finished. And tomorrow, after the executions, you and I will be married.'

'No,' she corrected. 'Tomorrow I will die with the rest of my family.'

'Ah, such dedication,' Lord Dorcon sighed. 'It does warm my heart.'

He reached down and caught hold of one of Kira's hands. 'I have appealed to the king for a wedding gift. If you behave yourself, your mother need not die tomorrow.'

Turning sharply, Kira looked up into his cruel face. 'What are you talking about?'

'Exactly as I said,' he responded softly. 'The king finds no joy in killing women. If you do as you are told, marry me without complaint and stand as a court lady serving me and the king, then your mother's life will be spared.'

'You're lying to me,' Kira challenged. 'It's a trick.'

'Perhaps,' he teased. 'But dare you risk it? Of course, your mother and sister must remain in the dungeons, but that doesn't mean their life will be miserable. If you behave yourself and do as you are told, then they need not suffer.'

'And if I don't?' Kira asked.

'Then Kahrin's stay at Lasser will become a pleasant memory compared to the future facing her and your mother.'

'What about my brother, Shanks and Paradon?'

'I'm afraid there is nothing I can do for them. Dane

and Shanks-Spar were knights of the realm who betrayed their post. Paradon used his powers against the king. Nothing can save them. Tomorrow morning, they all die.'

While he spoke, Lord Dorcon looked down to the pendant Paradon had given her, which was visible now that she was wearing a gown. Reaching for it, he inspected the pebble being clutched by the golden dragon's claw. When he tried to break the chain to remove it, he found it wouldn't give. Drawing his dagger, he attempted to cut if off her neck. When that also failed, he chuckled. 'A gift from your wizard friend?'

Kira said nothing.

'You may keep it. He will die tomorrow as well. It will be something to remember him by.'

Kira pulled it away from the evil knight and turned away from his awful eyes. She looked back down to the scaffold where her brother, Paradon and Shanks were destined to die.

'I shall be back for you in the morning,' he said lightly. The king's ladies will arrive early to prepare you for our ceremony. Then we shall stand together, watching the executions and miserable end to your small revolution. After that, the bishop will marry us.'

Lord Dorcon gave Kira's hand a final squeeze. 'Sleep

well, Kira, and dream of tomorrow.'

Once the door closed after him, Kira ran over to her waste bucket and threw up. When she'd emptied her stomach, she started to wipe her hand where he had touched her until the skin was raw.

Going back to her bunk, she threw herself down and started to cry.

CHAPTER
~39~

On the eve of their execution, Dane and Shanks heard more voices coming from out in the corridor.

'You know, if they are trying to keep us in isolation, they're not doing a very good job of it,' Shanks commented. 'There are more people down here than in the courtyard.'

'And each visitor worse than the one before,' Dane added. Almost as if he knew trouble was coming, he shivered. Then he and Shanks heard a familiar and unwelcome voice and his worst fears were confirmed.

'Open it,' Lord Dorcon ordered when he arrived at their cell.

When the door opened, several armed guards entered and drove both Dane and Shanks to the back wall. Lord Dorcon then entered and stood before the two of them.

Looking at Dane, Lord Dorcon smiled. 'Aren't you

going to congratulate me? After all, tomorrow I am going to marry your sister.'

'It'll never happen!' Shanks cried as he lunged at the tall knight. Blocked by the guards, Shanks was knocked to the ground.

'What's this?' Lord Dorcon taunted. 'Do I have a rival for Kira's affections?' He moved closer to Shanks, and kicked him while he was down. 'Kira is mine to do with as I please. We are going to be married and she will be a dutiful wife, or I swear she will suffer.'

'Kira will die before she marries you,' Dane spat.

Showing no anger, Lord Dorcon turned to him. 'My mark doesn't seem to have humbled you much. You do have another cheek, Dane. Think carefully before speaking or you'll be visiting the branding irons again before your execution.'

'You can't hurt me any more, Lord Dorcon,' Dane challenged.

Inhaling deeply, Lord Dorcon chuckled softly. 'Perhaps. But your mother and little sister are down here also. Perhaps they would like to meet my branding irons.'

The memory of the pain he suffered after being branded immediately silenced Dane from further comment. He couldn't risk Lord Dorcon doing it to them.

'What do you want from us?' Shanks demanded as he slowly sat up.

Crossing to him, Lord Dorcon knelt down to his level. 'All I want from you is your suffering. You must suffer for all the trouble you have caused me. Suffer for the humiliation. Your job now, Shanks-Spar, is simply to suffer.'

Straightening again, Lord Dorcon moved to the cell door. He called his men back and then reached behind himself and pulled a large velvet bag from his belt. Tossing it forward, it landed on the floor at Dane's feet.

'Something from your sister,' he said coldly as he turned and left the cell.

Shanks was the first to reach the velvet bag. Pulling open the ties, his trembling hand reached inside. Feeling the contents, he moaned.

'What is it?' Dane asked anxiously.

Saying nothing, Shanks pulled out the two long braids of red hair. There was no mistaking the colour or leather ties at the end. They were Kira's.

Falling to his knees, Dane reached for the braids. Throwing back his head he howled in agony, 'Kira!'

Far from their eyes, Lord Dorcon stood at the end of the corridor, waiting. When he heard Dane's pain-filled cry, he started to laugh and walk away from the dungeon.

CHAPTER
~40~

Dawn arrived, red and miserable. It was as though the sky was grieving for Kira and sending dark rain clouds that threatened to dump a deluge of water on the upcoming executions.

As Lord Dorcon had promised, the king's ladies arrived early to prepare her for the wedding. Kira said nothing as she was bathed and perfumed again. Two ladies wove flowers into her short hair while the others helped her into a gown of cream and gold.

A fortune in jewels was placed around her bare neck. As she looked at them, Kira wondered how many families could be fed from the value of those stones. Instead they were worn by someone who hated their very existence.

'Aren't you beautiful!' the ladies cried when they inspected their finished work. 'By far the loveliest bride in the whole kingdom. Lord Dorcon will be so pleased when he sees you! He will be the envy of all the knights!'

Kira wanted nothing more than to tell the ladies what she thought of their work. But fear for her mother and Kahrin stilled her tongue. Instead she let them draw the soft, beautiful bridal veil over her head and pin it in place with a garland of fresh summer flowers.

Not long after the ladies finished, Kira heard the sound of footsteps outside her door.

'Is my bride ready?' Lord Dorcon called into the cell.

'She is, my Lord,' the ladies all said together and they bowed their heads.

When Lord Dorcon entered the cell, he was struck once again by Kira's beauty. But seeing him in his ornate blue and silver wedding clothes only made her feel dead inside.

'Why, Kira, your loveliness steals my breath away!' he said as he crossed to her. He reached for her hand and gave it a light kiss. 'I do regret that your father isn't here to see this moment. I'm sure he would have a few good wishes for us.'

Kira knew he was toying with her. Trying to get her to say or do something that might upset him and make him go back on his promise to spare her mother.

Instead, she decided the time had come to play a few games of her own.

Curtsying gracefully, she bowed her head.

'Thank you, Lord Dorcon. You are far too kind,' she said in her sweetest voice. 'I'm sure he would.'

Her change of tack seemed to throw Lord Dorcon off. Taking a step back, he looked at her, searching for signs of tricks or betrayal. 'Ah, well, yes. I'm afraid it's time for the executions to begin. To spare you any undue pain, the king has granted us permission to watch from the tower roof rather than going below. After they clear away the bodies, it will be my distinct pleasure to escort you to our wedding.'

When he finished speaking, Lord Dorcon stepped closer and offered his hand. 'Shall we go, dearest? They are awaiting our arrival on the roof.'

Deep inside, Kira's heart was pounding so badly she could barely breathe. Her spirit was breaking. Dane, Paradon and Shanks were about to die. She was helpless to stop any of it. To try would be to seal her sister and mother's fate.

Fighting back the tears that were threatening to fall, Kira took in a deep breath and reached out to take Lord Dorcon's outstretched hand.

CHAPTER
~41~

Dane and Shanks hadn't slept all night. They knew everything they had fought for was now at hand. Their executions had arrived. If Tobias had been telling the truth, then this dawn would spell the end of King Arden and his cruel reign. If they failed, then they would all die, and Kira was condemned to marry Lord Dorcon.

As footsteps entered the corridor of the dungeon, Dane and Shanks looked at each other.

'For Kira and Elspeth,' Dane said quietly as he stowed one of his sister's braids in his top.

'For Kira,' Shanks agreed, doing the same with the other braid.

When the cell door opened, both Dane and Shanks were shocked to see several dragon knights they recognized from their class standing amongst the palace guards. Were these some of the knights Tobias had mentioned? Were they here to help? Unable to see any clues in their faces, both had to hope they were on their side.

After Dane and Shanks were placed in shackles, they were escorted from their cell. Standing silently in the corridor, they watched guards opening Kahrin's cell door.

'Dane!' Kahrin cried as she rushed out into the corridor and embraced her brother. 'Dane, please, let me go with you. I can't stay here. Please, I want to die with you!'

Dane tried his best not to let his own emotions overwhelm him as he hugged Kahrin tightly. Crouching down on one knee, he wiped away her tears. 'You can't, Kahrin,' he said softly. 'You must stay here and live. You mean the world to me. I can face this if I know you are going to live. If you come with me, I won't be able to do it, and what would Father think of me then? Please, you must live. One day you will be out of here, and when that happens, I want you to be happy.'

'I'll never be happy again,' Kahrin wept.

'Yes you will,' Dane said. Then he smiled gently. 'One day, long after we're gone, you'll be free. Then perhaps you will have children of your own and you'll tell them about us. About what we saw in the future world and then how we fought the evil twins so bravely in the past to rescue Elspeth. Tell them you rode on the back of a bright-blue, twin-tailed dragon called Jinx. Tell them all about us, Kahrin. That way, we'll never die.'

Kahrin hugged her brother again as she promised to remember all the adventures they'd had and how she would one day tell her children. Then as they parted, Dane saw the guards roughly hauling Paradon's unconscious body out of the cell.

'Wait!' Shanks said. 'If he's going to die with us, he's not going like this.'

Angrily pushing past the guards, Shanks approached Paradon. He caught hold of the arrow sticking out of the old wizard's chest and gently pulled it free. Throwing it to the ground, he shoved one of the guards away as he took the weight of the wounded wizard on his shoulder.

Seeing what Shanks was doing, Dane gave Kahrin a final hug and kiss and took his position on the other side of Paradon. When some of the guards started to protest, Dane angrily spat, 'What are you going to do about it? Kill us?'

'Leave them be,' the instructor called as he too was

released from his cell. 'For pity's sake, give us this last bit of dignity!'

Dane smiled sadly when he saw his instructor. As he approached, he said, 'I'm so sorry you got involved in all of this.'

'I'm not,' the instructor said. 'I'm fed up with King Arden and his foolish, wasteful war. I'd rather die now than live under him another day.'

'Silence,' one of the guards barked. 'Do you forget you're all going to your execution?'

'Of course not!' the instructor said. 'But I'm not going to spend my last bit of time alive singing the king's praises. If you have a problem with that, kill me now. Then see how the king likes it once he learns you've deprived him of his prize.'

'Dane?' his mother called.

'Go to her,' the instructor said. 'I've got your friend.'

When the instructor took over supporting Paradon, Dane ran to his mother's cell door. 'Mother,' he cried as he caught hold of her hand and pressed it to his scarred cheek.

'My beautiful boy,' she cried. 'Your father would have been so proud of you.'

'But we've failed.'

'No, my darling, you haven't. You tried. That's more than most people can claim. You found your sisters and did all you could for them. No mother could ever be more proud.'

Dane leaned closer to the window in his mother's cell door and pressed his forehead against hers. 'It's not all lost yet,' he whispered tightly. 'Pray for us, Mother. We are facing our greatest trial yet.'

'I will,' she whispered as she kissed Dane's cheek. 'I'll be here waiting for you. Save your sister, Dane. Don't let that monster have her.'

Kissing her back, Dane nodded. 'I will.'

'Let's go!' one of the guards viciously called. Crossing over to Dane, he roughly hauled him away from his mother's door. Dane was about to protect against the guard, when he felt the man secretly pressing the key to the shackles into his hand.

When Dane looked at him, the guard continued in his brash voice, 'You can't keep the people out there waiting. They've come to see an execution. We're going to give it to them!'

Still in shock, Dane stepped away from his mother's cell and took over supporting Paradon. He then watched as one of his other classmates caught hold of Kahrin's hand and led her over to their mother's cell.

He opened the door and Kahrin was finally reunited with her mother.

Seeing the two of them together again gave Dane the first bit of hope he'd felt since the awful morning at the barn.

Adjusting the weight of Paradon on his shoulder, Dane managed to let Shanks see the key to the shackles resting in his palm. 'You ready?' he mouthed quietly.

Shanks nodded. 'For Kira,' he whispered.

CHAPTER
~42~

Kira held on to Lord Dorcon's hand as he led her up the tower steps. He kept looking over to her and smiling. Each time he did it, every instinct in her body told her to run. Instead she tried not to look at him and concentrated on putting one foot in front of the other on the stairs.

Making it to the top of the tower, Kira was stunned to see the roof lined with knights in their dress armour. Seeing Lord Dorcon arriving, they stood at attention and raised their swords in the air in salute.

'For you, Kira,' Lord Dorcon said pleasantly as he led her forward under the sharp blades. 'Oh, and just in case you have any thoughts of leaping off the side of the tower, my men will stop you long before you do.'

Kira looked once again at the knights wearing Lord Dorcon's crest on their armour. She then turned back to Lord Dorcon. 'I would only try if you betray me and hurt my mother.'

He gave her hand a squeeze. 'You are about to become my wife, dearest Kira. Would I do something as underhand as that?'

Once again, the way he studied her made her feel sick.

'Now from up here, we can have a good view of the executions – but not too good. I wouldn't want to spoil our special day.'

She knew he was still toying with her. Even though her heart was breaking, she wouldn't give in to his goading.

As they approached the edge of the tower roof, Lord Dorcon released her hand. Grateful to be free of him, her heart sank when he slipped his arm around her waist to keep her from leaping off the side.

'Just in case you have any silly ideas,' he said.

Kira said nothing. At that very moment, she heard the trumpeters playing their horns to announce the arrival of the king and queen. Soon everyone in the courtyard was bowing and curtsying as the king and queen moved through the crowd. Taking their seats in the large outdoor thrones, they had a very up-close view of the scaffold.

Soon the trumpeters started playing again, announcing the arrival of the prisoners. As Kira stood on the tower roof, she leaned forward trying to see who was being led out.

'Careful, Kira,' Lord Dorcon warned as he held her tighter. Behind him, his men moved closer, ready to pounce should she try to jump.

Ignoring the tall knight pressed against her, Kira's eyes sought out her brother. Then she saw him and her heart cried out.

'No, Dane,' she moaned.

Down below, she watched as Dane and Shanks supported Paradon. Carrying him through the crowd of people, Kira saw them both holding their heads high. Following closely behind them, Kira saw the man Dane had described as his instructor.

'See?' Lord Dorcon said. 'Your mother isn't with them. I have kept my word, Kira. Will you?'

Kira had planned to stay silent, but seeing her brother and Shanks being led to the scaffold was more than she could bear.

'Dane!' she cried out.

Hearing her voice, both Dane and Shanks turned towards the tower. When he saw her in her wedding gown, standing next to Lord Dorcon,

Shanks called back, 'Kira!'

Unable to stand the sight of her brother and Shanks on the scaffold, Kira turned tearful, pleading eyes to Lord Dorcon. 'Please,' she begged. 'I'll do anything you ask of me.' When her eyes bored into his, she repeated, 'Anything. Please spare them.'

'Yes, you will do anything,' said Lord Dorcon coldly, 'if you wish to keep your mother and sister from that scaffold. But Dane and Shanks-Spar will die today, make no mistake. And you will watch! This is the price you must pay, Kira, for your betrayal of the king and me. Learn your lesson, my girl, and obey me!'

Her pleas were getting nowhere with the evil knight. Desperately turning back to the scaffold, she watched as guards moved forward to take Paradon from Dane and Shanks. The unconscious wizard was dragged forward. His head was then put on the block.

'No!' Kira howled.

'Stop it, Kira,' Lord Dorcon warned as he squeezed her tightly. 'Remember our arrangement. The crowd must see you've reformed and are obedient. If you defy me now, your mother and sister will suffer.'

Kira brought her hand up to her mouth and silenced herself as she watched Paradon being arranged for his beheading.

'No,' she whined weakly. 'Paradon . . .'

As the crowed hushed in sad anticipation, the executioner raised his large axe over his head.

Kira closed her eyes, unable to watch.

CHAPTER
~43~

Suddenly from behind them came the loudest dragon's roar Kira had ever heard in her life.

Turning quickly, she saw the sky was filled with birds of prey. But more than that, her eyes flew even wider at an impossible sight – Elspeth!

She was seated on the back of the kingdom's largest, wildest and most ferocious, twin-tailed purple dragon. It was Ferarchie. It was the Rogue!

Somehow, Elspeth had survived Lord Dorcon's arrows and made it up to the top of the Rogue's Mountain to get the monstrous dragon that lived there. Now as they drew near, Kira could see her amazing sister had her bow drawn and an arrow fited. As the huge purple dragon came in low over the tower, Elspeth released the arrow. It flew true to its target and struck the executioner in the chest. Falling backwards, his axe fell safely away from Paradon.

In that same instant, Dane, Shanks and the instructor burst free of their shackles and attacked the nearest scaffold guards. Disarming them, they caught hold of the men's swords and started to fight. Soon Tobias and his own men joined the battle against King Arden as they took on guards loyal to the king.

As Kira watched unbelieving, she heard Elspeth shout her wildest battle cry and bring the Rogue down to land in the crowded courtyard. She had him crush the royal thrones just as the king and queen started to run away in terror from the massive purple dragon.

Suddenly King Arden turned back and used his queen as a shield against the Rogue. In his cowardice, he shoved her into the dragon's snapping mouth. Tearing through the crowd, the king made it to the entrance doors of the palace. Quickly crossing the threshold, King Arden slammed the doors shut behind him – cruelly trapping all his people in the courtyard to face the wrath of the Rogue.

But the terrified and fleeing people of the courtyard were not the dragon's prey. Charging the closed doors, Elspeth directed Ferarchie to rip through the thick entrance to the palace in pursuit of the fleeing king.

Still in disbelieving shock, Kira heard a second roar, one she knew she would recognize anywhere.

'Jinx!' she cried excitedly. Turning, she started to jump up and down with pure joy at the sight of her blue dragon flying unsteadily towards her. The Rogue's other purple offspring was flying beside Jinx, roaring as he too approached the tower. He then flew over the top and landed in the courtyard beside his father.

'Impossible!' Lord Dorcon howled as he gazed down into the courtyard and saw Elspeth directing the Rogue to tear his way into the castle. 'Elspeth died. I killed her myself! I know I did!'

Breaking away from Lord Dorcon, Kira reached forward and caught hold of the dagger at his waist. Drawing it free of its sheath, she backed away from the evil knight.

'It's over, Lord Dorcon!' Kira cried triumphantly. 'You saw for yourself. That's my sister, Elspeth! I told you there was a prophecy! You didn't believe me. But look down there and watch as a girl dressed as a boy uses a twin-tailed dragon to tear down this wretched monarchy and heal the wounds of this suffering land. This is the prophecy, Lord Dorcon. It is fulfilled!'

Kira turned away from the evil knight and shouted down to her sister joyfully, 'You did it, Elspeth! It was never me! It was you all along!'

'No!' Lord Dorcon shouted. Then his eyes came to

rest fully on her and Kira saw murder rising in them. 'No, this isn't over, Kira. You're mine!' He took a large step towards her. 'No one's taking you away from me. No one!'

Raising the dagger to fight, Kira heard the other knights on the tower cry out and scatter as Jinx landed on the roof. Roaring in rage, he started to attack the guards. When they had fled, the blue dragon advanced on Lord Dorcon.

'Call off your monster!' Lord Dorcon cried as he backed away from Jinx. Losing his step, the tall knight stumbled.

Seeing him off balance, Kira cried out, 'For my father!' She lunged forward and shoved Lord Dorcon over the side of the tower. Howling in surprise and fear, he tumbled down the side of the tower until he hit the ground far below.

Watching for movement from the evil knight, Kira heard Jinx starting to whine.

'Baby!' she called. Running to him, she threw her arms around his thick neck. 'I thought you were dead!' Tears rushed to her eyes and her hands started to shake as she tried to check his many wounds. She could see they were packed with mud and healing herbs and starting to heal.

'How can this be?' she asked.

Beneath them, Kira heard the terrified cries of the people. She looked over the side and saw Elspeth directing the Rogue and his offspring to tear large chunks out of the palace walls; trying to make an entrance large enough for the huge dragon to pass through. Before long, Elspeth, Ferarchie and his offspring were able to enter the corridors of King Arden's palace.

Running back to Jinx, Kira quickly climbed up his wing and entered the saddlebox. She was grateful to see her bow and quiver of arrows sitting there, waiting for her.

Kira caught hold of the reins, and gave a light tug. 'Fly, Jinx!'

With joy unmatched, Kira felt Jinx tensing and then flying assuredly off the side of the tower. Taking him over the courtyard, Kira put the reins in her mouth as she fixed an arrow in her bow and prepared to open fire on the king's guards.

But as she watched, she was uncertain whom she should shoot at. Down below, guard fought guard. She sought out Dane and Shanks in the struggle, and watched as they too fought side by side *with* other guards.

If she were going to help, she realized it would not be with her bow. Instead she caught hold of the reins and directed Jinx down into the centre of the courtyard. As they landed, the crowds of villagers were crying and trying to run away from the dragons and attacking birds of prey.

Standing tall in the saddlebox, Kira pulled off her bridal veil and started to shout at the fleeing people. 'I am Kira, daughter of Captain Darious! Don't run from me. This is your chance at freedom! Take it! Rise up against King Arden. End First Law. End the war. End your starvation. It's up to you! If you want freedom, you're going to have to fight for it!'

As had happened so long ago at Lasser Commons, Kira watched the fleeing and frightened people stop running and start to listen to her.

'I can't save you. You have to save yourselves,' she cried. 'Use your bare hands if you must, but fight for your families. Your daughters are waiting to return home. They can't while that tyrant Arden is king. It's up to you! You can free yourselves, or you can be slaves. The choice is yours.'

As she stirred the people into revolt, Kira heard the Rogue's enraged roars echoing from deep within the palace. Turning in the direction of the sounds, she saw the walls of the palace trembling then start to crumble from the inside. Soon the huge purple dragon tore away another section of the wall. As the Rogue and his offspring emerged from the wreckage, the people and guards alike cried in terror at the sight of Elspeth astride the monstrous purple dragon.

Climbing up to stand on the Rogue's high back, Elspeth threw back her head and howled triumphantly. 'King Arden is dead!' As proof, she angrily threw down the king's jewelled crown.

Watching her sister standing tall on the Rogue's back, dressed in her boy's clothing, holding her bow high as her twin braids flew wildly in the wind, Kira's heart filled with pride. 'It was always you,' she repeated quietly to herself. 'The prophecy was all about you. Elan would be so proud.'

Kira directed Jinx to move closer to the Rogue. She climbed down from the blue dragon and ran as close to Ferarchie as she dare go. 'Shadow!'

'It's all right,' Elspeth called to her as she ordered the Rogue to lower himself further so she could climb down his side. As Kira watched her sister struggling to climb down his massive wing, she realized just how big Ferarchie truly was.

Finally Elspeth made it to the ground. Racing

forward, both sisters embraced. Kira could hardly speak as her joy and relief all welled up.

'I thought you were dead!' she cried.

Hugging her tightly, Elspeth also sniffed. 'I was. Onnie saved me.'

'Onnie?'

Appearing from the pouch on Elspeth's back, Kira saw the red fox. Without hesitating, she excitedly leaned forward and kissed the soft red fur of his head. 'Onnie, thank heavens you're alive!'

'We're both alive,' Elspeth cheered.

'We're all alive!' Dane shouted as he dropped his sword and embraced both his sisters.

'Kira!' Shanks called as he joined them. When he saw the change in her appearance, he smiled brightly. 'Hey, I really like your hair!'

Relieved to see him again, Kira turned and threw her arms around the knight. Shanks hugged her back tightly and then suddenly kissed her right on the lips. When he finally let go, he stood back and put his hands on his hips. 'So what's all this I hear about you marrying Lord Dorcon?'

'You married Lord Dorcon?' Elspeth asked. 'What happened? I was only gone a few days!'

Laughing and crying at the same time, Kira turned

to her sister. 'Thanks to you, I didn't. And please don't ever mention that man's name to me again!'

Around them the fighting for control of the kingdom continued. But as the four stood together watching, they could see that the people were starting to win back their freedom.

'Elspeth!'

Turning at the squealing voice, everyone saw Kahrin and their mother running with Tobias and pushing through the crowds to reach them. Once again, tears were shed at the joyful reunion.

As hugs and kisses were exchanged, Elspeth started to hang back. She didn't know how her mother would react to the big change in her. But then her mother saw her and opened her arms. 'My little Elspeth,' she cried.

Running into those arms, Elspeth found she was much taller than her mother, but suddenly that didn't matter. They were a family again.

'May I join in all this fun?'

'Paradon!' Kira squealed as she saw the wizard being supported by two dragon knights. Running to him, she threw her arms around his neck.

'Hey, take it easy on him, Kira,' Dane warned. 'He doesn't look too steady on his feet.'

Suddenly remembering his terrible wound, Kira's

eyes flew open wide. 'How? You were hurt?' She then looked back at Elspeth. 'And you were dead! I know you were. How is this possible?'

Still very weak, Paradon chuckled lightly. 'Arrows can't kill wizards. But they can hurt us. We can't heal with them left in. So when Shanks removed the arrow in my chest, I finally start to heal.'

Elspeth then stepped forward as Onnie climbed out of his pouch and into her arms. 'It was Lord Dorcon who actually saved us. He was the one who pulled the arrows out,' she explained. 'Onnie says when his wizard's blood mixed with mine it was enough to heal us both.' She then dropped her eyes as heavy sadness rose. 'But we couldn't save Harmony. She's dead.'

Kira nodded. 'I know. I'm so sorry. She fought bravely for you.'

'So did Jinx and Rexor,' Dane offered.

'Wait . . .' Kira added in confusion. 'What about Jinx? He left me. I thought he was going to die.'

Elspeth put her arm around Kira. 'Onnie and I were alive, but we were very, very weak. When we discovered we couldn't save Harmony, I called out to Jinx, hoping he'd survived the fight. He came back to us and took us to the Rogue's Mountain.'

'Where you got Ferarchie,' Kira finished.

'And Ferblue,' Elspeth added.

'Ferblue?' Kira repeated. Then she realized Elspeth meant the Rogue's other offspring. 'Where did you get that name?'

Elspeth shrugged. 'Well, his father is Ferarchie, his mother was Blue. So I put the two together and got Ferblue.'

Kira's eyes trailed over to the young, purple twin-tailed dragon standing beside his father. He was pulling back the skin from his teeth and growling viciously at people who came too near, but doing no more than that. Then Kira glanced back to Jinx and saw no aggression towards Ferblue or the Rogue. 'I thought the Rogue would kill Jinx if he ever saw him again.'

'I ordered him not to,' Elspeth explained. 'Just like I told them not to kill the people here at the palace unless they tried to hurt us.'

Kira and the rest of the family turned and looked back at the massive Rogue, sitting beside his offspring and waiting for Elspeth. As they studied the people and guards at the palace, they continued to grumble and growl, but did not attack.

'I can't keep them here long,' Elspeth said. 'It's not fair for them. They're wild dragons that hate people.

They belong on the mountain.' She paused before adding. 'So do I.'

'You hate people?' Kahrin asked.

Elspeth shook her head, but then added, 'I don't hate them. But after living so long on the mountain, I've come to realize I don't feel comfortable around them. Onnie and I are just like the Rogue, we're better off away from people.'

'Shadow,' Kira said quickly, 'you can't go back to the mountain. We need you here.'

Elspeth smiled at her sister and gently shook her head. 'No you don't. You can do just fine without me. Besides, Jinx wants to stay with you, and I know Rexor will be glad to get back with Dane. You can all come up to see us any time you want. The Rogue knows to let you back on the mountain. He won't attack.'

'No, Shadow, please stay!' Kira cried.

'Let me go, Kira. It's what I want.' She then looked at Onnie. 'It's what we both want.'

'But I'll miss you so much,' Kira said softly.

'And we'll miss you too,' Elspeth said. 'But it's not for ever.' Giving her a final hug, Elspeth kissed her forehead. 'Onnie and I are still very tired and weak from our wounds. We're going back up there to recover. Once we're better, we'll return. We need to find Paradon's granddaughter so she can finally turn Onnie back into a man.'

Unable to stand on his own, Paradon clung to the guards supporting him as he nodded. 'Of course we will. When you're ready, we'll use the Eye to find her.'

After saying her goodbyes to the family, Elspeth gave a special kiss to Jinx. She then stepped through the parting crowd and slowly made her way back to the Rogue. Giving Ferblue a reassuring pat on the snout, she approached the Rogue's folded wing.

Kira watched in overflowing pride and wonder as the Rogue turned his huge head back to Elspeth to gently nudge her up on to his wing. When she climbed the rest of the way on to his back, Kira smiled.

Her little big sister was seated on the back of the largest and most vicious dragon in the entire kingdom, tamed only for her. Elspeth waved a final time to her family as she ordered the Rogue and Ferblue into the sky.

EPILOGUE

For the next few days the kingdom entered a time of great celebration.

The damage to the palace caused by the Rogue and Ferblue was being repaired, while the new guards hunted down those still loyal to the king. Once they were captured, they were driven from the kingdom and banished for ever.

No one was in charge at the moment, but there was talk of public elections. Though still disorganized, a new and honourable government was starting to form, one whose first job would be to formally end First Law. Soon emissaries would leave to meet with King Casey in the hope of brokering a peace between the two warring lands.

Food was still scarce, but what was left was gathered together and distributed amongst the people as they prepared to leave the palace and return to their homes.

With luck, there was still time to plant some crops before the end of the summer.

During the days after the demise of King Arden, Kira stayed close to her mother and family. She was well aware that no one had found Lord Dorcon's body at the base of the tower. Dane and Shanks insisted the evil knight was dead and suggested that his men had hidden his body to keep the threat of him alive.

Kira wanted desperately to believe them. But even as the time passed, she couldn't shake the feeling that he was very much alive. Though she told no one, Kira felt that Lord Dorcon was out there, somewhere, planning his revenge against her and the family.

Spending time with her mother, Kira was profoundly grateful to have at least one of her parents still alive. At her mother's gentle coaxing she kept many of the gowns given to her by Lord Dorcon and the king. Feeling more than a little awkward dressing as a woman, she laughed openly and teased Shanks mercilessly when she caught him staring at her.

As the sun started to set on the final banquet, Paradon had recovered enough strength to cast a spell that filled the tables with food. People quickly got over the fact that the spell had gone wrong and the food was all the wrong shapes and colours. It may have looked strange, but it tasted delightful.

Soon pipers struck up merry tunes as the newly freed people of the kingdom started to dance.

Seated at the banquet table with her family and Paradon, and with Jinx resting quietly behind her, Kira watched as Tobias came up to the table. He had a girl with him that bore a strong family resemblance.

'Toby!' Shanks called as he stood and greeted his friend. As always, he ruffled Tobias' hair.

Grinning from ear to ear, Tobias greeted everyone at the table. He then drew the girl forward. 'Kira, this is my sister, Anna. She's heard all about your adventures and really wanted to meet you. Like you, she's loved dragons all her life. I was hoping you might let her meet Jinx.'

Also standing, Kira smiled at the girl who couldn't have been much older than she was. Looking at her sleeves, Kira noticed she wore black ribbons, which meant she had been married but was now a war widow. It also explained how a young girl like her had managed to escape being sent to Lasser.

'Hi, Anna,' Kira said as she offered her hand. 'I'd love you to meet Jinx. He's not great with strangers, but once you get to know him, he's a real sweetie.'

Shanks looked at Dane and nudged him. 'Jinx

a sweetie?' he repeated. 'Where does she get this stuff? Dragons aren't sweet, no matter how tame they become.'

Dane started to laugh, but his eyes lingered on Anna. 'Don't tell me, tell Kira.'

'Kira,' Shanks insisted. 'Jinx is not sweet. He's a dragon. He's big and he's blue and he has twin tails. But he's still a dragon. That's all.'

Kira gave Shanks her most charming smile, which caused the knight to blush. Laughing at his discomfort, she teased, 'You're just jealous because he still doesn't like you!'

'I don't care if he likes me or not,' Shanks argued. 'Dragons aren't sweet.'

Kira chuckled again, then turned to Anna. 'Ignore him. He's just scared of my Jinx.'

'But I'm not,' Dane suddenly offered as he stood up. 'I like Jinx. And Rexor. He's my dragon. He was hurt but he's getting better. I'll show you if you like.'

Kira guided Anna over to her brother and introduced him. As Dane offered his hand, she noticed him turning his face away so Anna wouldn't see Lord Dorcon's brand. It struck her as strange because Dane never appeared bothered about his scarred face before.

'You don't have to hide your face from me,' Anna

said shyly. Reaching forward, she caught hold of Dane's chin and gently turned his face so she could see the scars burned deep into the skin of his cheek.

'Toby told me what Lord Dorcon did to you.' As she tilted her head to the side, she smiled. 'It's not that bad. The way Toby described it, I didn't think you'd have any face left, but you look fine to me.' Suddenly realizing what she had said, she put her hand over her mouth as her face went red.

Kira watched her brother blush under the compliment.

Just before the moment became too awkward, the pipers started another tune. Kira gave Dane a light punch. 'Why don't you ask Anna to dance?'

The colour in Dane's cheeks turned even brighter. But he offered his hand to Anna. 'Would you like to?'

When Anna nodded, they stepped out on to the grass and joined in the dance.

'How about you?' Shanks asked Kira. 'Want to dance?'

Kira smiled. 'In a moment. Why don't you ask Kahrin first? I know she'd love to.'

Shanks shrugged and playfully reached for Kahrin's hand. 'C'mon, Kahrin, let's show them how it's done.'

As Kira watched Shanks lead her sister on to the

grass, she quietly left the table and stepped back to Jinx. Standing beside her beloved blue dragon with her arm draped over his neck, her eyes trailed up to the sky and the direction of the Rogue's Mountain. She smiled. Elspeth and Onnie were up there and very much alive.

They had been on such a long and seemingly endless journey together, starting from the very first day when Lord Dorcon arrived on their farm, to the final fulfilment of the ancient prophecy.

Many times she doubted they would survive. Many times they fought side by side and many times they suffered for each other. But finally in the end, they triumphed over an evil king.

Looking over at her family, Paradon and Shanks, Kira knew, whatever else they faced in the coming days and winters of their lives, they would always get through it – together.